Solo Leveling

- VII -

CHUGONG

YEN ON

NEW YORK

Solo Leveling VII

CHUGONG
Translation by Hye Young Im and J. Torres

SOLO LEVELING Volume 7
© Chugong 2017 / D&C MEDIA
All rights reserved.
First published in Korea in 2017 by D&C MEDIA Co., Ltd.

English translation © 2023 by Yen Press, LLC

Yen On
150 West 30th Street, 19th Floor
New York, NY 10001

Visit us at yenpress.com ◊ facebook.com/yenpress ◊ twitter.com/yenpress
yenpress.tumblr.com ◊ instagram.com/yenpress

First Yen On Edition: March 2023
Edited by Yen On Editorial: Won Young Seo, Payton Campbell
Designed by Yen Press Design: Wendy Chan

Yen On is an imprint of Yen Press, LLC.
The Yen On name and logo are trademarks of Yen Press, LLC.

The publisher is not responsible for websites (or their content)
that are not owned by the publisher.

Library of Congress Cataloging-in-Publication Data
Names: Chugong, author. | Im, Hye Young, translator. | Torres, J., 1969– translator.
Title: Solo leveling / Chugong ; translation by Hye Young Im and J. Torres.
Other titles: Na honjaman rebereop. English
Description: First Yen On edition. | New York, NY : Yen On, 2021.
Identifiers: LCCN 2020047938 | ISBN 9781975319274 (v. 1 ; trade paperback) |
ISBN 9781975319298 (v. 2 ; trade paperback) | ISBN 9781975319311 (v. 3 ; trade paperback) |
ISBN 9781975319335 (v. 4 ; trade paperback) | ISBN 9781975319359 (v. 5 ; trade paperback) |
ISBN 9781975319373 (v. 6 : trade paperback) | ISBN 9781975319397 (v. 7 ; trade paperback)
Subjects: GSAFD: Fantasy fiction.
Classification: LCC PL994.215.G66 N313 2021 | DDC 895.73/5—dc23
LC record available at https://lccn.loc.gov/2020047938

ISBNs: 978-1-9753-1939-7 (paperback)
978-1-9753-1940-3 (ebook)

10 9 8 7 6 5 4 3 2 1

LSC-C

Printed in the United States of America

CONTENTS

1
THE NEW PRESIDENT OF THE HUNTER'S ASSOCIATION

1

THE NEW PRESIDENT OF THE HUNTER'S ASSOCIATION

An executive meeting was held in order to fill the vacant seat of the president of the Hunter's Association of Korea. More than thirty leaders, including the vice president, directors of all the branches, and the heads of each department filled the large conference room. Each person possessed sociopolitical power equal to those in high-level government positions or those on the board of the largest corporations, yet they all looked concerned. The air was tense as they deliberated on the situation at hand.

"We must choose the next president of the association."

Finally, the crux of the matter. Looks of apprehension flashed across everyone's faces following the vice president's declaration. A few people gulped audibly.

It was time to decide the fate of the Hunter's Association.

They were acutely aware that, as the control tower for all the hunters in Korea, the Hunter's Association having any instability within it meant instability for the country, especially with both the number of new hunters and spawning gates on the rise.

"Well then......"

The vice president, who was presiding over the meeting, closed the file folder in front of him, making it clear that whatever was written in the report could not compare in importance to his next words.

"Following an extensive discussion with the board of directors, we are recommending Director Jinchul Woo be named as the new president of the association."

This was the first time Jinchul was hearing about this. His head whipped around to face the vice president, his eyes clearly asking, *Why me?*

The vice president pulled the mic closer as his eyes remained on Jinchul. "Director Woo has a wealth of practical experience and knowledge from working as President Go's right-hand man. He also possesses the strength needed to lead other hunters."

This was true. President Go had highly valued Jinchul, who had elected to work for the association despite being courted by large guilds. He was an A-rank hunter so powerful that, had his magic power evaluation been slightly higher, he would've been the second S-rank hunter to join the association after President Go. He had four years of practical experience under his belt and was a top-tier A-rank hunter.

There were murmurings among the group when Jinchul's name was first brought up, but they soon died down as the vice president explained the board's choice. There was no other candidate better suited to lead the legion of hunters working for the association.

Jinchul himself was unable to accept the endorsement. "I'm lacking in several areas needed to fill this role. There are many others who rank above me. Besides, aren't I too young?"

Jinchul was in his mid-thirties. Though he had amassed invaluable experience in the four years he'd dedicated to the Surveillance Team, he was still way too green to become the head of the organization. At least, that was his opinion.

"Vice President, there's you and the various members of the board of directors, not to mention the other directors." Jinchul looked each of the prominent people in the eye before turning to the vice president again. "How could you think I'm good enough to replace the late President Go with all these great people here?"

The vice president turned his head and let out a quiet sigh. He had expected resistance, but he hadn't expected the pushback to come from Jinchul himself.

The vice president shut off his mic. He had already revealed the official position of the board of directors, so he would now unveil the actual reason they'd recommended Jinchul. Everyone in the room pricked up their ears.

The vice president explained, "No one else, myself included, has the influence you have on Korea's strongest."

A member of the Hunter's Association of Korea referred to as "Korea's strongest"—everyone knew exactly who the vice president was talking about.

"He's proven his power in Korea, Japan, and the US. It's already the case to an extent, but it's clear that, going forward, the Hunter's Association will not be able to function smoothly without him."

A national-level hunter had the power to mobilize a whole country, and yet Jinwoo Sung had brought such a hunter to his knees. What kind of influence could the mere Hunter's Association have on such a hunter? Their option was to politely ask him for favors and await his answer. They needed someone able to approach Jinwoo just like President Go had when he asked him to rescue the Jeju Island raid team from certain death.

Currently, Jinchul was the closest person to Jinwoo within the association. That was good enough to make him the next president.

No one on the board of directors had been able to object to the vice president's logic when he first nominated Jinchul to them. Similarly, everyone in the large conference room started nodding along with his reasoning.

"We cannot compel you to do as we ask any more than we can Hunter Sung."

The vice president had made himself crystal clear: The hunters held all the cards here.

"But please give our offer some serious consideration."

In the brief silence that followed, all eyes were on Jinchul. Their stares seemed to needle at his skin as he cautiously opened his mouth.

"I......"

* * *

"OMG," Jinwoo blurted out. Though it was frequently used by Jinah, Jinwoo never thought he'd use that expression until now. His fingers sped across the screen as he scanned the article on his cell phone.

Jinchul Woo Named President of the Hunter's Association, Successor to the Late President Gunhee Go!

Seeing Jinchul's name trending had made Jinwoo worry that something bad had occurred, but after seeing the good news, he heaved a huge sigh of relief. To think Jinchul Woo, someone he considered a close acquaintance, had risen to become president of the Hunter's Association. He beamed, feeling genuinely happy for Jinchul, as he turned off his phone and tossed it gently over his shoulder.

The ant soldier standing behind him barely caught it. He watched the ant tuck the phone in his bag, then gave him a warning.

"Your predecessor did a much better job. You've got some big shoes to fill."

Jinho was preoccupied with his duties as vice president of their guild, so this ant had been selected as the luggage carrier in his stead. The ant bashfully bowed his head.

"Good." Jinwoo patted the ant soldier on the shoulder and smiled. Then he turned around, ready to resume hunting after lunch. However......

"Ugh...... These again?"

Jinwoo rubbed his forehead as he took in the sight of the dense thicket of trees before him. What had previously been a village destroyed by the giants was now a forest reminiscent of the Amazon. One didn't need to be a hunter to find the area suspicious.

Oddly enough, animals didn't seem to question anything. There were traces of half-eaten animal carcasses strewn about the place. Jinwoo clicked his tongue at the flies swarming around animal bones.

He then picked up a stone from the ground and threw it.

Whoosh!

This was no ordinary stone. It wasn't a stone flung by any old S-rank hunter but one flung by Jinwoo Sung.

Crack!

The stone became lodged in the face of one of the tree-type magic beasts, and its eyes shot open. Its face contorted as it rose to its full height and ran toward Jinwoo.

Graaaah!

Apparently, even plants got angry when struck. Jinwoo summoned a Demon Monarch's Dagger and dashed to meet it. The massive tree swung its branches at him.

So slow......

Jinwoo took advantage of its slow speed to examine the tree's face while avoiding the two branches it swung in lieu of fists. On the other hand, the tree was unable to follow Jinwoo's movements.

Awful reaction time, too.

Every time a branch struck the ground, it left a deep dimple, but Jinwoo sucked his teeth in disappointment.

It's not that strong considering its size.

The tree-type magic beast looked strong because of its huge body, but its destructive power was terribly weak when compared to giant-type magic beasts of a similar size. However, the tree-type beasts had one huge advantage to make up for all their shortcomings.

Jinwoo gripped his dagger tightly and stabbed the magic beast's body again and again.

Gyaaaaah, gaaah! Contrary to its never-ending screams, the tree didn't go down easily.

Mutilation!

The dagger hacked into the tree like a spray of bullets.

Shk-shk-shk-shk-shk-shk-shk-shk-shk!

Gyaaaaaaaah!

The tree squeezed its eyes shut and randomly swung its limbs against Jinwoo's flurry of blows. Jinwoo deftly avoided them as he approached the tree. He returned the dagger to the inventory and concentrated mana into his fist.

Jinwoo threw a single punch.

Crack!

The tree doubled over and was sent flying.

Gyaaah!

The magic beast flailed on the ground while screeching in pain but managed to drag its broken body toward Jinwoo with one hand.

"Whoa......"

Tree-type magic beasts were incredibly durable. They had been newly discovered in Japan and displayed amazing stamina. This particular one finally stopped moving only after Jinwoo struck it dozens more times.

Gah... With one last outburst, the dead tree spewed putrid sap from its mouth.

"Ugh." Jinwoo covered his nose.

The awful stench was more annoying in Jinwoo's book than its resistance. As the one ant soldier diligently extracted essence stones from the fallen tree, Jinwoo glared at the remaining trees.

That many more to go......

It hadn't been that long since the dungeon break had occurred, but these magic beasts had already established a veritable forest. Jinwoo frowned as he gauged the situation. But man was an intelligent animal, and having already discovered their weakness, Jinwoo had a card up his sleeve.

I figured this would be the case, so they're ready to go.

Jinwoo gleefully summoned a few select soldiers. "Come on out."

Fang and three mage soldiers emerged as if they had been waiting for his call. It had definitely been worth keeping these four with him while he'd sent his other shadow soldiers out to battles in other locations.

"Begin!"

The mages and Fang, who had finished enlarging his body, rained down fire at Jinwoo's command.

Fwoooooom!

Boom! Ka-boom! Ka-boom!

The trees screamed as they caught on fire, their bodies twisting in agony.

Gyaaaah!

Gyah!

Graaaaaah!

Despite not being dry wood, the mana-powered fire easily burned them down. Even the foul-smelling sap evaporated quickly from the heat, allowing Jinwoo to comfortably watch things unfold from an adequate distance. He smiled as everything went exactly according to plan. The system messages kept coming.

[You have defeated an enemy.]
[You have defeated...]
[You have defeated...]

Countless notifications poured in. The magic beasts' ability to spawn quickly was bad news, but it worked in his favor because of the experience points he racked up. Sure enough, that *ping* sound seemed to ring clearer than usual.

[You have leveled up!]

Now, that's what Jinwoo was talking about! He brought up his stats to check his gains.

Stat window.
Ping!

[Name: Jinwoo Sung]   [Level: 133]
[Job: Shadow Monarch]   [Title: Demon Hunter
                         (and 2 others)]

[HP: 78,330]   [MP: 136,160]
[Fatigue: 3]

[Stats]
Strength:	Stamina:	Agility:	Intelligence:	Perception:
308	307	316	321	298

(Available ability points: 0)

Jinwoo had reached level 133 in no time thanks to his soldiers taking care of raids all over Japan. The many magic beasts pouring out from gates had been a boon.

Most of his stats had exceeded 300, with his perception stat being a mere two points shy.

I'll pour everything into perception after tomorrow's daily quest.

Satisfied, Jinwoo closed the stat window.

There was still the matter of the coming war the King of Giants had spoken of, as well as the grand plan President Go had mentioned, but what was the use of worrying over it? He just needed to be ready for whatever was coming. His current priority was to keep leveling up.

Beru, who had been leading the ant army into battle far from Jinwoo, suddenly reached him.

My liege...... If I may, I would like to ask something of my king.

"Hmm?"

What could this be about? Puzzled, Jinwoo sent a message back. *What's up?*

* * *

"......don't have anyone who can help you, I can be reached through the Hunter's Association of Korea."

The Hunter's Association had received a flood of inquiries after Jinwoo's interview aired, most of them from the top hunters in the world. Some of them even visited Korea in secret to consult with Jinwoo.

Lennart Neirmann, Germany's strongest hunter, was among them.

They got a prominent S-rank hunter and even one of the national-level hunters. I've got no chance against something like that.

He was a humble man and incredibly perceptive. Instead of being paralyzed with fear, Lennart decided it would be more prudent to put his faith in Jinwoo and the countermeasures the Korean man claimed he had in place. And so he made his way to Korea. Lennart arrived at Incheon Airport and breathed in the Korean air.

So this is the scent of Korea......

Excited at visiting Asia for the first time, he cheerfully asked the customs officer, "Is this the land of Jinwoo Sung?"

"Pardon? Oh, yes......"

When the flustered customs officer nodded, Lennart flashed a smile. Soon, he'd be able to talk with the most powerful hunter in the world. Lennart had narrowly missed a chance to talk to Jinwoo during the International Guild Conference banquet, so his heart raced at the prospect of meeting him here.

As he took some deep breaths to try to calm down, the hulking man right behind him lost his temper.

"Get outta my way if you're gonna take your sweet-ass time."

Lennart instantly scowled. How dare the stranger be so rude to one of the best hunters in the world?! He took off the sunglasses he'd been wearing as a precaution and turned around, determined to teach this man some manners.

"Hey! Look me in the eyes and say that again." Lennart frowned at the man who was a head taller than he was.

The man removed his sunglasses in turn. "I said... Get. Out. Of. My. Way."

Lennart froze as soon as he recognized who it was, then managed to force out, "P-please go right ahead."

Thomas Andre shoved Lennart aside with his wide shoulders and made his way to the front of the line, leaving Laura to apologize to the German hunter.

The customs officer felt like he was suffocating as he laid eyes on Thomas, a national-level hunter considered to be the strongest in the world. With such a towering stature, his nickname "Goliath" was more than fitting.

Thomas noticed the officer's face growing pale. He put his sunglasses back on and smirked. "Is this the land of Jinwoo Sung?"

* * *

My liege...... If I may, I would like to ask something of my king.

Beru, who was currently leading the army of ant shadow soldiers far from Jinwoo, made contact out of the blue. What could his most powerful soldier have to say?

What's up?

Jinwoo replied telepathically.

Beru cautiously asked, *If it pleases my liege, I would like to request that prey be driven toward my location.*

Driven toward Beru? By "prey," Beru was referring to the magic beasts that had escaped into their world via dungeon breaks. Beru was expressing his desire to take care of the magic beasts all by himself. Greed, despite holding the rank of general same as Beru, couldn't bring himself to look Beru straight in the eyes, so this wasn't about his ant subordinates revolting against him. Jinwoo pondered the possibilities before it hit him.

Could it be……?

I sense something similar to the time my whole body went through a metamorphosis, and the more prey I defeat, the stronger the feeling grows.

Jinwoo's hunch was right on the money. Metamorphosis—in other words, leveling up. Beru had stood on the front lines and fought more enemies than any other soldier ever since he first joined the shadow army, and finally the day had come for him to level up. Considering how much stronger high-rank soldiers such as Igris and Iron had become by leveling up……

That's great news!

Even before becoming a shadow soldier, Beru was already powerful enough to toy with S-rank hunters. Likewise, his rank was currently the highest among the existing soldiers.

That means I'll get to see what rank comes after general.

Jinwoo was intrigued to see how this promotion would affect Beru. He replied to the anxiously awaiting ant.

Sure.

Thank you, my king. Then I shall return the ant soldiers to you.

No, hang on.

A smile spread across Jinwoo's face, though Beru couldn't see it, since they were miles apart.

My soldiers.

Jinwoo's army, now approximately 1,200 strong, responded at once to his call. Igris led the knights, Fang led the high orc unit, Jima led the nagas, No. 6 led the giants, Tank led the ice bears, and Greed led the remaining soldiers. With the entire army's attention solely on Jinwoo, it was like he could practically hear them all roaring. The tension radiating from them was palpable.

Jinwoo relished in it as he issued his command.

Everyone, withdraw.

......!

Return to me.

The shadow army began moving as soon as he gave the order. Soldiers returned to shadow and quickly converged from all over Japan to gather by Jinwoo's feet.

My king...... Why did you withdraw us all?

Jinwoo grinned at the surprised ant.

You and I will handle the rest of the magic beasts together.

That was the best way to hasten Beru's progress. Known as power leveling, it was a strategy used by gamers where a high-level player would help a lower-level player level up quickly. Similarly, Jinwoo was planning to fight beside Beru to maximize the efficiency of hunting and drive up Beru's experience points. With all the dungeon breaks, leveling Beru up would be a piece of cake if they toured together. It would be less efficient than deploying shadow soldiers to those areas, but Beru took priority.

My king......

Overcome with emotion, Beru couldn't finish his sentence. Jinwoo raised an eyebrow. Beru's voice had become increasingly expressive over time, no doubt influenced by all the TV dramas he'd been watching in the shadows while assigned to protect his mother and sister.

Once the last shadow soldiers arrived, Jinwoo asked, "By any chance, is there any other soldier who can sense when your level is about to go up?"

There was no answer, of course. Leveling up was a difficult feat in and of itself, but a soldier would need to have excellent perception in order to sense it. There was a reason Beru was the only soldier capable of informing Jinwoo about the timing of his leveling up, or so Jinwoo assumed, but......

Vwoooom......

Another shadow soldier rose to join them, dashing Beru's dreams of hunting alone with his master. Although Beru looked disappointed, Jinwoo's face lit up.

"Excellent."

Igris knelt to his liege as usual. Jinwoo usually felt a little uncomfortable at Igris's extreme formality, but it had been a while, and he welcomed the familiar sight. Jinwoo had also been looking forward to Igris leveling up for some time now.

"Then let's begin." He smiled as he summoned a Demon Monarch's Dagger.

Sprouts were already emerging from the remains of the tree-type magic beasts they'd burned down. The spawn rate was truly terrifying.

Gyaaaaah!

Gaaah!

There were an additional forty dungeon breaks to take care of after this. If they were to handle everything among the three of them, there was no time to waste.

* * *

Jinho felt more at home in the Ahjin Guild headquarters than in his actual home, but at this very moment, every minute felt like an hour. Jinho checked the clock on a wall.

It was 4:10 in the afternoon, which meant more than two hours had passed since that man had arrived.

Jinho swallowed nervously, then peeked at the unannounced visitor, worried that he'd swallowed too loudly. He ended up making eye contact with the man, who grinned at him over his sunglasses.

Jinho forced his stiff facial muscles into a semblance of a smile and hurriedly looked away. He broke into a cold sweat and picked up his cell phone to try calling his boss again, but his attempt was in vain.

Riiing, riiing!

It had been two days since Jinho last heard from Jinwoo, and it wasn't about to change anytime soon.

"......"

"......"

Jinho pressed his lips together, and the wonderful employees who had chosen to work for the Ahjin Guild because they saw potential in the organization followed suit. Within the awkward atmosphere, they stayed silent as if they had planned it together. Who could blame them for doing so? Anyone in this situation would act the same way.

The man sitting in the corner of the office was simultaneously one of the most powerful hunters in the world and the hunter with the worst temper in the world. In addition, he had been badly beaten up and sent to the hospital by their guild president. None of them could dare laugh or chatter away in the presence of Thomas Andre.

The number one hunter in the world had visited the Ahjin Guild to meet with Jinwoo. As a result, Vice President Jinho and the other guild members were dying inside. Just as Jinho debated calling Jinwoo one more time......

Shhhf.

The office's automatic doors slid open. Everyone's gazes snapped toward the entry to see who it was.

Jinho's eyes widened. He excitedly leaped out of his seat and spoke with a desperation that reflected what the rest of the staff members were feeling.

"Boss!"

* * *

No wonder the building's been mobbed by reporters......

Jinwoo met the gaze of the grinning Thomas Andre. Judging by the look on his face, it didn't appear that Thomas held a grudge against Jinwoo. So why had he come all the way here?

Jinho intercepted Jinwoo before Thomas could. "Boss! Why was it so hard to reach you?"

"I was a little busy."

"Now that you mention it, your clothes......" Jinho paused.

Jinwoo's clothes were covered in the evidence of his many battles. The sight reminded Jinho of their giant-killing adventures.

If the boss was so preoccupied with hunting these past two days that he couldn't call me, then......

How many magic beasts had lost their lives this time? It gave Jinho chills just thinking about it.

At that moment, Thomas leisurely got up and strode over to Jinwoo. He was so tall that he shortened the distance between them in a few steps, coming to a stop right in front of the Korean hunter.

Oh no......

They wouldn't fight in here, would they?

The guild employees nervously held their collective breath, unsure of the relationship between their boss and Thomas. Their hearts beat so loudly that Jinwoo's ears began to ring.

"Mr. Sung." Thomas held out his hand. Jinwoo shook it, returning the greeting with a smile.

Thomas's smile faded, startled by a sudden realization.

How in the world......?

The American sensed that Jinwoo had changed somehow. It was subtle, but this wasn't the same man he'd met before. Perhaps it was a change in demeanor? Certainly, Jinwoo's clothes were much messier than in their first confrontation or in the subsequent meeting at the banquet. Yet regardless of the man's appearance, Thomas felt a sort of toughness radiating from Jinwoo, a firm steadiness that he'd carried before but that seemed more pronounced now.

Is it even possible?

No way. As far as Thomas knew, that was impossible. His keen perception detected the change in Jinwoo from leveling up, but he didn't have a way of articulating what it meant. The handshake ended before he could figure it out.

"What brings you to Korea?" Jinwoo inquired.

"Oh." Thomas snapped back to his senses, grinning once more. "Didn't you promise me that we'd have a meal together once my hand recovered?"

Thomas held up his healed left hand and gave him a wave. "Also......"

Jinwoo checked the time. It was four thirty in the afternoon now—too late for lunch but too early for dinner.

"There's still a lot of time left before dinner, so… Pardon me for a minute." Jinwoo excused himself and quickly approached Jinho. Since Thomas wasn't here for any important business, he decided to take care of something more urgent. "Could you find me the biggest gate that's open in Seoul?"

Jinho's eyes widened at the request. "Is anything fine as long as it's big, boss?"

"I want a high-rank gate even if it's already booked."

"Gotcha." Jinho's fingers flew over his keyboard until he found the information he was searching for. His face lit up. "There's a dangerous A-rank gate, boss."

"Really?"

"But the Hunters Guild already claimed it."

The news didn't deter Jinwoo.

"That's fine."

Jinwoo wasn't concerned about who owned the raid permit. Rather, he was relieved that things would most likely go smoothly, since he had acquaintances in the guild. He was about to leave the office with a spring in his step but doubled back to say good-bye to Thomas.

"I have to take care of some business, so let's talk about dinner later after I come back."

"……"

Jinwoo was off like the wind, leaving behind a flustered Thomas Andre. In a daze, the American could only stare after Jinwoo before breaking into a loud guffaw. "Ha-ha! Oh geez……"

Thomas didn't really have a choice in the matter. Although it was inconsiderate behavior to a guest who had come from afar, Thomas had been the one to show up unannounced. He should've known Jinwoo would be busier than even himself.

"Well then… You can reach me here." Thomas gave Jinho the phone number of the hotel he was staying at before leaving the office.

"Whew…" Relieved, Jinho let out a sigh of relief, then flinched in surprise at the sudden presence he felt next to him. "Oh, you were still here?"

Lennart had arrived at the guild office way before Thomas had dropped in. Unfortunately, Lennart didn't speak a lick of Korean, but it was painfully obvious that the vice president of the Ahjin Guild had forgotten about him until now.

"I made an appointment and everything......"

Lennart was treated as a VIP in Germany, but he now lowered his head, feeling small. After all, what could he say after even Thomas Andre left empty-handed without protest? Both magic beasts and hunters had but one life.

"......"

Downcast, Lennart heaved himself to his feet and wrote his contact number in tiny writing next to Thomas's.

* * *

The elite strike squad members of the Hunters Guild were in the middle of raid prep, but everyone stopped to stare at Jinwoo as he entered the scene.

Haein, who had received a phone call in advance, was the only person not taken aback at his presence. "What do you mean you want to 'borrow' a dungeon?"

"Exactly that. I want to borrow a dungeon if possible." Having not seen her in a while, Jinwoo was pleased to see her.

Haein, however, thought it ridiculous that his first phone call after a long period of no contact was about borrowing a dungeon. She was about to berate him, but she couldn't bring herself to do so after seeing Jinwoo's bright smile. At a loss for words, she averted her eyes and hesitated as Jongin, who had also been expecting Jinwoo, dashed toward them.

"Hunter Sung!"

Jinwoo had explained his proposition before his arrival. No guild master would refuse an offer to exterminate all magic beasts but the boss of the dungeon without touching anything else. Jongin, who had been concerned that his people might get injured in the high-rank gate, accepted Jinwoo's offer with open arms, and though they tried not to show it, the strike squad felt the same way.

Jinwoo headed for the gate but stopped and turned around when he felt someone grab his sleeve. It was Haein, her cheeks beet red. She murmured to him, "What're you planning to do inside?"

"I need to test something. My minions are going through some changes."

At the mention of his minions, Haein recalled the two she'd fought in the association's gym, Igris and Beru. They had been too overpowered to be considered minions, strong enough to put the life of an S-rank hunter of her caliber in danger. What kind of changes to such minions would require a test run?

Curiosity got the best of Haein, and she quietly asked, "Then…can I go inside with you?"

It wasn't a totally altruistic offer, and Jinwoo shook his head immediately. "I'm going to let them run wild, so it'll be too dangerous."

Jinwoo gave a firm answer, his eyes completely serious. Haein nodded and withdrew without protest. He passed through the gate, leaving a disappointed Haein behind.

[You have entered the dungeon.]

There was the usual message. Jinwoo summoned Beru from where he'd been waiting in the shadows.

Come out.

* * *

The Hunters Guild strike squad scrambled to get inside the dungeon once Jinwoo left.

"Hey, no pushing!"

"The dungeon isn't going anywhere, guys! No need to run!"

What in the world was the great Jinwoo Sung testing out that he needed to borrow another guild's gate, despite the increased difficulty of A-rank dungeons as of late? The hunters scanned the dungeon interior with inquisitive eyes that quickly filled with shock. The remains of crushed magic beasts left a bloody trail of carcasses that continued into the dark recesses on the opposite side of the cave. They were at a loss for words, not daring to go deeper inside.

"L-look over there......" One of the hunters elbowed another hunter standing next to him.

The other hunter turned to look at what his guildmate was pointing to without a second thought. His mouth dropped at the gruesome sight.

What in the world had happened for a dead magic beast to have been smashed into the ceiling? Considering how dungeons were made up of much stronger materials than regular caves, the scene was astonishing.

"I guess I won't be eating dinner tonight......"

The faces of hunters with weak stomachs grew pale as they took in the magic-beast massacre. Even more unbelievable was that Jinwoo had wrapped everything up in less than ten minutes.

A shocked female hunter murmured to herself, "Hunter Sung...... He really doesn't give off that kind of impression, but......"

The farther they went, the more disturbing evidence of violence they saw. This was the first time she'd seen the walls of a dungeon destroyed like this in her five years as a hunter.

One of the male hunters agreed with her. "Is this what they mean by, like, *unleashing your inner beast* or something?"

But Haein shook her head. She was sure that this destruction hadn't been caused by Jinwoo. She had witnessed Jinwoo's fighting style several times up close. The Jinwoo she knew finished off his enemies with a clean kill. It was practically art. When Haein had first seen him in action, she'd gotten lost in how beautiful and fluid his moves were. That meant......

Which of his minions is capable of—?

She was suddenly struck with a memory of the monstrous ant minion who had opened his mouth wide and roared at her, sending chills down her spine. It had been savagery incarnate!

Jinwoo said his minion had gone through changes, but just what kind of changes had it gone through?

Haein left her flabbergasted colleagues behind and ran out of the dungeon to try to get some answers, but Jinwoo was already gone.

"What's the rush......?" Haein grumbled as she looked around for Jinwoo. She had so many questions for him, and yet...

I'm sure there will be another opportunity.

She let out a sigh so gentle a butterfly wouldn't have felt it. She then slowly turned around with a small smile.

* * *

Jinah snuck toward her mom, who was doing dishes, as quiet as a cat.

Clink, clink.

Kyunghye either didn't hear Jinah or pretended not to notice her approaching, and as soon as Jinah got close enough to hear her mother breathing, she tackled Kyunghye into a big hug.

"Mom!"

Kyunghye didn't seem surprised in the slightest, and responded with warmth in her voice. "Are you bored, my dear?"

"Yeah, super bored. Jinwoo hasn't been home in a few days, and you won't play with me."

While her mom was asleep in the hospital, Jinwoo had stepped up to fill her shoes. Not only was he the breadwinner but he also did the housework so that Jinah could focus on her studies. He wasn't any old sibling but also a parent and a friend to her. Since he was regularly out of the house due to how busy he had become, Jinah missed him terribly. Everyone in Korea knew his name now, but who cared about that if *she* never saw him? Jinah looked to her mother for comfort from the loneliness she felt at the absence of her brother.

"But I'm happy because you're here." Jinah nuzzled Kyunghye's back and grinned.

Kyunghye chuckled as she continued to do the dishes. For a time, Jinah silently stuck to her mom like a cicada clinging to a tree.

"Mom, I think we should move."

Kyunghye's hands froze for a moment, and then she started up again, still with a smile. "You want to move to a different apartment, honey?"

"Yeah."

"Oh dear. I still like this place, though."

"Why would anyone want to live in this old dump?"

Kyunghye's hands never stopped doing the dishes as Jinah whined to her.

It wasn't like Jinah wasn't aware of the truth. She knew exactly why her mom didn't want to move. Jinwoo already made more money than most people could only ever dream of, but she stayed here in a rented apartment for one reason only. She was waiting just in case her supposedly deceased husband, the father of her children, ever returned.

Jinah herself no longer had any memories of her dad, so she felt like it was a waste of time. On the other hand, Jinwoo had never brought up the idea of moving ever again after hearing his mom's reasoning.

"I still like our home here."

Jinah puffed out her cheeks and let her mother go at her mother's gentle rebuttal. "Hmph."

"Don't be like that— Oh!" Kyunghye spun around. "Can you bring in the laundry I hung to dry outside, my beautiful darling?"

"You only call me 'beautiful' at times like this, you know."

Not that Jinah minded it. She hummed as she stepped out onto the balcony where the laundry was hanging. In her mom's absence, Jinah had become a pro at laundry and was making quick work of it, but she suddenly paused.

The sky had darkened above her.

"Huh?"

Was it about to rain? She looked up without much thought, and her jaw dropped at what she saw. The laundry basket fell from her hands.

"M-Mom!"

* * *

President Jinchul Woo's hands were sweaty. He looked down at his clammy palms and rubbed them on his poor dress pants. When was the last time he'd been this nervous? Venturing into a dungeon close to a dungeon break might have been less nerve-racking than this.

"Don't be so nervous, President Woo." The high-ranking government official who had invited Jinchul to the Blue House smirked.

How could anyone have a proper conversation with a leader of a nation if they were *that* on edge? The government official sympathized with how Jinchul felt a heavy burden at being appointed to such a high position at a young age, but as the one who had invited Jinchul, he hoped that the new association president wouldn't make any blunders.

"I'm sorry." Jinchul nodded with a stiff smile.

The government official patted the back of his hand to encourage him. Soon, the door to the private room opened, and the man of the hour walked in with his staff.

"Mr. President!"

"Mr. President."

Jinchul and the high-ranking government official rose from their seats.

"Oh, please sit. No need to get up. I'm not that special."

President Myungchul Kim broke the tension with some humor as he took a seat. Jinchul and the official followed suit.

President Kim's eyes zeroed in on Jinchul. "You must be very busy with the association, President Woo."

"Oh......not at all."

The bags under Jinchul's eyes betrayed his words. It was hard to believe the late President Go had managed so much work while battling for his health, and Jinchul's respect for President Go had grown greater even after his passing.

In any case, Jinchul was hoping to remove himself from this uncomfortable situation as quickly as he could. "Excuse me, Mr. President… but may I ask why you called me here?"

"Mr. Woo! My apologies, sir—"

The government official was appalled at Jinchul's direct manner of speech, but the president stopped him.

"Come now, it isn't right to keep President Woo too long, since he's a busy man."

Speedy discussions and clear points—that was how President Kim preferred to go about matters.

"Then I'll get straight to the point. President Woo, I have asked you here because……"

In that instant, Jinchul, with his sharp perception, realized that the president of Korea was gauging his reaction. He had a hunch that President Kim was about to ask him for a very troublesome request.

Sure enough, President Kim gave an embarrassed chuckle. "I've heard that you and Hunter Jinwoo Sung are quite close."

Jinchul quickly corrected him on the matter. "It's true that I personally know Hunter Sung, but we're merely acquaintances."

"Ha-ha. Is that so?"

"Yes, sir. The late President Go was the one who had quite a good relationship with Hunter Sung." Jinchul nodded as he recalled President Go expressing his desire to have a drink with Jinwoo.

After giving it some thought, President Kim continued. "Still, you are able to reach out to Hunter Sung, correct?"

"Ah…… Yes, sir."

"In that case, I'd like to ask a favor of you, President Woo."

And there it was. Jinchul reluctantly asked, "And what favor is that, Mr. President?"

President Kim smirked. "Since he's a well-known public figure now,

I would like to use Hunter Sung as a PR ambassador for Korea. We can use a catchphrase like, *Hunter Sung's Korea Is a Safe Korea.*"

Jinwoo Sung was a Korean hunter who had punched the lights out of a national-level hunter and someone for whom the Hunter Command Center bent over backward. Naturally, politicians around the world had to keep an eye on Jinwoo. President Kim's master plan was to use his standing as president to get Jinwoo on his side before anyone else. Step one was making Jinwoo a PR ambassador for Korea, and the goal was to establish a good relationship with the hunter, which would grow to be a powerful card in the president's hand as Jinwoo's fame rose higher. President Woo of the Hunter's Association would be the bridge to connect them.

Of course, Jinchul wasn't born yesterday.

He made me come all the way here to pitch...this?

His nerves vanished as he began to feel angry at the realization that they were trying to rope him into this ridiculous scheme so soon after he'd stepped into the role.

......President Kim underestimates me.

After all, Jinchul Woo was not Gunhee Go. The late president had acted for the association as a barrier and shield from politics, and they'd chosen him as their pawn as soon as the defenses fell.

As furious as Jinchul was, he also felt relieved. President Go had always said that the purpose of the Hunter's Association was to create an environment that allowed hunters to focus on their work, which benefited both the hunters and the public in general. Remembering President Go's words brought an unbidden smile to Jinchul's face.

President Kim laughed, misunderstanding Jinchul's smile as a positive sign. "Ha-ha-ha! President Woo understands what I'm saying, unlike someone else. I'm counting on you, okay? After all, this isn't just for my sake, right?"

It wasn't difficult to figure out who he was referring to by "unlike someone else."

Jinchul gritted his teeth. "The late President Go was an absolute gentleman."

"Yes, of course. A true gentleman, and rather uptight as well."

"I'm quite different from President Go."

"Ha-ha-ha! Indeed you are. The association needs change like this. We can't be stuck in the olden days forever, right?"

Jinchul shot him a cool smile. "So how long do you think it would take for me to kill everyone in this building, including the guards?"

"H-how dare you......!" The government official stood abruptly, but the hostility emanating from Jinchul stopped him in his tracks.

The two men weren't hunters, just average people. To them, an A-rank hunter could be considered an even greater threat than a magic beast. What chance did a human who couldn't even hold their own against a tiger or a bear have against an A rank?

"A few hours? No, it wouldn't take more than a few minutes." Jinchul calmly continued even as he watched the color drain from their cheeks. "Then, how many people do you think you would need to stop me if I went on a rampage? Well, I suppose you could stop me somehow if you summon every soldier and police officer in Seoul, and they manage to resist until my magic power runs out."

Jinchul's calm demeanor as he said such horrible things frightened President Kim further.

"Y-you...... Why are you......?" President Kim was unable to speak properly due to the intense pressure of Jinchul's hostile energy.

"But what if Hunter Sung went on a rampage? How many people would you need to stop him?"

Chills went up President Kim's spine as he imagined Jinwoo, a man who killed giants with his bare hands, hunting humans instead.

Satisfied that he'd gotten his message across, Jinchul reined in his hostile energy. "That sort of thing doesn't happen, because hunters are dedicated to their work."

Hunters had their domain, and politicians had their own. Making sure society was functioning properly was the mandate set by the late President Go.

Jinchul looked straight into President Kim's fearful eyes and declared, "I have no intention of damaging the pillars of the Hunter's Association established by the late President Go. And I trust I have your full cooperation."

How could he object? With Jinchul's stance made clear, President Kim quickly stammered, "O-of course the hunters should do their work hunting beasts. I didn't think this through and said things I shouldn't have."

Jinchul rose from his seat as the pale-faced President Kim kept nodding to show his support. Even after he left, President Kim and the government official could not get up for quite some time after.

"......"

"......"

Once again, they were reminded of just how scary hunters could be.

*　*　*

"Did something good happen in there, President Woo?" asked the driver.

"Do I give off the impression that something good happened?"

"You do, sir."

The driver was a rookie from the Surveillance Team. The sight of them had Jinchul smiling as he reminisced about his own first few years.

"It's because for the first time, I feel like I did something right as the president of the association."

Jinchul leaned back in the seat President Go used to occupy. He thought again of how the late president would go to bat for the hunters and had no qualms about taking the heat from the powers that be.

......*It went well.*

Jinchul was used to being a target because of the intense look in his eyes and his large frame. If this was one of his duties as president of the Hunter's Association, he would gladly take the hot seat. He had steeled himself to some extent as soon as he accepted the position.

"Where to, President Woo?"

"......The association."

Jinchul was dying to go home, but all the work he was supposed to do had been put on hold in order to rush to the meeting. He still had a mountain of things to take care of.

"Understood." The driver stepped on the accelerator as if he'd read Jinwoo's mind, and the car pulled out from the Blue House.

How much time had passed? Jinchul had fallen asleep from staring out the window. As he opened his eyes now, all he could see were endless lines of cars on the road. Seoul was always congested, but how was the traffic this bad at this hour on a weekday?

Has another gate appeared in the middle of the road?

Jinchul worriedly scanned his surroundings, but the air felt too strange for that to be the case. Drivers had gotten out of their cars, and pedestrians on the street and crosswalks had all stopped. Everyone was looking up at something in the sky. Even Jinchul's driver was craning his neck to look up through the windshield.

What in the world is going on......?

Wide awake, Jinchul shook the young man's shoulder.

"Hey. What's going on?"

"P-President Woo." With a quiver in his voice, the driver leaned to the side and pointed up. "O-over there......"

Jinchul was stunned. Was he seeing things? No, that wouldn't explain how everyone else was also looking up at the sky with identical facial expressions. Jinchul didn't want to believe that what he was seeing was real, and he flung open the car door to join the other drivers on the road.

His eyes weren't lying. Horrified, he stared up at the thing floating in the sky.

"How......? How could this be happening?"

* * *

There was a spring in Jinwoo's step, as he was very satisfied with the results of the test run. Beru had gotten strong, stronger than Jinwoo had expected. While unfortunate that Igris hadn't been able to level up, the results were gratifying nonetheless.

The Hunters Guild members were likely gobsmacked by what had transpired inside the dungeon. Jinwoo chuckled as he imagined Haein's jaw dropping in shock. He'd wanted to catch up with her, but alas, guests awaited him.

He debated who to contact first and went with Thomas. Jinwoo had a good idea why Lennart wanted to see him, but he couldn't fathom why the world's number two hunter would drop by Korea without any notice.

Thomas answered right away.

"Mr. Sung!"

Thomas spoke quickly, worried that Jinwoo might hang up on him.

"I come bearing some fantastic gifts for you."

Gifts? When Jinwoo half-jokingly remarked that Thomas should've opened with that earlier, Thomas was silent for a beat. He then replied, sounding like he was reining in his emotions.

"......I'm glad that you're excited about them. Where can we meet? I would like to hand you these presents first."

"Wherever is convenient for you."

"Then could you please come to me? It's somewhat dangerous for me to walk around with these things."

Dangerous gifts? Jinwoo raised an eyebrow before confirming that he would and hanging up.

They're not bombs......are they?

Of course not. It'd be more efficient for a national-level hunter to get the job done themselves than to explode a bomb. Jinwoo regretted not asking what kind of items they were.

At that moment, Beru addressed Jinwoo.

My king.

Yeah?

Could I perhaps have a bout with that foreigner?

......

Jinwoo was tempted for a moment but quickly shook his head, as if he was trying to shake the thought. It wasn't even worth considering. Although Jinwoo wanted to know how much Beru had grown, he couldn't very well let him fight Thomas. He neither wanted Thomas to get hurt nor Beru to be destroyed, and knowing their personalities, the fight wouldn't end with just a few bumps and bruises.

Still……

That he'd even considered it was a testament to Beru's growth, and it was clear that Beru also wanted to appraise his new abilities.

Beru.

I await your sage counsel, my king.

You'll have a chance to test your strength soon, so be patient.

I will keep your wise words with me.

And stop watching so many historical dramas. They're making you sound cheesier and cheesier.

I shall do as you comma—

Just say yes. Y-e-s, yes.

Yes.

Having said everything he wanted to say to Beru, Jinwoo merrily headed to his meeting with Thomas.

* * *

"Oh, Mr. Sung! You have no idea how long I've waited for this moment." Thomas ushered Jinwoo into his hotel room with much enthusiasm.

Receiving presents might feel good, but Thomas was of the opinion that giving presents had its own charm. Ever since Jinwoo had requested a dagger, he'd been dying to gift Jinwoo with the best weapon in the guild's storage room that just happened to be lying idle. Thomas hadn't made the trip out here for any old reason. He couldn't wait to see how the hunter he personally acknowledged as the best in the world reacted to these beauties.

With a snap of his fingers, his bodyguards brought in a box with a cloth draped over it.

Truth be told, Jinwoo had been feeling rather indifferent toward the present, as he wasn't in want of anything. However, he perked up as the bodyguards drew closer.

What's this......?

Vmmm, vwooooom......

His magic power was resonating with whatever was in the box. Thomas gleefully noticed Jinwoo's expression shift.

That's what I'm talking about!

Thomas had accurately predicted that Jinwoo would recognize the daggers as his weapons, and the weapons would recognize him as their master. This was the moment his prediction would be validated. These weapons might have bided their time in the darkness of the Scavenger Guild storage room for this very moment.

Clack.

The box was placed on the table between the two S-rank hunters.

"This is to repay you for showing mercy to my guild and me, Mr. Sung."

Thomas carefully slid the cloth off to reveal a transparent case holding two daggers stabbed into a giant scale.

Jinwoo wondered if *daggers* was the correct term for them. The daggers' blades were shorter than swords but longer than the typical dagger. Yet it wasn't the length of the weapons that caught Jinwoo's eyes but their color. They were as white as snow. The weapons weren't made of any kind of metal but of some different type of material. They reminded Jinwoo of his very first dagger, Kasaka's Venom Fang, which he'd acquired in an instance dungeon. Thanks to that, he deduced that they were fashioned from the fang of a magic beast. And there was only one dead magic beast whose body parts could emit this kind of energy.

"Kamish......"

Thomas shook his head and applauded. "It's impressive that you correctly guessed what these guys were made of at a glance."

Jinwoo was right, but that raised another question. "Aren't the remains stored at the Hunter Command Center......?"

"We surrendered Kamish's remains to the US government upon request because we knew we could leverage them for things better than money." Thomas grinned as he recalled the raid against Kamish. "But I got to keep Kamish's biggest and sharpest fang as a souvenir. Pulled it out myself when the bastard bit me."

No awakened being had been capable of crafting a dragon's fang into a weapon......except one. Thomas explained that since the craftsman who had created these masterpieces had died of old age, however, no other weapon would ever be forged with the dragon's remains.

"At that time, the fang was too short for a sword, so the craftsman made it into these daggers. Looks like it was the right choice after all." Thomas seemed happy as he told Jinwoo about what had happened in the past. He slowly lifted up the case and pushed forward the dragon scale that the daggers had been stabbed into. "These are yours now."

The greatest weapons were finally united with the greatest warrior. Thomas tried to stay calm as he watched Jinwoo's reaction.

Jinwoo pulled out one of the daggers.

Shiiing...

The dagger easily slid out, as if it had been waiting for this moment.

Ping!

A notification sounded, and Jinwoo swallowed hard. Soon, the dagger's stats popped up in front of him.

What?

Jinwoo couldn't believe what he was seeing. It wasn't possible. He summoned the Demon Monarch's Dagger, his main choice of weapon, in order to compare them.

[ITEM: DEMON MONARCH'S DAGGER]
Acquisition Difficulty: S
Category: Dagger
Attack Power: +220
A dagger acquired from Balan the Demon Monarch. When you use both Demon Monarch's Daggers together, the set buff will be applied.

Set Buff: Two in One: Extra attack power equal to the current strength stat will be applied to each dagger.

Jinwoo's strength stat was over 300, so his attack power would be over 500 with the set buff. The set buff alone made it very useful. However, it couldn't compare to the new dagger. He was floored as he stared at the difference between them.

......*Are you kidding me?*

2

KOREA IN CRISIS

2
KOREA IN CRISIS

Jinwoo's gaze was fixed on the daggers made from the fang of Kamish the dragon. He could hardly believe what he was seeing on the info screen.

[ITEM: KAMISH'S WRATH]
Acquisition Difficulty: ??
Category: Dagger
Attack Power: +1,500
A dagger of the best quality made by a master craftsman from the sharpest fang of a dragon.
A weapon with no equal, the dagger's strength can be amplified by the user's own ability due to its superior sensitivity to mana.

All Jinwoo could see was the attack power.

That's the dagger's attack power: 1,500?

The dagger's base attack was 1,500 before possible enhancements. He couldn't wrap his head around it. Since a higher attack power meant an easier time cutting into enemies, fighting with this dagger would probably feel like slicing through butter.

Wait a minute. Is there any other dagger at a similar level?

Jinwoo eagerly pulled up the system shop, not caring about all the eyes on him. The daggers weren't worth comparing to with their usually limited attack power, so Jinwoo searched through the swords instead.

Oh......

The system shop's weapons had always been of excellent quality, but even its most expensive sword was barely above one thousand.

Numbers-wise, it's like I'm holding a sword in each hand!

He felt the heft of the dagger in his grip and sensed an overwhelming urge to slice something, anything.

Thomas noticed the shift in his expression and laughed awkwardly. "Oh my, Mr. Sung. Even if I increase my defense power with an enforcement skill, that dagger will cut right through me. You don't want to kill me with the weapon I just gifted you, do you?"

Jinwoo had no intention of doing that. He chuckled at Thomas's feigned dismay, then focused on the dagger again.

It's sensitive to mana?

In order to find out what being sensitive to mana, or magic power, meant, Jinwoo sent a tiny bit of his own to the dagger.

"Whoa......!"

Bodyguards were supposed to keep silent and not make any unnecessary sounds, but one of them couldn't help but gasp. He quickly slapped his hand over his mouth, but with everyone's attention on Jinwoo, nobody registered his mistake.

"Oh my God......" Despite having witnessed many things in his lifetime, Thomas couldn't help but be astonished by the black aura radiating from the dagger.

The dagger is responding to my magic power......

It wasn't just an aura that was coming out of the dagger. The hefty weight in his hand disappeared instantly, as if it were a mere illusion, leaving a dagger as light as a feather.

Wow......

It was a weapon that adjusted its weight based on the user's fighting style.

Vmmm, vwoooom......

Kamish's Wrath shuddered as if greeting its new master. Jinwoo squeezed the handle as his heart raced.

Ba-dump, ba-dump.

He wasn't sure if this desire was coming from himself or the dagger, but he wanted to fight someone and swing around his new weapon. Jinwoo calmed himself down and stabbed the dagger back into the scale.

Shhhk.

The dagger stopped vibrating, and Laura and the bodyguards exhaled in relief as the black aura dissipated.

Thomas glanced at her.

Still think I made a bad call?

Laura shook her head at the clear question in Thomas's gaze. His decision was absolutely right as long as those two daggers pointed at magic beasts instead of humans. The weapons had found their rightful master. Although Laura was an ordinary human being with no sensitivity to magic power at all, she recognized this at once.

Thomas was delighted that he'd been proven right. "How do you like my gifts, Mr. Sung?"

The most intense expressions of emotion were often shown in gestures instead of words. Jinwoo quietly gave him a thumbs-up.

"Ha-ha-ha!" Thomas slowly clapped as he laughed.

The daggers would represent the friendship between the two men, and Thomas had no regrets at parting with such priceless items if it meant entering Jinwoo's good graces.

Jinwoo didn't feel like it was a fair exchange. "Are you sure I can have them for free?"

"Free?" The smile faded from Thomas's expression. "It's a small price to pay for my life and the lives of my guild members."

In other words, *Shut up and accept them.* Having already received explanations from Laura about the hidden meanings of Thomas's words, Jinwoo laughed.

"In that case, I graciously accept."

"It's my pleasure."

The heartwarming moment was shattered when Jinwoo and Thomas froze simultaneously. Before Laura and the bodyguards could start to panic at the identical looks on their faces, Thomas spoke up.

"Mr. Sung, just now......"

Jinwoo gave a short nod. Chills had run down both their spines because of something situated in the sky. Jinwoo and Thomas shot out of their chairs and rushed to the window.

"......"

Jinwoo groaned, and Thomas's eyes popped out of his head and jaw dropped as they took in the sight of a massive gate facing the earth.

"I can't believe this. I've never seen such a huge gate in my life."

Thomas had been one of the first hunters to awaken, but in his many years, he had never seen a gate of this size before. Even Kamish's gate hadn't been quite so large.

However, Jinwoo had actually seen a similar gate once before in the data the angel statue had presented: the gate the winged soldiers had rushed out from. The one from that memory was identical to the one currently hovering over Seoul. Jinwoo shuddered as he recalled the sky turning black from the sheer number of soldiers.

Was this the source of the incredible amounts of dark matter gathering around Seoul that scientists observed?

Jinwoo was at a loss for words, as were the Americans in the room. A heavy silence fell over the space.

The humongous gate silently shook, as if it were going to swallow everything in the world.

* * *

Those who knew that a newly formed gate wasn't in any danger of a dungeon break gathered below, taking pictures with their cell phones of the gate that blackened the sky.

It was both the first gate to ever appear in midair like this as well as the largest gate of all time. Although there was no telling what creatures it contained, people couldn't resist their curiosity. Among the crowd were foreign reporters, who were busy filming the inquisitive swarm of people.

"Yes, I'm standing under the gate covering the sky of Seoul, South Korea......"
"The gate you see now is the biggest ever recorded since magic beasts first appeared......"
"As you can see, many people have come out to look at the gate. However, the grim expressions on their faces say it all......"
"......this is Nick Falwell from BBN News."

They reported on the situation in their respective languages with solemn expressions.

Japan, which had continued to keep a keen interest in the goings-on of their neighbor, started a special news program dedicated to the gate in the skies of Seoul. They brought on an expert, Dr. Norman Belzer, who had been monitoring the strange phenomenon for some time, and as the host finished introducing him, the doctor held up his microphone.

"I have warned people about the large mass of energy gathering in the sky for a while now. The huge gate appearing over Seoul is just the beginning, and I predict we will see more of these horrifying gates in many countries."

The host shuddered. "Excuse me? Are you saying that you're seeing the warning signs in more places?"

"That is exactly what I would like to emphasize."

Dr. Belzer went on to give the same lecture he'd given the hunters at the International Guild Conference. Because his topic of research presented real-life danger to people, he felt he had a duty to inform others of it. Seoul was only the beginning. There were eight other regions where dark matter was coalescing.

The studio audience gasped and moaned as Dr. Belzer revealed the names of nine locations, along with aerial photographs. While some folks were relieved that Japan wasn't one of the nine locations, others were shocked by the crisis brewing around the world.

The host asked the somber Dr. Belzer, "You have studied gates and magic beasts for a long time, correct?"

"That's right."

"In your opinion, what is the wisest way to handle this situation, Dr. Belzer?"

The audience in the studio and the viewers in front of their TVs awaited his answer with bated breaths. Unfortunately, he didn't have a solution for them.

"We can only pray......" Dr. Belzer looked at those seated in the audience. "Let us pray that this unprecedented situation won't end in tragedy."

As the mood in the studio grew heavy, he remarked, "However, there is a silver lining."

The host brightened at the doctor's declaration right before the end of the show. Perhaps there would be a way to end the broadcast on a positive note.

"What is it, Dr. Belzer?"

"Luckily, the gate is over Korea."

Did the doctor have some personal grudge against Korea? His unexpected statement stirred up the shocked audience. The producer of the show was aghast, worried that Dr. Belzer's comment might spark an international conflict. Thankfully, Dr. Belzer explained himself before the misunderstanding got out of hand.

"Korea has a hunter who has stopped several international disasters."

That hunter's name was quite well-known in Japan as well.

"Yes, I'm referring to Hunter Jinwoo Sung, who took care of the ant-type magic beasts on Jeju Island and defeated the giants in Japan."

Strangely, the strongest hunter in the world resided where the dark matter was most concentrated, and Dr. Belzer didn't think this was a coincidence.

"If Hunter Sung can't stop the gate, no one can. From the rest of the world's point of view, we should be thankful that this gate appeared in Korea of all places."

Should people be thankful or extend their sympathies to Korea?

Dr. Belzer emphasized his point once again to a confused audience. "Koreans may think I'm being cruel in the face of this crisis, but the world needn't lament Korea's situation."

Were the show producer's worries not unfounded after all?

Dr. Belzer seemed to be playing with the frazzled producer's mind at this point, as he proclaimed, "If we ever get to the point where we need to mourn for Korea, there won't *be* anyone left to mourn at all."

* * *

The largest recorded gate until now had been Kamish's gate in the US, but this new gate was easily ten times that size. Its rank was obvious even without an evaluation, but the association stuck to protocol and sent up a helicopter. Everyone on the job was a hunter, as regular employees physically couldn't withstand such large amounts of magic power.

Takakakakaka!

As the pilot, copilot, and two staff members flew toward the gate, they couldn't help but feel as if they were being sucked into a black hole.

One of the employees inside the vibrating helicopter gazed at the massive black circle and asked his colleague, "Sir, have you seen anything like this before?"

They had to rely solely on the light coming from the chopper because the sun had already set, but the darkness did nothing to hide the magnitude of the gate.

The senior employee shook his head. "No, and I'll bet no one else has ever seen a gate this size before, either."

The whole world was in a panic because of this single gate being both an unprecedented size and location. Had they known that even Thomas Andre had been taken aback at the sight, this wouldn't have been a topic of discussion in the first place.

While the employees were trying not to let their fear get to them as they stared at the gate, the helicopter began slowing down as it approached its destination.

The copilot announced, "It's too dangerous to get any closer."

The employees nodded in understanding and prepared to evaluate the gate's rank. Usually, they would go right up to the front of a gate, but that wasn't necessary this time. As soon as they turned on the mana meter, it overloaded and died. As expected, their instruments couldn't handle the amount of magic power coming from the gate.

"Sir."

At the senior employee's nod, the junior employee opened a line of communication to the Hunter's Association in order to report on the result of the evaluation.

Just then, the senior employee spotted something in the distance and yelled, "Look out!"

His colleague flinched and looked around. "Wh-what is it?"

"I think I saw a magic beast right outside......!"

"What? A magic beast? Already?"

It should have been impossible for a magic beast to escape from a gate that was less than a day old, but the senior employee was a high-rank hunter. His perception was much better than anyone else's in the helicopter, and sure enough—

"Over there!" He pointed at what he had seen earlier.

At that moment, Jinchul's urgent voice came over the junior employee's headset.

"What? What are you talking about? Sangwon! Sangwon Yoo! What's going on?"

"P-President Woo, it's a magic beast! A huge magic beast has been sighted near the helicopter!"

"What?!"

"But it doesn't appear to be any ordinary magic beast......"

"You don't stand a chance against a magic beast in the air! That's not what I sent you in to investigate. Land right now!"

"N-no, that's not it, President Woo...... Someone is riding the magic beast!"

"What are you talking about? How could a person ride a magic—?"

Jinchul paused as he recalled a man who did indeed ride a magic beast.

"Sangwon...... Can you see the face of the person riding that magic beast?"

"Stand by. Oh, yes, I can just about make out his face."

"By any chance, is it Hunter Jinwoo Sung?"

"Excuse me?" Sangwon pressed his face against the window and squinted. He then exclaimed, "S-sir, how did you know that?!"

* * *

"Kreeee!"

Jinwoo rode Kaisel the winged dragon up toward the gate. As Kaisel flew directly under it, Jinwoo noted that it was like looking into a bottomless black lake rather than a gate. Its size was overwhelming, and an ordinary hunter would've found the staggering amount of magic power coming from the gate unbearable, but Jinwoo was unfazed.

Judging that it was too dangerous to stick around, the association's helicopter hastily retreated at a lower altitude.

Jinwoo watched them go before heading closer to the gate. The opening faced the earth, and he was now close enough that he could touch. With the black membrane still intact, he had no idea what it was like inside.

......

If he poked it, would he penetrate the surface or would he get sucked in like with a red gate? It was possible he'd be able to take care of it before the dungeon break occurred. Expectantly, Jinwoo placed his hand on the gate's membrane.

Huh?

He had never experienced anything like this in his time as a hunter. The black membrane was as hard as a wall and prevented Jinwoo's hand from going through the gate.

If this was some ordinary wall, I could break through, but......

He pushed against the wall with all his might, but it wouldn't budge.

Knock, knock.

Jinwoo pursed his lips as he knocked on the membrane.

Something's different.

He hadn't heard of a gate that an awakened being couldn't go through. Since this gate was unlike any other, would the inhabitants also differ from the usual magic beasts?

Whatever they are......

Jinwoo had family and friends he needed to protect, so he had no intention of letting whatever was in there anywhere near them. He had increased stats and intrepid soldiers on his side.

""""Raaaaaah!""""

His army roared in response.

Ba-dump.

Jinwoo felt a mix of unease and excitement. He'd never felt this way before. He'd always assumed that there was a reason why he had been chosen as the Player and granted this power by the system. Maybe it was to deal with this.

I'm being silly......

Jinwoo laughed at how emotional he'd suddenly gotten and took his hand off the gate.

At that moment, his phone began to vibrate in his pocket. The phone call was one he'd been waiting for from the Hunter's Association of Japan.

"Hello? Hunter Sung?"

"Yes, this is he."

"My apologies, but it's hard to hear you. Should I call back another time?"

Jinwoo smirked at the buildings below him. At this distance, they looked like tiny toy blocks. "No, that's fine. I'm somewhere high up. Is this about my request?"

"Oh, yes. I scanned all of Japan via satellite just now, but……"

Uncharacteristically, the representative from the Hunter's Association of Japan seemed to be at a loss for words. Had something bad also happened in Japan?

Jinwoo never would've guessed what the representative said next.

"There is no gate. Not a single new gate has spawned in Japan."

……!

After defeating the giants, Jinwoo had spent most of his time raiding dungeons in Japan, so this hit him like a bolt out of the blue. "Not one?"

"Yes, that's right. I contacted hunter-related organizations in other countries in case this was an isolated case, and I discovered that……"

The representative hesitated, then continued, clearly vexed.

"Ever since that gate appeared over Seoul, all others have disappeared."

It had been three hours since the appearance of the monolithic gate. What were the odds of every single gate in the world vanishing during that three-hour window?

……*That can't be a coincidence.*

Stunned, Jinwoo wordlessly stared at the black mass above him.

The representative cautiously probed him.

"Um…… Excuse me, but may I ask why you wanted me to locate the highest-rank gate we had?"

"……" Jinwoo didn't know how to answer that. How could he explain that he wanted to try out Thomas's gift of 1,500 attack power before this gate opened?

"Even if tomorrow the world would go to pieces, someone still has to plant an apple tree, you know?"

"Oh…… Apple trees. I see. Such a great saying."

Jinwoo was about to hang up after giving his vague answer, but the representative had something to get off his chest.

"Um, Hunter Sung?"

"Yes?"

The representative faltered as if embarrassed, then confessed.

"I was never a fan of Korea. As you know, those ants from Jeju Island were a real headache for the Hunter's Association of Japan for the past few years. As a Japanese person and an employee of the association, I didn't hold Korea in the highest regard."

Jinwoo quietly listened to what the man had to say.

"However, it was you who changed my mind. Korea saved us. I am truly grateful to both you and your country."

The representative began to sob.

"From the bottom of my heart, I hope that Korea doesn't go through the horrors we experienced."

Giants crushing humans underfoot, cities burning, screams echoing, and the never-ending despair. It hadn't been long since that waking nightmare, and the representative had experienced it firsthand. No one should ever have to go through that.

Jinwoo replied softly, "That won't happen."

That wasn't a promise but a declaration. He had consistently pushed himself in the pursuit of leveling up for this very reason, and it was time to show the fruits of his labor.

The employee chuckled at his answer.

"Ha-ha! I never thought I'd ever be jealous of Korea, but I envy them for having you, Hunter Sung."

"No need to butter me up. I've got nothing else going on besides hunting magic beasts, so I'll keep visiting Japan as long as magic beasts show up there."

"Whoops, you got me. I can't slip anything by you, can I? And here I was, trying to score some points with you."

The representative was thankful that Jinwoo had lightened the mood with banter, and he bid the Korean a sincere farewell.

"Please keep in touch."

"I will."

Jinwoo tucked his phone back in his pocket, then inspected the gate before him. It was eerily quiet like the calm before a storm.

If the time line for a dungeon break hasn't changed......

There were about six days left. Jinwoo's eyes shone in the dark of the night.

"......Let's head down."

"Kreeee!"

With a flap of his huge wings, Kaisel began his descent.

* * *

The public also noticed the change the next day. Gates had disappeared, and no new ones had spawned after the monolithic gate appeared in the skies above Seoul. No one knew if this was good or bad, but there were those who welcomed the news, including President Woo and the Hunter's Association of Korea.

After apprehensively listening to the report, Jinchul came to a decision. "Let's summon all the hunters in Korea to Seoul."

"Sir? That's too risky."

"If there's an undetected gate and a dungeon break happens, then......"

"How about summoning half of the hunters and leaving the rest where they are?"

As he continued to receive opposition, Jinchul slammed his hand on the conference room table.

Bam!

Everyone cowered at the display of rage by such a high-ranking hunter.

Jinchul bared his teeth. "Do you think we have the luxury to take *what ifs* into account?"

Everyone in the meeting room fell silent as Jinchul waved a hand toward the outside of the room and bellowed at them. "This is an unprecedented situation. Even if we pour every resource into stopping this fucking thing, there's still no guarantee we'll win!"

He looked around the room. "I'll take full responsibility for any damage that occurs in other areas, whether that means giving up everything I own or laying down my life to fight."

After this clear display of his resolution, no one dared argue with him.

Leaders have been known to kill their own squadmates in a dungeon if they didn't fall in line during life-and-death situations, as insubordination could lead to an entire squad's demise. It would be a crime outside of a dungeon, but dungeons followed different rules. Raids were wars with people's lives on the line, not playtime. And now, war was about to break out not inside of a dungeon but on their own turf. Time was of the essence, and Jinchul wasn't a slipshod hunter who would waste precious seconds hearing out the opposition.

"Summon all our hunters to Seoul immediately. Do not excuse anyone who is able to fight."

Under Jinchul's orders, every single Korean hunter converged in Seoul.

* * *

It was a rather unusual sight. The roads of Seoul were congested because of the citizens leaving the city and the hunters coming in to protect it. At the Hunter's Association's and government's urging, residents in the areas directly under the hovering gate were evacuating to avoid the inevitable destruction.

As they watched the evacuation on TV, Jinwoo turned to his mom. "Shouldn't you and Jinah go somewhere else, too?"

"Our neighborhood isn't in the evacuation zone."

It appeared Kyunghye had no plans to leave Seoul. Their run-down apartment building was on the outskirts of the city, so the magic beasts would have to get past the defensive line of hunters to reach them. That would mean that Jinwoo would have failed on the front line. Kyunghye had faith that the flames of this crisis would never get far enough to reach them.

Jinwoo returned her smile and dropped the matter.

Kyunghye and Jinwoo were sitting on the floor in front of the couch, around the coffee table, while Jinah sat on the couch hugging her knees. She looked down at her brother.

"You don't have to go?"

They'd put out an official call for hunters, but Jinwoo was already based in Seoul, so it didn't apply to him.

"That's only for the hunters coming from outside of Seoul. They need to report to the association once they arrive."

"Oh." Jinah nodded as she accepted a plate of apple slices from her mother.

Truthfully, Jinwoo was feeling jittery about staying put and doing nothing at this time. He wanted to level up, but there were no magic beasts, and he hadn't received any more keys to instance dungeons since he got rid of the Architect. Jinwoo's family may have been happy that he was spending more time at home, but the man himself was itching to train.

Should I skip the daily quest and go to the penalty zone?

While it was enticing, it wasn't necessarily a good idea. Like the gate in the sky, he also had no idea what monster would await him in the penalty zone.

The risk may be low, but......

There was a one-in-a-million chance that it could put him out of commission. No need to go out of his way to take another risk at this very moment. And so he dismissed the idea. He'd have to find another way to test Kamish's Wrath, but what?

Jinwoo was deep in thought when footage of the Hunter's Association building on TV caught his eye.

Now, there's an idea.

Jinwoo's eyes sparkled, and he couldn't stop the smile spreading across his face.

Riiing, riiing!

The other party picked up quickly, as he always had.

"Yes, Hunter Sung. This is Jinchul Woo."

"I should call you President Woo now, shouldn't I?"

Jinchul gave an embarrassed laugh.

"You can call me whatever you like. I'm in over my head, so it still feels rather awkward to be called president."

After their brief greeting, the amusement faded from Jinchul's voice.

"Did something happen? I can't help but be worried that you're contacting me out of the blue."

With the association currently in crisis mode, Jinchul had been keeping his ear to the ground, so of course a sudden phone call from the nation's most influential hunter would put him on edge.

"It's nothing serious, but......"

Jinchul gulped nervously.

"Not serious" by Hunter's Sung's standards could mean a disaster by ours. Heck, the odds of it being an emergency are higher *the more nonchalant he* is.

Jinchul attempted to calm his nerves and listen attentively during Jinwoo's brief pause...but it truly was nothing serious.

"May I use the association gym?"

* * *

Despite his busy schedule, Jinchul personally escorted Jinwoo to the Hunter's Association's gymnasium.

"As you can see......this is the current state of it."

Jinwoo frowned. He had wanted to use the gym as a quiet place away from prying eyes, but it was already packed to the brim with hunters.

Seeing the weapons in their hands, Jinwoo belatedly recalled the association's stockpile in the storage of the gym. "Are you providing weapons to the hunters who don't have proper gear?"

"Yes. After all, President Go had prepared them for a time like this."

Jinwoo nodded. This was what he wanted to show those who had criticized the Hunter's Association for wasting money on weapons that the association seemed to be hoarding.

The tension was palpable as the hunters donned their borrowed equipment. At that moment, a heavyset hunter made eye contact with Jinwoo while struggling to get his arm into a piece of mana-coated armor.

"Huh?" In his shock at seeing the world's greatest hunter right before his eyes, he blurted out, "Hunter Jinwoo Sung?"

"What?"

"Hunter Sung is here?"

The hunters looked over their shoulders, and sure enough, there stood Jinwoo next to the president of the Hunter's Association, watching them.

A hush fell inside the gym, and the air grew heavy. The man before their very eyes was at the top of their field, and his overwhelming presence wasn't something that could be conveyed through TV screens. Their hearts began to pound as they set their eyes on the best of the best.

Ba-dump, ba-dump, ba-dump!

The hunters grew excited. Some shot him envious looks while others gazed upon him with admiration.

It finally sank in why Jinchul had called him here to talk instead of explaining the situation on the phone. The hunters gathered here were low-rank hunters who couldn't afford expensive gear. Being suddenly summoned here must've been mentally taxing for them, so the new president of the Hunter's Association wanted to embolden them by introducing them to their strongest ally.

Based on the lively look in their eyes, the plan had worked. Jinchul had led the Surveillance Team for a long time, and the quick-witted thinking that came from his experience brought a smile to Jinwoo's face.

Jinchul sheepishly rubbed the back of his neck as Jinwoo caught on to him. "So, Hunter Sung, why did you need the gym?"

Jinwoo summoned an item from his inventory while pretending to take it out of his pocket. "I'm going to use this."

Jinchul cocked his head at the seed the size of a plum in Jinwoo's hand. "And......what is this?"

"If you plant this in the ground, a magic beast resembling a tree will spawn. There is something I need to try out on a magic beast."

"Did you say a *magic beast* would grow?" Jinchul's eyes widened as Jinwoo nodded.

A tree-type magic beast had spat out this seed as it let loose a dying screech. If the seed wasn't destroyed, another magic beast would grow out of it. Tree-type magic beasts had a high defense and formidable stamina, so it was inefficient to hunt them again and again. Jinwoo had destroyed all the seeds except the one expelled by the dungeon boss, keeping it in his inventory just in case he saw an opportunity to use it. Because their skin was tough to cut through, as if they had iron armor on, Jinwoo had named these magic beasts Ironclad Trees.

It'll be the perfect guinea pig to test out my new daggers.

The problem was......

"People will panic if they see this magic beast, especially in these times." Jinchul spoke with concern.

Jinwoo agreed. "That's why I need somewhere private, quiet, and durable......"

No one outside the Hunter's Association could access the gym, and it was reinforced to allow hunters to train without worry. Jinwoo turned back toward the other hunters. Many of them gripped their association-issued weapons tightly as they peeked at him, finding encouragement at the sight of him.

"But since it's like this......" Jinwoo clicked his tongue, disappointed.

He could go to an uninhabited area of Japan, but it was too far to fly there for that sole purpose, and he didn't want to waste the Shadow Exchange skill. Who knew what might happen during the two hours he was over there?

Jinwoo was about to leave when Jinchul made up his mind. "Okay."

"Pardon me?"

"I will clear this afternoon's schedule and make the gym available to you. Considering how much you've done for us, you couldn't even call it special treatment."

The late President Go had gone so far as to amend laws for Jinwoo, saying that they couldn't ask a hunter of Jinwoo's caliber to put his life on the line for them if they weren't willing to do at least that for his sake. The least Jinchul could do as President Go's successor was let Jinwoo borrow the gym.

"Are you sure that's okay?"

Jinchul had to grin at Jinwoo's concern. "I may not look it, but I'm the person in charge of this organization. I'm the one who decides whether the gym is open or closed."

He then clapped his hands to get everyone's attention before calling out, "Who's in charge of the gym?"

"Me, sir!"

As Jinwoo watched the staffer hastily make his way toward them, he realized that whether one was qualified for it or not, securing a higher position was the way to go.

* * *

Thomas watched the Seoul streets congested with cars evacuating the city from his hotel room window in a luxury hotel.

Laura approached him from behind with her packed suitcase. "Will you stay here, sir?"

"Yeah." Thomas tapped the window, pointing at the gate. "How could I leave with that big, beautiful thing there?"

"It's certainly huge, but beautiful......?" Laura was used to Thomas's eccentricities, but she was taken aback that he would call something so ominous and grotesque beautiful.

Thomas turned around to look at the perplexed manager.

"That which makes my heart race is beautiful." He put his hand on his chest to feel his heartbeat. Ever since he'd laid eyes on the gate, his heart had continued to pound loudly. "That fire-breathing dragon, this humongous gate, Hunter Sung's power...... They're all beautiful to me."

Thomas was not your average man. Laura chuckled as she shook her head.

Thomas let his hand drop and smirked. "Even if I did go back to the US, what would I do with no more gates spawning?"

"But......the Hunter Command Center is worried about you."

Worried about Thomas, she said. Thomas laughed at the prospect of someone being concerned for his safety. "Just hearing that makes me laugh. Besides, there's no safer place in the world than wherever Hunter Sung is."

Laura couldn't refute that. It was no longer a secret that the Hunter Command Center had asked Jinwoo to protect the top-ranked hunters of the world. Thomas smiled at the speechless Laura, then turned back to the window and the monolithic gate quietly vibrating in the sky over Seoul.

"If that thing isn't stopped here, there's no future for humanity anyway."

If Jinwoo couldn't end things here, the same disaster would happen eight more times. Then who could stop those? Thomas? Zhigang Liu of China or the other national-level hunters? No way.

"That's why I want to see it with my own eyes." Thomas continued while smiling at Laura's reflection in the window. "This will either be the end of human history or a new beginning."

* * *

Jinwoo walked to the middle of the large, empty gym.

Here is good.

He put the seed on the floor and poured water on it. He had confirmed several times that this was all a magic beast needed to grow. No soil or even sunlight was needed.

Krik, kriiiiik!

The seed quickly transformed into a tree, accompanied by the sound of cracking bones.

"Whoa."

No matter how many times he witnessed this, it was always a sight to see. Tree-type magic beasts had an incredible vitality that allowed them to survive even in the harshest environments.

Jinwoo withdrew to a safe distance.

Graaaaah! Gaaah!

The sapling kept growing, and in less than five minutes, it had transformed into a huge magic beast whose head nearly grazed the ceiling of the gym.

Graaaaaah!

Jinwoo ignored the tree's screech echoing inside the gym and summoned the recently upgraded Beru.

Come out.

Beru emerged from the ground.

My king!

His visibly changed appearance caught Jinwoo's attention. Instead of an insect's exoskeleton, he wore fitted black armor that made him look much sturdier than before. But that wasn't all. The black smoke coming from Beru's entire body was more intense. Instead of a haze, it was now reminiscent of burning flames. His power was overwhelming!

Jinwoo opened Beru's stat window.

[BERU LV.MAX]
Marshal Rank
The marshal acts as the leader of the army, of which there can be only one. If more than one soldier reaches the marshal rank, a hierarchy must be decided.

The only ones who can possibly challenge the marshal rank are Greed and Igris, who are close to leveling up to the general rank......

Jinwoo imagined it would be fun to watch the three soldiers battle for the top position, then gestured at the tree in front of them with his chin.

"Beru, attack it with your full power."

Following his king's order, Beru expanded his body and howled.

"Skraaaaaaaah!"

It was the roar of a true beast. Beru's armor also transformed to fit his augmented frame. Once he was twice his normal size, he stomped toward the tree, then broke into a run, aiming full tilt at the Ironclad Tree.

Bam!

Beru's eyes widened. The tree should've snapped in half, but he'd managed only to dig a hole as deep as his wrist. This flustered the soldier who had previously ripped S-rank magic beasts apart like they were nothing. But Ironclad Trees were known for their defense power against physical attacks and their resistance to damages that weren't magic-based.

This was good enough for Jinwoo. Satisfied with the result, he ordered Beru to stand down.

"Step aside."

Beru drew back as Jinwoo called up the two Kamish's Wrath daggers from his inventory.

Vwoooom.

The daggers appeared in his hands.

Okay.

Gyaaaaah!

The Ironclad Tree whirled around, looking for the opponent who had punctured its stomach; its eyes landed on Jinwoo instead and lumbered toward him. Seeing how slow it was, Jinwoo realized this magic beast really had nothing going for it except its high defense. That being said, its defense was nothing to laugh at.

How well would Kamish's Wrath work against it? Black energy spread out from the tips of his fingers and wrapped around the daggers.

I need brute strength.

As soon as he made the call, the two daggers became as heavy as a thousand weights, so heavy that Jinwoo's arms and shoulders strained to hold them up.

Time to see what 1,500 attack power can do.

The blades of the two daggers began to quiver as if channeling Kamish's wrath. As the Ironclad Tree had managed to make its way to Jinwoo, he stared it down and spun the daggers around to hold them in a reverse grip.

Let's take it easy.

He made a diagonal slash with his right hand.

Swish!

The sound of the air splitting was followed by the thud of something hitting the floor.

"……Hmm?"

The Ironclad Tree looked down. One of its thick, armlike branches had been cleanly lopped off and now lay on the ground. The magic beast discovered a wound bleeding tree sap and let out an ear-piercing roar.

Gyaaaaah!

The tree might have been in pain, but Jinwoo was bursting with joy. He stared with amazement at the dagger that had easily sliced through the branch that had been as wide as a post.

Wow.

All it had taken was a gentle swing of the dagger. Jinwoo could hack at the tree with the Demon Monarch's dagger for eternity, and it still wouldn't do this type of damage to a regular tree, much less the boss. It was like slicing through butter. The dagger also felt great in his hand.

Vmmm……

It'd been a while since he'd been this excited about a weapon.

My king!

Beru called out urgently to him from his vantage point.

I know.

Jinwoo's response was relaxed as he glanced up. The Ironclad Tree had gone from upset to enraged. With its right appendage missing, the magic beast raised its left branch to try and crush Jinwoo, but it was already too late.

Another quick slice of Kamish's Wrath and……

Shk!

Gaaaah! The Ironclad Tree screeched, having lost both arms.

Awesome.

Jinwoo nodded. He had verified what the daggers could do when swinging them around lightly. Now it was time to test how they performed when used to their full potential.

The daggers respond excellently to magic power because they're made from dragon's bone, right?

Jinwoo squeezed the dagger and poured mana into it. Then more mana. Then even more. When he focused every drop of his magic power into his right hand, he could see the black aura surrounding the blade practically exploding.

From Beru's point of view, it looked like the aura distorted everything in the area. How was that possible?! Beru stumbled back instinctively. Though his mind knew that it wasn't aimed at him, the sheer power forced him to retreat a few steps. Beru looked at his trembling hands.

My liege......

When it came to emotions, Beru had only ever felt loyalty toward Jinwoo, but for the first time, he learned how it felt to pity someone.

The Ironclad Tree was unaware of its fate as it bellowed. *Gyaaaaaaah!*

Its bloodshot eyes were focused solely on Jinwoo. Its mouth was a gaping maw as wide as the building's entrance. It heaved its huge body forward to try to swallow Jinwoo whole.

Jinwoo unleashed the concentrated magic power from the tip of the dagger.

Go!

He held nothing back, just as he had ordered Beru. Jinwoo threw his whole body, from his toes, legs, hips, shoulders, and even wrists into the attack. And the result was......

What?

He realized something was very wrong.

Ack!

Shhk, shhk, shhk, shhk, shhk, shhk!

The black aura had shot from the tip of the dagger, slashing everything in front of it like the claws of a ferocious animal swiping the air. Jinwoo's enhanced eyesight allowed him to see the exact hundredth of a second the aura ripped the Ironclad Tree apart.

Shit!

The unstoppable power of the dagger left horrific marks on the gym's floor and walls behind the tree.

"Damn......" Jinwoo was speechless.

Klak!

Tmp, tmp......

Little chunks of concrete tumbled from the large slash in the wall until the entire thing came crumbling down, unable to withstand the damage.

Rrrrumble!

Thud!

The walls of the gym had been reinforced with magic power so that hunters could train without holding back, yet one side of the wall had collapsed from the single hit. Jinwoo looked at the rubble on the ground, appalled.

"Is this what the system meant by the strength of the weapons depending on the user?"

These magic-powered daggers made from dragon remains were the real deal.

My liege! Beru was so overcome with emotion by his king's display of power that he flung himself to his knees in front of Jinwoo. *Your humble servant cannot contain his awe at your might and power!*

"......"

Unfortunately for his mother, who loved historical dramas, Jinwoo was this close to banning them in the house. Still, he understood why Beru was so riled up. Jinwoo's own heart was racing at this unimaginable power.

These were the traces of Kamish's Wrath. Would a blow from a dragon large enough to block out the sky cause this much destruction? Jinwoo sucked his teeth as he took in the Ironclad Tree's gruesome remains, the collapsed wall, and the gouged-out floor.

I should name these daggers Dragon's Claw instead of Kamish's Wrath.

Of course, the daggers were this powerful only because Jinwoo was wielding them.

At that moment, a message popped up.

[Would you like to change the name of Item: Kamish's Wrath to Item: Dragon's Claw?]

Jinwoo was caught off guard by the system's unexpected response.

I can change the name?

He quickly canceled the order and breathed a sigh of relief when he saw the name hadn't changed.

"Whew."

That was a close call. The craftsman would roll over in his grave if the name was changed to a cringey name like Dragon's Claw. Jinwoo couldn't help but laugh at the system's ever-so-literal interactions.

In any case, he was more than satisfied with the power of his new weapons. Their sharpness and destructive power were on an entirely different level from his previous ones. Jinwoo smiled as he looked between them and then returned them to the inventory.

Now that the practice run is done......

It was time to clean up. As he came off the high of the power of his new weapons, his heart ached at the sight of the collapsed wall of the gym. He'd only meant to borrow the gym for an afternoon and had ended up destroying it. What to do......?

Jinwoo pondered his next course of action and then called Jinchul. "President Woo, please stay calm and hear me out first. I have about three hundred ants who are excellent at manual labor, so......"

* * *

It had been three days since the gates disappeared. Jinwoo had kept himself busy with raids before then, but now he had nothing but free time. Instead, he lay in his bed, and like a bored student spinning a pen, he used Ruler's Authority to spin one of the Kamish's Wrath daggers.

He was interrupted by Jinah, who suddenly barged in on her way to the bathroom. When she opened his bedroom door, he sent the dagger back to inventory and pretended to do something else.

"You were spinning a dagger again, weren't you?"

Technically, he was training his Ruler's Authority skill, but from a doting little sister's point of view, it just looked like he was playing a dangerous game.

"Nope."

Jinah squinted at her brother. He had gotten rid of the evidence, so although he was acting suspicious, she couldn't prove anything. As an ordinary human, there wasn't much she could do to catch her S-rank brother in a lie if he was going out of his way to look innocent.

She stared at him through narrowed eyes for a few moments before eventually sighing. "Jinwoo."

"Yeah?"

"If you're that bored, why don't you get out of the house? You haven't taken a day off in a while."

She sounded like a mother nagging her son.

Jinwoo chuckled and closed his eyes. "What would I do?"

"Can't you make plans with someone? Like with a friend?"

A friend, huh? Jinwoo opened his eyes again as the words stuck in his head. Many people came to mind, but one stood out.

She was probably in the same boat as he and every other hunter, forced to take a breather right now, and he still hadn't made good on his vow to treat her to a meal for accidentally getting a glimpse of her in the shower through his shadow soldier. He usually couldn't see her because they were both so busy, so this was the perfect opportunity. She might be spinning a dagger just like Jinwoo because she was bored out of her mind, for all he knew.

"Good idea, sis."

Jinah flinched as Jinwoo suddenly bolted up from bed and strode over to her.

"H-huh?"

"Excuse me." Jinwoo passed his sister en route to the bathroom.

She caught the unfamiliar look on his face and called after him. "Wait, where are you going?"

Jinwoo grinned at her. "On a date."

* * *

"Enough."

Haein stopped swinging her wooden sword. She had practiced her swordsmanship until her white training uniform was soaked through with sweat. She turned around to face the master of the dojo, an older man in a similar uniform who was missing an arm. He gestured for her to sit down, and Haein did so, kneeling politely as she put down her wooden sword.

The old man was her swordsmanship teacher. As an S-rank hunter, she was nearly unmatched physically, but she still needed to train skills that played to her strengths. Hence, Haein had chosen this quiet *kumdo* dojo to practice the way of the sword whenever she had had time.

Her teacher, Chiyul Song, who was proud of her for never wasting a single day, sat down across from her. "I sense much hesitation in your sword lately, Haein."

His words compelled Haein to look up, her face grim.

Chiyul made eye contact and continued softly. "I'm concerned that you may have developed fear in your heart."

"......"

Haein said nothing, but she didn't have to. In addition to running a dojo, Chiyul went on raids as a hunter whenever the association requested his assistance, so he understood her fears.

No one had ever seen a gate like the monolith before. There was no telling what kind of terrifying creatures would come out of it. Even the strongest people knew fear. In fact, the strong felt a fear in their bones that ordinary people would never know.

Chiyul let his eyes shut and slowly nodded as he reflected on his past. "Of course you're scared. Why wouldn't you be? I've been there. I can't compare the magic beasts I've met to the magic beasts you've encountered, but that time I lost my arm......"

At that moment, the phone that Haein had tucked away in the corner so she wouldn't be disturbed began to ring.

"How can a hunter not answer her phone?"

"I'm sorry, master." Haein bowed in apology and ran to pick up.

As Chiyul waited for her to wrap up her call so he could finish his story, he noticed a delighted look on her face.

Hmm......?

Haein tried her best to hide it, but because she was usually rather expressionless, Chiyul caught the change in her expression.

Haein walked back to Chiyul after hanging up and cautiously told him, "Master, um...something came up, so I have to go."

Her cheeks were flushed. Seeing her eyes lit up, Chiyul realized he may have made the wrong assumption. The hesitation he had seen in her sword hadn't come from fear.

"Of course. Get going, then." Bewildered, Chiyul nodded and gave her leave.

"I'll be off." Haein left with a spring in her step.

Chiyul gave a bemused smile as he watched her go. "I see...... So that's it."

Ha-ha.

Chiyul wondered who was lucky enough to garner the affections of such a charming and sincere young woman. Seeing his esteemed pupil so happy gratified him as well.

* * *

"Isn't that Hunter Jinwoo Sung?"

"What, where?"

"Damn...... It really is Jinwoo Sung!"

The amusement park was packed with weekend visitors who recognized Jinwoo and gawked at him in amazement.

"Who's the woman with him? His girlfriend?"

"Wait a minute...... Isn't that Hunter Haein Cha from the Hunters Guild?"

"Seriously?! Whoa!"

"Those two are dating?"

Jinwoo was accompanied by a woman with a short and neat hairstyle that allowed her to move freely.

Not used to having so much attention on her, she lowered her head and murmured to Jinwoo, "Do you like these kinds of places?"

Jinwoo answered with a smile. "Not particularly, but I've always wanted to come to a place like this at least once."

Gone was the ice-cold glare he had when killing magic beasts. The man next to Haein had an impish grin on his face, and she couldn't help but notice how her heart sped up at the sight. Jinwoo was an outstanding S-rank hunter, so there was no way he didn't notice her racing heart, either. She flushed at the realization.

She asked another question in an attempt to distract him. "So why me......?"

"Because you're the only friend I have."

"Pardon?"

When had Jinwoo and Haein become friends? Haein looked up at him as she tried to recall, and Jinwoo smiled mischievously when their eyes met.

"That's what you said to that weird statue, right......?"

Oh, that. The day she had entered the double dungeon to save him, she'd said something to that effect to the angel statue inside.

"What is your relationship to Jinwoo Sung?"
"......We're friends."

Jinwoo was most likely referring to that.

"You were listening to us?"

"More like, I overheard you. My hearing is better than most."

It was slightly mortifying that instead of helping him, he'd ended up coming to her rescue. That was one of many times he'd saved her life.

"By the way...... What was the deal with that strange dungeon?"

Jinwoo had promised to explain it to her someday, but he didn't think the time was right just yet. "I need to process some of my thoughts first. I still don't fully know what's what right now, but I'll tell you once I do."

Haein nodded in understanding. As the conversation came to a lull, Jinwoo looked around them.

"Over here! Please look over here, too!"

"I'm a big fan, Hunter Sung!"

People had gathered around the couple like a swarm of bees, holding up their cell phones as if they'd run into celebrities on a busy street. In fact, most of them were more familiar with Jinwoo's face than they were with most of the A-list celebrities out there, since he had been shown on every TV channel after the appearance of the monolithic gate.

Normally, Jinwoo would've shrugged it off with a smile, but he didn't want anything to interrupt this day off with a friend.

Come out.

His hardworking, unpaid bodyguards, Igris and the thirty elite knights, emerged from the shadows and surrounded Jinwoo and Haein in a circle. Igris especially got to work, admonishing individuals taking flash photography with a wag of his index finger. Haein was flustered by their escort of knights.

"Doesn't this just draw more attention?"

"As long as we can't see the crowd, you know?"

Haein found herself nodding at the strangely persuasive logic of his statement. She did feel more relaxed shielded from the mob.

When was the last time she'd left her house to do something fun? Haein had become a hunter two years ago, and she had never felt fully comfortable with taking a day off in that time. Mostly, she worried that her colleagues would get hurt when she wasn't on the job. At the same time, she worried about doing a bad job on every raid she participated in. Haein was always nervous and tense in some way. However......

It's different when I'm with this man.

She could depend on him. When Haein was with Jinwoo, she could forget about work and her colleagues' expectations, and she felt like she could go back to being a regular woman living her life.

Haein took a step closer to Jinwoo without realizing it and blushed.

He smells nice......

Looking at Haein's content expression, Jinwoo had just one regret.

I should've done this sooner.

He scanned the various attractions and pointed at a drop tower.

"Do you wanna go on that?"

"Sure."

At the quick agreement, Jinwoo pointed at another ride.

"What about that one?"

"Okay."

"Or the one beside it?"

"That looks good, too."

"Are you up for all of them?"

"Yes, I am."

Jinwoo gazed down at the blushing woman next to him and chuckled.

Huh, I guess I wasn't the only one who wanted to come here.

He was relieved that she seemed to be enjoying herself. He gently grabbed her by the wrist and led her to the nearest ride.

"Then let's go on all of them."

* * *

Unfortunately, the ride wasn't as fun as he had hoped.

"Eeeeek! Eeeek!"

"Ahhh!"

Jinwoo had snagged a front seat, but while everyone behind him screamed their heads off, he watched the goings-on of the park as it zipped by.

Hmm? That kid's gonna drop his ice cream. Oh dear, I knew it. Wait, is the food court over there? But it's too early to eat dinner......

Jinwoo was bored. As soon as the roller coaster started going at full throttle, his surroundings began to move like a slow-motion video. He could probably ride this roller coaster standing up if he wanted to.

......

He tried very hard not to yawn as he looked over his shoulder. Behind him were Igris and a few other soldiers who had wanted to go on the ride, and behind them were civilians screaming with glee. Their facial muscles expressed their thrill and enjoyment. He could hear their hearts beating so hard, they sounded like they were about to explode.

Jinwoo put his hand on his chest to feel his own heart. He gave a wry smile as he felt his usual heartbeat. Leaping up with all his might to smash his fist into the humongous stone statue—now, *that* was thrilling.

And that time I was chased by those centipedes in the Penalty Zone?

That had been ten thousand times scarier than this. Jinwoo shook his head to get rid of these thoughts.

Look at me thinking about monsters when I came all this way to have fun.

He couldn't believe himself. And judging by the expression on his companion's face, she was in the same predicament. Jinwoo chortled and pulled Haein out of her thoughts.

"You aren't enjoying this, are you?"

"Oh...... No, I am."

He appreciated that he didn't have to yell, since she also had heightened senses.

"So how come you didn't scream once?"

This was the fifth ride they had been on. Every ride had claimed to be full of thrills, but Haein hadn't even let out a surprised "oh." Haein was an S-rank hunter as well, and though she wasn't as powerful as Jinwoo, she was above and beyond ordinary people.

Jinwoo was relieved to see that it wasn't just him. At that moment, he was filled with a desire to show her the world through his eyes. Beru detected Jinwoo's intention and tried to stop him.

My king...... That might be dangerous for this woman.

It's okay. If Haein falls, you make sure to catch her no matter what. And if you miss her......you know what'll happen, right?

......As you wish, my liege.

With no one else to stop him, Jinwoo turned to Haein. "Never mind these rides. Do you want to try something super fun?"

"Something......super fun?"

As soon as the roller coaster stopped, Jinwoo led an intrigued Haein to the main plaza.

"Wow!"

People were amazed by the sight of the black knights guarding the couple, but their exclamations soon turned to screams.

"Ahhh!"

"What is that?!"

The shadow soldiers pushed back the crowd to make space for a huge black magic beast that rose from the ground. It flapped its wings and roared at the sky.

"Kreeeee!"

It was the first time Haein had seen a winged dragon this close. Her reaction wasn't much different from the onlookers'.

"O-oh my goodness......!" Haein stared at the creature in front of her.

Jinwoo gestured to her. "Quick, hop on."

She seemed thrown for a loop as she spotted him already astride the winged dragon.

"You......you want me to get on that?"

"Mm-hmm."

He impatiently lifted her up using Ruler's Authority.

"Oh!" Haein was caught off guard by the pull of the invisible force.

But that was only the first of the reactions Jinwoo was expecting from her. It was merely the beginning. Haein's jaw hung open as she was situated behind Jinwoo.

He gave an order to the dragon. "Let's fly."

"Kreeee!"

As if he had been waiting for this moment, Kaisel flapped his enormous wings and launched into the sky. Haein gulped as she looked down at the people getting farther and farther away. This sensation was incomparable to riding a roller coaster.

Her arms naturally wrapped around Jinwoo's waist. When they were high enough that the onlookers were out of view, Haein yelled.

"O-over there!"

"Pardon?"

"Why is that ant following us?"

Jinwoo craned his neck down and saw that Beru was closely following behind Kaisel. Jinwoo couldn't help but laugh at seeing Beru's face scrunched in concentration.

"He's a lifeguard!"

"Sorry?"

"Hang on tight. The real ride starts now."

"What?!"

But there was no need to explain further. Jinwoo felt Haein's arms tighten around his waist.

If I was an ordinary man, she would've folded me in half.

It was a testament to how frightened she was. On the other hand, Jinwoo was excited that his plan was going swimmingly so far.

"Kaisel! Maximum speed!"

"Kreeee!"

As Kaisel shot off, Haein screamed for the first time that day.

* * *

The small dragon split the air as he sped along.

Whoosh!

Kaisel took the couple to places only S-rank hunters could go. They ventured inside a rainy, windy storm cloud. They flew dangerously close to a high mountain and over an endless field of snow. Of all the places they went, the best by far was watching the sun set over the ocean. Kaisel slowed down, and the ocean breeze caressed their cheeks as the two watched the sun disappear into the horizon against an orange-colored sky. Haein's eyes shone like the crimson-tinged sky as she took in the marvelous sight.

A question suddenly struck her. "Jinwoo."

"Yes?"

"Why did you even bother with the amusement park?"

"That amusement park......" Jinwoo took his time in collecting his thoughts. "That's where I lost my father to a gate."

"Oh."

If Jinwoo's father had failed to close the gate and a dungeon break had happened, the amusement park would no longer be there, but thanks to his sacrifice, it was open and thriving. At first, Jinwoo had resented his father for leaving his family behind. But somehow, seeing other families having fun there was comforting. And that was good enough for him.

"I always wanted to go there at least once."

In response, Haein simply hugged him without saying a word. He could feel her warmth on his back.

"Thank you."

Surprised, Jinwoo tried to look back at Haein, but she was clinging too closely to him.

"What?"

"I wanted to......make sure to properly thank you. You've helped me in so many ways."

Jinwoo could sense her sincerity as her body rested on his back, her breath ghosting over his neck and her heart causing a ruckus.

Yes, that was good enough.

Jinwoo smiled softly as he directed Kaisel to reverse course.

"Where are we going now?" Haein sounded disappointed that they were heading back.

Jinwoo answered, "There's something I want to show you."

* * *

After flying a great distance, they landed in Japan. It was a restricted area, so not only were there no humans around but there were also no animals, as they'd fled from the presence of magic beasts. Kaisel landed in a wide, forested location where they couldn't hear even the tiniest creature breathing.

"Kreeee!"

Kaisel lay flat on the ground to let them dismount. Jinwoo landed on the ground and turned around to help Haein.

"Be care—"

Haein gently landed next to him and rolled her shoulders back before he could extend a helping hand. Jinwoo laughed at himself for having forgotten what she did for a living.

"Where are we......?" Haein had just experienced something beyond her wildest dreams, so she looked around with heightened expectations. However, there was nothing to see other than an endless expanse of trees.

Jinwoo placed on the ground a blanket he had purchased from the system shop. "It won't be any fun if I tell you, so come here and lie down first."

"I'm sorry?"

Had she misheard? But there's no way she, an S-rank hunter, could've heard wrong. Plus, Jinwoo himself had already sat down.

"C'mon, hurry."

Jinwoo rushed her as if there was nothing odd about this, but Haein's heart felt like it was about to explode out of her chest.

"Are......you serious?" She checked again.

Jinwoo nodded without a moment's hesitation. He made sure Haein was reluctantly approaching before fully lying down. Soon, she made up her mind and lay down next to him, ramrod straight.

"I'm......ready." Haein had her eyes squeezed shut.

"Then open your eyes."

Haein cautiously opened her eyes at Jinwoo's instructions, and he wordlessly pointed at the sky...and the stars.

"Oh......"

Haein unconsciously let out a sigh as she gazed at the sea of stars above her. Beautiful. There was no other word to describe it.

Pleased with her reaction, Jinwoo explained. "I saw this night sky when I came here to deal with a dungeon break."

Tired, he'd lain down to get some rest, but he couldn't fall asleep because it had been too bright. Annoyed, he had opened his eyes to this array of starlight, his chest welling with emotions.

"I thought about how nice it would be if I could stare up at this night sky with someone."

That night, it had been just him and the stars in the quiet of the forest. He had hoped to share this sensation, this moment with another.

And now......he felt at ease having someone close to him who felt the same way he did. Jinwoo felt like a blight that had been in his heart was gently melting away.

Hmm......?

Haein placed her hand on top of his.

"May I......hold your hand?"

As if she wasn't already. A smile bloomed on Jinwoo's face, and he turned his hand over to interlock his fingers with hers. Her hand, cold yet soft to the touch, fit perfectly inside his.

Countless stars shone down ever so quietly over the entwined couple.

3
THE KING OF BEASTS

3

THE KING OF BEASTS

The next day, a tabloid that had long since replaced their coverage of celebrities for gossip about hunters printed a rather provocative headline.

Jinwoo Sung and Haein Cha Spotted at Theme Park—Birth of the Ultimate Power Couple?

Accompanying the article were pictures taken by cell phones of Jinwoo and Haein at the amusement park and riding off to an unknown destination on the back of a magic beast.

Because Jinwoo and Haein had requested that their private lives be protected by the association, newspapers weren't normally allowed to report such information. However, considering the size of this scoop, this particular tabloid decided to publish the article regardless of the consequences.

The article blew up. The public had grown tired of the nonstop news about the monolithic gate, but the gossip involving two prominent S-rank hunters revived them. People were keen to read more about the

best male hunter in the world and the best female hunter in Korea, and
news about the couple traveled like wildfire online.

᠌└If Jinwoo Sung and Haein Cha get married and
have a kid, Jinwoo Jr. should be able to defeat all the
magic beasts, right?
└Jinwoo Jr. LOL
└They haven't officially announced that they're
dating. You're jumping the gun SMH
└Based on your logic, Jinwoo Sung's parents
would be superpowerful. OP is just a troll who
doesn't know how a person awakens as a hunter.
└Yeah, but who isn't hoping that they're really
dating?
└I hope it's real. Their surroundings would be
destroyed if they ever got into an argument. LOL

└I live in a suburb of Seoul and I thought the world
was doomed when I saw that gate hanging over
Gangnam. But hearing about hunters going out on
dates and having fun is reassuring and makes me
think we still have hope.
└Same.
└I wish they'd stop reporting about the gate at
this point.
└Hunter Sung and Hunter Cha, please do something about that massive gate or monolithic gate
or whatever it's called!

"Tsk, tsk." President Yoonho Baek of the White Tiger Guild clicked
his tongue as he set down the tabloid.

That explained why he'd noticed a difference in the way Haein looked
at Jinwoo versus others. The news itself wasn't why he was irked.

"This headline is totally stupid. What do they mean by the 'ultimate power couple'?"

Manager Sangmin An noted the president's displeasure. "What's wrong with it, sir? I would think those two are more than qualified for that title."

"It doesn't matter which woman Hunter Sung has by his side. They'd still be the most powerful couple! This headline is pointless."

After contemplating Jinwoo with other partners, Sangmin had to concede that point. Even if Jinwoo went out with that one female hunter still in high school, they'd be unbeatable, in large part because Jinwoo himself was overwhelmingly strong.

"You're right, President Baek."

"I told you."

Sangmin nodded as he took a sip of his instant coffee. He turned his gaze out the window. "Oh geez, the air pollution from fine dust keeps getting worse. I'm scared to even open a window these days."

Sangmin frowned and went to close the half-opened window, but President Baek held out a hand to stop him.

"Wait."

"Pardon?"

President Baek opened the window all the way and stuck out his hand. "This...... This isn't fine dust."

The smog that covered Seoul wasn't the usual fine-dust pollution but a bone-chilling mist.

"How strange."

It was the middle of fall, so it shouldn't be nearly this cold.

President Baek shuddered, and he stared out the window with Eyes of a Beast activated. "I......I have a bad feeling about this."

* * *

Jinwoo woke up first. Haein must've been exhausted from yesterday, as she didn't stir. When was the last time he'd woken up next to someone like this?

Jinwoo carefully got up and ventured into the woods.

It was definitely around here......

He washed up in the stream he'd luckily stumbled across the last time he was there. On the way back to Haein, he stopped in his tracks as something caught his eye.

What's this......?

It was a sapling with newly sprouted buds. That in itself wasn't anything special, but instead of green leaves, its leaves were a shiny silver color. It was unlike anything else on earth, and it exuded a very small amount of magic power that would've been hard to detect by anyone other than Jinwoo.

This tree isn't of this world.

Since its magic-power signature was different, he concluded it wasn't a magic beast. Upon closer inspection, Jinwoo noticed other silvery leaves poking out of the ground in the vicinity. They were a stark contrast from the surrounding trees with leaves that were steadily drying up.

The dirt......is changing.

Was this also part of the Rulers' plan? Or was this an aftereffect of the magic beasts? Jinwoo dug up some soil, gave it a sniff, and rubbed his fingers together as he let it fall back to the ground. He could smell weak magic power from the soil as well. Earth was already imbued with magic power, and humans may be the only creatures to not realize this.

At that moment, Jinwoo sensed from a distance that Haein had woken up. He dusted off his hands. While the changes were worrisome, he had something much more important to focus on at this very second: to reassure Haein that he hadn't vanished in the middle of the night.

He made no attempt to hide his approach, and she let out a small sigh of relief as soon as she caught sight of him.

He greeted her with a smile. "Did you sleep well?"

For some reason, her cheeks flushed, and she avoided making eye contact as she replied. "......Yes."

When he shot her a puzzled look, she looked tentatively back at him. "Where did you go?"

Jinwoo pulled off the towel around his shoulders and dried his wet hair. "I went to wash up."

Speaking of, he realized that she must also want to get cleaned up, as even the slightest ocean breeze left hints of salt on one's body.

But I can't let a lady wash up in a place like this......

Jinwoo grinned when a solution that would allow them to both bathe and get something to eat popped into his mind.

"I know a hotel with a fantastic breakfast nearby! Would you like to grab a bite there?"

Haein remained tight-lipped as she nodded in acquiescence. Jinwoo held out his hand to help her up before summoning Kaisel.

"Kreeeee!"

Haein tilted her head as she watched Kaisel spread his wings. "Didn't you say it was nearby?"

"It would take me about five minutes if I ran at full speed...... Then shall we run there together?"

Five minutes at Jinwoo's full speed. Haein climbed onto Kaisel without another word.

It's nice that she catches on quickly.

Jinwoo settled into the spot in front of her, and Kaisel rose into the sky.

Koreans had gotten used to seeing Kaisel on TV, but how would the Japanese hotel staff react to seeing a dragon with their own eyes? Jinwoo hoped that the chef wouldn't be too traumatized as Kaisel headed in the direction of the hotel.

* * *

It appeared out of nowhere. The first person to encounter it was a middle-aged man exiting the Hunter's Association headquarters after being evaluated as a B-rank awakened being.

Thwump.

He stopped as it seemingly appeared out of nowhere and bumped his shoulder.

"Huh?"

The middle-aged man's eyes trailed up the shadow cast on the ground to come face-to-face with a hulking man standing nearly seven feet tall. He was clad in some kind of leather and had a bestial air about him. Or rather, he seemed like an actual beast. His sheer size made him stand out, so the two men quickly drew people's attention.

"Are they going to fight?"

"Wow! That guy is huge! Even Dongwook Ma would have a tough time against him."

"Is that older man out of his mind? Is he trying to get sent to the ER?"

With so many people watching him, the middle-aged man felt like a heavy silence had suddenly fallen on the bustling street. Normally, he would've apologized and just walked away. But he was a different man now. The man who used to pander to his superiors and get ignored by his subordinates was no more.

I'm a B-rank awakened being now.

B-rank hunters were up there in power. He didn't need to grovel at this normal civilian who probably thought it was okay to push people around because of his size.

He gently put his briefcase on the ground and spoke forcefully. "Hey! You should apologize when you bump into someone!"

As his heart began to pound in his chest, he could feel magic power coursing through his body. His cells seemed to be telling him that he was alive. It was time for him to start his new life as a hunter.

The bestial man stood there quietly, seemingly pacified by the other man's mettle.

Encouraged by his opponent's reaction, the middle-aged man continued. "Do you think this is over if you just stand there? When you do something wrong, you should own up to it and ask for forgi— A-ahhhh!"

The bestial man roughly grabbed the middle-aged man by the head and lifted him up off the ground to the screams of onlookers.

"Guh! Ohhh!"

Veins began to pop out of the middle-aged man's head as the beast of a man squeezed. A bear. No, a tiger. What kind of predator, whether it be a lion, shark, alligator, or poisonous snake, could instill this kind of overwhelming fear in humans? The instinctual terror the human felt in front of a creature at the top of the food chain made him wet his pants.

"Agh...... Gah......"

And eventually, blood and brain splattered everywhere to the sound of something shattering.

Crack!

"Ahhhhhhhh!"

But the bestial man didn't stop there. He started devouring the corpse splayed on the ground.

"H-he's eating him!"

"Wh-whoa!"

"What the hell......? What's he doing?!"

The man's feeding frenzy was over in a flash. He wiped bits of human flesh from his mouth as he straightened up. There wasn't a trace of sanity in the man's eyes. They were clearly the eyes of a beast.

Some people had run away screaming, but there were still plenty of curious onlookers watching the beast's barbaric display. The beast roared at the crowd in an indecipherable language.

"Hear me, lowly humans! From this moment forth, I shall hunt you!"

Tears streamed down the faces of trembling onlookers, paralyzed by the thunderous roar.

The beast's sharp fangs were in full view, giving him an almost regal visage.

"I will tear your flesh with my fangs and claws!"

It was the King of Beasts. The Fang Monarch gnashed his teeth, his bellow shaking the entire street.

"Stop me if you can!"

* * *

President Woo caught wind of the horrifying creature that had appeared out of nowhere in downtown Seoul. "How many victims?"

"It's impossible to get a body count at this point."

It had first been sighted in the neighborhood of Myeong-dong and was traveling in a straight line, killing every human it laid eyes on.

"If it continues on the same path, it's heading for—"

"The Hunter's Association." President Woo bit his lower lip and clenched his fists tightly. "We've already got our hands full with that gate...... Where in the world did this monster come from?"

However, this was not the time to lose one's cool. They had to focus on trying to stop the creature.

"What's Hunter Sung's status?"

"We can't reach him."

"Dammit......" President Woo cursed inadvertently.

He had just received a report that the monster had easily annihilated one of the guilds that had been sent out to intercept it. The one good thing was that it was moving slowly, almost as if it was waiting for something. But nonetheless, it was all too obvious that the number of victims would increase astronomically the longer they couldn't stop it. That they couldn't contact the most powerful weapon in their arsenal was the worst-possible case.

If it comes to it, then I'll step in......

As he gritted his teeth in determination, good news arrived.

"Mr. President!"

Jinchul jumped out of his seat at the sight of the employee bolting into the room without so much as a knock.

"Were you able to contact Hunter Sung?"

"Not yet, sir. But we just received word that a renowned hunter was in the vicinity and is going to engage the monster!"

"What? Who?"

"It's......!"

* * *

Lennart, Germany's strongest hunter, sensed the monster approaching as it left a trail of blood.

Can I......do this?

As a hunter, he was unable to ignore the cries of innocent people. Based on the Hunter Command Center's point system, Lennart ranked twelfth in the world. Seeing people's expressions of relief as they recognized him made him feel responsible for their safety. It wasn't a matter of whether he could. He *had* to do it. It was his duty as a hunter.

Perhaps......

It might have been fate that Lennart was in Seoul to stop the monster.

Face grim, Lennart had unbuttoned the top few buttons on his shirt and taken a step toward the beast when a deep voice came from behind him.

"Get out of my way."

* * *

As soon as Jinwoo had entered an area with cell service, his phone started ringing nonstop.

The Hunter's Association?

He frowned when he saw the caller ID. Had something bad happened in the short interim he'd been away? He quickly answered his phone.

"H-Hunter Sung?"

"Yes, this is Jinwoo Sung." Jinwoo replied cautiously, the urgency in the other party's voice putting him on edge. "What's the matter?"

"Um, so... Actually, the president will fill you in. I'll put you through to him right now."

A matter that needed the president's direct involvement? Jinwoo realized the gravity of the situation as he waited for Jinchul to come on the line. Jinchul picked up without delay and rapidly spoke.

"Hunter Sung! Why was it so hard to reach you?"

"I didn't have reception until a minute ago."

The forest of trees had been polluted by frequent dungeon breaks, so cell phone reception was practically nonexistent in the area. Jinwoo hadn't thought it would be a problem, since he had placed a shadow soldier with everyone he wanted to protect.

Did that massive gate open?

But there were at least two days left before that was supposed to happen. Jinwoo ran through different possibilities in his mind, but before he could ask, Jinchul quickly and efficiently relayed the emergency.

"A monster has appeared and is on a rampage in the middle of Seoul!"

Jinwoo had been feeling rejuvenated after his short break, but now his heart dropped. "How large is the group of magic beasts?"

"It's not a group. There's only one."

Just the one?

Hunters from all over Korea were gathered in Seoul presently, and they were waiting with bated breath for the possible dungeon break from the monolithic gate. Additionally, the association had distributed weapons to the hunters who hadn't had sufficient gear.

But they still can't handle one magic beast that appeared out of nowhere?

Jinwoo listened with bewilderment as Jinchul continued his explanation.

"A guild went after the bastard and was decimated in a heartbeat. It doesn't appear to be an ordinary magic beast."

"What's its location?"

"It appears to be near the Grand Hotel in Seoul."

Could it be a mere coincidence? His mouth went dry at the mention of the luxury hotel Thomas Andre was staying at. His bad feeling was proven correct when Jinchul anxiously told him:

"I just got a phone call that Hunter Andre is facing off against it."

That couldn't be right. Jinwoo had left a shadow soldier with Thomas just in case, with the order to signal him right away if he sensed anything odd. He hadn't heard a peep from the soldier despite Thomas single-handedly battling a creature that had wiped out an entire guild.

...... Wait a minute.

Something was very off. The signals from his soldiers in Seoul were very weak, like something was interfering with them.

What's going on?

An overpowered new enemy, a national-level hunter as its opponent, and a bunch of jammed signals. Could it be?

Jinwoo pressed Jinchul as one possibility popped into his mind. "President Woo, does that monster have a shadow?"

"Pardon?"

"I need to know if that monster has a shadow."

Jinchul's voice paused before hurriedly answering his query.

"Oh my goodness...... You're right, Hunter Sung. I've just confirmed through a photograph that the monster doesn't have a shadow."

Shit. Recalling that the ice elf who had attacked President Go was also missing a shadow, Jinwoo yelled, "Don't let Thomas engage that monster!"

Thomas Andre had probably been the target from the start.

"Sorry? But he's already......"

Time was of the essence. Jinwoo didn't need to hear any more. He activated Shadow Exchange with the soldier assigned to Thomas.

Ping!

A hologram-like message popped up with an unpleasant alarm.

[The designated shadow soldier cannot be found.]

Jinwoo tried several more times, but the result was the same.

Ping, ping!

[The designated shadow soldier cannot be found.]
[The designated shadow soldier cannot be found.]

How was this happening? Jinwoo was stunned.

My soldier......is gone?

The shadow soldier he had strategically placed for the express purpose of using Shadow Exchange had vanished into thin air. Jinwoo was unable to sense his presence anywhere. He could clearly tell that the connection between him and the soldier attached to Thomas had been severed. It was a similar sensation as when Jinwoo would send a soldier back to the void. A shadow soldier had been forcibly terminated.

Confused, Jinwoo blurted out, "What the hell is going on?!"

* * *

A deep voice came from behind Lennart. "Get out of my way."

Lennart was hit with déjà vu, but his reaction was the complete opposite of the previous incident.

"Thomas Andre!" His face brightened at the sight of the man large enough to block out the sun.

Thomas strode past Lennart, and even those who had been screaming and fleeing the scene slowed in their tracks as they recognized the great national-level hunter.

"He's that American hunter......"

"Th-Thomas?"

"Goliath! It's Goliath!"

Even Lennart, a fellow hunter at the top of the field, felt his heart pounding excitedly as he watched Thomas advance, so the civilians who were running away as if they were being pushed by the beast's horrifying aura were ecstatic.

"Yes......!"

"Thank God for Thomas!"

Some people collapsed to the ground as their legs gave out in sheer relief.

Thomas barked at the hunters who had been rendered immobile by the beast's staggering power. "Don't just stand there, you idiots! Clear everyone out of the area!"

The bellow of a national-level hunter snapped them back into action. Those who understood English rushed to evacuate the remaining civilians from the area, and Lennart joined them. Thomas stood in the middle of the road, acting as a barrier as the beast leisurely approached them.

Thomas removed his sunglasses and narrowed his eyes. "......"

The beast was covered in blood. Although he had the appearance of a human, he was definitely something otherworldly. Thomas growled as he took in the sight of body parts of the creature's victims strewn about in his wake.

"This beast didn't know his place and went too far."

As if to mock Thomas's fury, the beast bared his fangs, displaying bloodred teeth with pieces of flesh stuck in them.

A rabid animal should be put down, no?

Thomas leveled a cold glare at the beast. "Enforcement."

His muscles became armor-like, and his already hulking frame grew larger. Now bigger than the beast, the man they called Goliath charged at the creature to test his power against him. Those watching Thomas from afar were reminded of a tank as they felt the ground shaking with each heavy step.

The beast smacked his lips at his new prey, then made his move as well. The two huge men were face-to-face in no time. They sized each other up for a moment before the two beings, both strong enough to smash concrete as easily as a block of tofu, let their fists driven by magic power fly.

Pow, pow, pow, pow, pow, pow!

The other hunters were astonished by the show of brute strength. A single punch would mean instant death for them, yet both the beast and Thomas continued to exchange blows without bothering to defend themselves.

I can do this.

Thomas was sure of it.

Ka-pow!

His next punch knocked the beast's head sideways. It was thrilling to feel his left fist connect. After losing to Jinwoo, Thomas's confidence had waned slightly, but his head was back in the game.

Pow, pow, pow, pow, pow, pow!

After gradually pushing the beast back with a barrage of blows, Thomas used a punch at full swing to bring the beast sprawling.

Ka-pow!

Craaaaaack!

The beast skidded across asphalt, splitting the road in two, before finally crashing into a building. The hunters watching the fight were cheering in delight, but Thomas himself wasn't pleased.

No. The attack......wasn't as effective as I thought it'd be.

He could still sense the beast's hostility coming from under the debris of the building.

Swoosh!

Shwoop!

Hunks of metal shot out like missiles through the thick cloud of dust swirling around them. Thomas kicked aside the cars flying at him, then drew the hiding beast toward him using the skill Gravitation.

Woooom!

As soon as the thrashing beast was right in front of Thomas's nose, the hunter pulled out his most powerful skill.

"Demolish!"

The muscles of Thomas's arms expanded until they looked like they were about to burst. He slammed both fists into the ground.

Ka-boom!

A horrific shock wave struck the beast.

"Argh!"

The beast was thrown up in the air, landing unceremoniously. Without missing a beat, Thomas leaped on top of him and delivered another round of punches using the skill Heavy Blow.

Pow, pow, pow, pow, pow, pow!

"Yeaaaaaah!"

The people who had been anxiously watching the fight between Goliath and the beast cheered. The other hunters were grinning from ear to ear. From everyone's vantage point, the fight was over. It was an indisputable victory for Thomas, as expected of the strongest national-level hunter.

However, Thomas had broken out into a cold sweat despite being the one who had his opponent on the ropes.

What's this?

The closer he got to victory, the more it felt like anxiety was tightening around his throat. Each strike hit its mark, and the target wasn't resisting, but......why was Thomas feeling uneasy despite absolutely dominating in the fight?

And then it hit him: the eyes. It was the beast's eyes. His gaze hadn't changed throughout their fight, showing no reaction to the thrashing he was receiving. He seemed to be egging Thomas on to do his best.

Incensed, Thomas raised his clenched fists high in the air. His shoulder muscles expanded as an incredible amount of magic power gathered in his shoulders, arms, wrists, and fists. This would cinch it. Could the beast survive being directly hit by Demolish? Thomas swung his arms down with all his might.

"Demolish!"

He saw the exact moment his opponent blinked, his eyes transforming from those of a human to those of a beast. The beast easily blocked his strongest blow with a single hand.

"......?" A chill ran down Thomas's spine as he stared at his immobilized hands.

"This is an impressive show of power for a mere puppet of a Fragment."

Thomas frowned at what sounded like growls. "What?"

That was when the creature's black hair turned white and began to grow longer. His nails transformed into claws, his teeth sharpened, and white fur covered his entire body.

A werewolf?

But a white werewolf had never been observed in the last ten years.

"What......what are you?"

Thomas shuddered at the frightening amounts of magic power in front of him. Instead of answering, the beast tightened his grip and crushed the bones in Thomas's hands.

Crack!

"Arghhhh!"

Everyone was taken aback at one of the most powerful hunters in the world letting out a cry of anguish. A news helicopter circled overhead, capturing footage of Thomas writhing in agony. A national-level hunter had set out to put an end to a monster that showed up in Seoul, the city everyone had their eyes on because of the monolithic gate. It was hard to believe that that same hunter seemed to be losing.

"But how......?"

Everyone watching the battle either with their own eyes or on a monitor desperately prayed that wasn't the end, but their hopes were dashed as the beast grabbed Thomas by the wrist and slammed him down.

Blam!

This time, the beast was the one to straddle Thomas.

"Argh!"

The man known as Goliath tried to resist the beast with his broken hand as he coughed up blood, but he didn't stand a chance against the beast's true form. The beast pushed Thomas's head into the ground and howled toward the sky.

Graaaaaah!

The terrifying sound pierced the ears of everyone who heard it as it echoed across the entire city like thunder. Beasts didn't pick fights. They hunted prey. The roar contained an incredible amount of magic power that forced other hunters one by one to their knees.

The beast snickered. "Are you scared?"

Predators delighted in the feat of catching their prey. Thomas wasn't giving up, though. He struggled to make a fist with his broken hand and countered with a punch.

Pow!

The beast didn't even flinch. As he searched the beast's emotionless gaze, Thomas was reminded of a wall that endlessly stretched out toward the sky. He had experienced this feeling once before. How strange that the beast's eyes reminded him of Jinwoo.

Why......?

Thomas lost his train of thought as the beast threw punches that knocked his head from side to side.

Ka-pow!

"Gah!"

That was only the beginning.

Pow, pow, pow!

The beast's punches rained down on Thomas in a reversal of earlier. He attacked nonstop, as if demonstrating what a proper attack was.

Pow, pow, pow, pow, pow, pow!

While the beast hadn't reacted to being punched, Thomas yelped with each blow he took.

"Ack!"

The beast relished the pain he was inflicting, but he suddenly spotted something behind Thomas.

"......?" The beast pulled back, intently observing Thomas's shadow. "I see there's a rat hiding here."

Shlup!

The beast plunged his hand into Thomas's shadow and grabbed ahold of something.

Shoop!

The beast pulled out an ant shadow soldier, thrashing in vain against the powerful grip around his throat.

"Skraaaaah!"

Soldiers of the Shadow Monarch couldn't be eliminated through ordinary means, but the one gripping the ant's neck was rather extraordinary. As a higher being, the Fang Monarch was able to focus his spirit energy and erase the ant soldier from existence.

"Gaaah!" The ant soldier let out a scream, turning to ash as it was sent back into the void.

The beast smirked at the gray ash scattering in the wind.

Meanwhile, Thomas had managed to stand up and position himself behind the beast to put him in a secure headlock. It wasn't over until the very end, and despite his broken hand, Thomas's arms and shoulders were still in working order. The pressure he applied was strong enough to crush a metal post.

"Huff, huff!" Thomas tried to regulate his quickening breath as he focused on the attack. There was no turning back. He wouldn't get a second chance if he let go now. He narrowed his eyes and clenched his jaw.

Kriiik, crack!

He heard the unpleasant sound of bones breaking. If it was coming from the beast's neck, Thomas would still have hope.

......Yes!

But soon, the adrenaline wore off, and Thomas screamed as he belatedly felt the pain.

"Arghhhhh!"

The beast had grabbed the arm around his neck and shattered it. The beast then took hold of Thomas by the head and bashed it against the ground.

Wham!

Those watching the scene unfold on screens had to turn away after seeing Goliath's arm flopping around. It was an awful sight, but the gruesome scene didn't end there. The beast leaped on top of the prone body of Thomas and started feasting on his flesh and bone with sharp, knifelike teeth.

"A-ahhhhhh!"

Although Thomas desperately fought back, it seemed hopeless. Blood gushed out, and pieces of flesh flew everywhere.

"Gyaaah!"

The hunters keeping the civilians away stumbled back at the ghastly sight. The hopeful civilians had long since scattered, frightened out of their wits.

But one hunter shot out of the crowd and slammed himself into the beast.

Whud!

Drunk on victory and distracted by the taste of his loot, the beast was thrown by the surprise attack.

Thomas recognized Lennart hovering over his body and attempted to warn him. "R...... Run......"

But Lennart shook his head. "I'm a hunter, too."

Though he was weaker than Thomas, Lennart had sworn an oath to himself when he decided to become a hunter: He would never turn his back on an ally. While Thomas wasn't a guildmate, Lennart counted him as a distinguished ally, since they shared a common enemy. No matter what Thomas thought of him, Lennart could not back down.

Still......just looking at him gives me the chills!

Lennart's legs quivered as the beast snarled at him, furious that his meal had been interrupted.

Thomas saw that the German hunter was trembling and spoke with much difficulty. "You'll......be......killed......"

Lennart was acutely aware of that. He hadn't brought his gear with him, and his best attack skill, Charge, had barely pushed the beast back. Titles like "Germany's strongest" or "the twelfth hunter in the world" meant little in this situation.

No regrets.

Even if this meant the end for Lennart, he'd make the same call again and again. Better to die honorably than to live cowardly.

This was the right decision.

This was the right decision.

Lennart kept that in mind as death barreled toward him.

This was the right decision.

The beast was in front of him in a flash, maw opening impossibly wide to devour him. Lennart threw a punch with everything he had.

As he did, his life flashed before his eyes. It had been one without many difficulties, thanks to the power he'd been blessed with. He'd lived a good life, hadn't he? Lennart smiled contentedly as he looked down the beast's throat.

This was indeed the right decision. He had lived a proud life until the end. He closed his eyes, expecting he'd never open them again, as the beast swallowed his head.

Ka-pow!

Lennart's eyes shot open at the sudden *bang* in front of him.

What?

The beast had been blasted dozens of meters away, tumbling to the ground from Lennart's punch. The asphalt road was cracked, cars were pushed away, and some streetlights were bent.

"Huh?"

Had he possessed a power he hadn't been aware of? In a daze, he looked down at his fist and finally realized someone else was standing beside him.

"Oh!" Lennart's voice hitched, and he cried out in joy. "Hunter Jinwoo Sung!"

* * *

He'd cut it way too close. If Jinwoo hadn't placed a shadow soldier with Lennart back when he'd visited the guild office, Jinwoo likely wouldn't have made it here in time. Once Jinwoo had confirmed the shadow soldier attached to Thomas had vanished, he had tried Shadow Exchange with the only other soldier in the area. Who knew it'd be the one attached to Lennart? Thanks to that, he was able to save both men.

Jinwoo heaved a sigh of relief after hurriedly inspecting Thomas's injuries. They were quite serious, but Thomas would live. Lacking the energy to speak, Thomas could only look up at Jinwoo, who nodded at him wordlessly, thankful that the American had bought him some time.

When Jinwoo turned around, he was greeted by an emotional Lennart. "Hunter Sung!"

"Thank you for stopping the beast. Could you please take Thomas somewhere safe?" Jinwoo politely asked Lennart in English.

Lennart nodded enthusiastically. That would be a piece of cake compared to fighting the monster. "Of course! I've got this." Lennart carefully helped Thomas up and rushed off.

Jinwoo turned his attention to the beast who was slowly getting up. Intense hostility radiated from him, and he was clearly on another level from other magic beasts.

I knew it......

His hunch was correct. This bastard had the same energy as the ancient ice elf Jinwoo had encountered. He was one of the Monarchs aiming for the hunters. But unlike the ice elf, there was no panic on his face. Despite the interruption, the beast seemed calm, even relaxed.

Why is that......?

For a creature that looked halfway between a human and a wild animal, he was unexpectedly composed.

As Jinwoo pondered this, the beast emerged from the rubble. He sloshed something around in his mouth before spitting out broken teeth. The beast couldn't hide his surprise.

"So it's true. The shadow bastard's scent is mixed with the human's scent." The beast sniffed the air, fascinated. "But how is a mere human able to channel this much power from a higher level of existence?"

I leveled up, asshole.

Instead of answering, Jinwoo unsheathed Kamish's Wrath. He had tons of questions for these so-called Monarchs, but he decided to save the interrogation until after he'd finished the beast off. Fury rolled from Jinwoo as he swept his eyes over the remains of victims strewn all over the street.

An unforgettable voice came from next to the beast. "The Architect has probably found a way. The Shadow Monarch and the Architect have been in cahoots for a while now."

The light fog around them gathered like smoke, coalescing into a humanoid figure.

Is that......?

The ancient ice elf. The Frost Monarch, who had been concealing his presence in the fog, finally revealed himself. It was no wonder Jinwoo had noted that the fog surrounding the whole city was an unnatural phenomenon as soon as he came into contact with it.

Another voice came from behind him. "Does that mean I can eat this human, then?"

Jinwoo looked over his shoulder for the source of the shrill woman's voice and was met with an incredible sight.

Bzzzzzzz.

Insects poured out from the sewers and came together in a swarm that transformed into an imposing woman. "I've always wanted to know what another Monarch tasted like."

Jinwoo's expression grew dark as enemies appeared on all sides. His shadow soldiers hadn't been silenced to prevent him from disrupting their hunt but to hide their numbers. It was a trap laid in order to catch Jinwoo.

Emergency notifications from the system popped up in front of him.

[The Frost Monarch, King of the Snow Folk, has designated you as an enemy.]

[The Fang Monarch, King of Beasts, has designated you as an enemy.]

[The Plague Monarch, Queen of Insects, has designated you as an enemy.]

Three enemies on a whole other level revealing themselves at once had the dormant Black Heart pumping wildly.

Ba-dump, ba-dump, ba-dump!

This is......

This was good. Jinwoo smirked. The villains thought they had him surrounded, but he wasn't alone. In fact, the Monarchs were the ones who were surrounded. Jinwoo focused his perception so as not to miss a single move made by the Monarchs as he summoned his army.

Come out!

4
THE MONARCHS' PINCER ATTACK

4

THE MONARCHS' PINCER ATTACK

Whether it be New York, London, Shanghai, or Paris, this was the day metropolises around the world came to a halt. People stopped in their tracks, unable to take their eyes off screens broadcasting breaking news about the disaster happening in Seoul, the capital city of Korea.

It was already on people's radar due to the appearance of the massive gate, so word of the attack quickly spread. Networks in different countries interrupted their regularly scheduled programming to broadcast the live stream. Viewers were aghast at the aerial footage of the blood-drenched streets of Seoul. If a bustling metropolitan city like Seoul was in such a state, there was no hope for the rest of them. The tragedy felt way too close to home.

That was most likely why Thomas Andre's appearance had been so reassuring. Excited foreign correspondents who were busy filming chanted the American hunter's name as loud as possible. Viewers put their hands together and cheered for Thomas as one. People on the streets rooted for him as he'd seemed to gain the upper hand.

"Harder! Yeah! Get him!"

"Destroy him! Destroy the bastard, Goliath!"

"Let's goooo!"

But silence fell when Goliath's fist was crushed, his arm snapped, and his blood and his flesh splattered against the ground. Hands that were raised victoriously toward the sky fell limp. Some shed silent tears as they watched the greatest warrior in history being overwhelmed.

It was as if time had ceased. Stunned, everyone seemed to have collectively stopped breathing. They prayed to wake up from this nightmare, but Thomas's agonized screams continued through the speakers. Their faces fell in despair.

Just when all hope seemed lost, a hunter with European features suddenly barreled toward the beast and knocked him back. And he wasn't the only one to pop up out of nowhere. A hunter with black hair appeared out of thin air next to him.

Viewers and reporters alike had no idea what was going on. What had just happened? Who were those two people? Because of the speed and distance at which it had occurred, the cameras couldn't capture the mystery hunters' faces. But the black soldiers filling the street were unmistakable.

"It's Hunter Jinwoo Sung! Hunter Sung has appeared!"

"No need to see his face! No need to confirm his name, either! We know exactly who that is! Those black soldiers! That's Hunter Jinwoo Sung without a doubt!"

"Goliath has fallen, but Hunter Jinwoo Sung has taken over! Hunter Sung's minions have surrounded the monsters!"

"Yeahhh!"

As the soldiers in black crowded the streets of Seoul, viewers around the world threw their hands in the air with joy. Having already lost one national-level hunter, Americans had been the most devastated at Thomas's defeat, so they were more exhilarated than anyone. Their cheers were loud enough to shake the country.

The video of Jinwoo on the Jeju Island raid had gotten more than two billion views, so there wasn't a soul who didn't know who he was. The whole world chanted Jinwoo's name.

"Hey, I know that other guy! I know exactly who he is! It's Lennart Neirmann from Germany!" But even the person trying to show off his knowledge quickly joined in on chanting Jinwoo's name.

The entire world was focused on Jinwoo Sung.

* * *

Jinwoo's shadow army encircled him and the three Monarchs. Here, on the street cloaked in shadow by Monarch's Domain, the army's morale was at an all-time high.

Jinwoo inspected each Monarch's reaction in turn. They looked amused.

The female giant made of insects scanned the street and snickered. "So this is the new shadow army?"

"They are large in number, but they're a disorganized mess." The Frost Monarch sniffed and stepped forward.

Hwoooo......

He took a deep breath and blew a bone-chilling wind throughout the area.

Kriiiik!

In an instant, everything aboveground froze, including the shadow army.

No way!

Jinwoo could only stare, astonished. The Monarchs were able to neutralize Jinwoo's soldiers in the blink of an eye. Jinwoo had experienced this once before when he had fought Balan, the Demon Monarch of White Lightning, in the Demon's Castle instance dungeon. However, he had faced only one enemy back then. This time, he was facing three simultaneously.

Jinwoo tried in vain to free his soldiers from the ice by summoning them.

"Your soldiers cannot make a single move inside the prison I've created."

Having imprisoned the shadow army, the Frost Monarch seemed

confident of their victory. However, the setback hadn't abated Jinwoo's rage.

"You." He pointed the blade of Kamish's Wrath in his right hand at the Frost Monarch. "You, if no one else, will die today."

The combat power of the shadow army was but a useful tool to Jinwoo. It was unfortunate that Jinwoo was unable to utilize them, but that didn't mean he had any intention of letting the Frost Monarch leave with his life. He had a score to settle with the asshole.

"......" The Frost Monarch grimaced, as if the shoulder wound Jinwoo had previously inflicted was aching. "You worm!"

He swept his hands up, and golems rose from the ice covering the ground. At the same time, the Queen of Insects whistled, and the corpses strewn throughout the area begin to wriggle around.

Crack, kriiiik, crack!

The corpses twisted and turned, rearranging their bones and joints until they transformed into four-legged creatures that crawled like spiders.

Are they undead creatures?

No, they weren't undead. The remains were being controlled by strange parasites that had entered their brains. Detecting the magic power of the insects moving within the corpses' skulls, Jinwoo turned to the Queen of Insects.

"Did you think that we killed these humans for no reason?"

The Queen had planted the egg of a special parasite in each human the beast had killed. Golems and parasites. Realizing he would be unable to convert his enemies' armies into shadow soldiers, it dawned on him how extensive the Monarchs' preparations had been.

"Whew......" He took a deep breath.

As the golems and the corpses made their way past the frozen soldiers and toward Jinwoo, the hunter focused on his heartbeat.

Ba-dump, ba-dump, ba-dump.

He had endured countless dangers to come this far. He closed his eyes. Jinwoo's extremely keen perception picked up on every single movement from the enemy, however small.

He could do this, just as he'd done countless times before.

Here they come.

When Jinwoo opened his eyes, the human spiders were upon him. Time slowed down as the Kamish's Wrath daggers slashed through the air.

Shk, shk, shk, shk, shk!

The human spiders that had leaped at him were sliced in half in midair.

Whack!

Jinwoo kicked away a golem trying to punch him, jumped into the air, and searched for his primary target: the Frost Monarch. The annoyed Monarch was pointing at Jinwoo and screeching at the golems, but the slow hunks of ice were no match for Jinwoo's speed.

Jinwoo used Ruler's Authority to hurl his own body toward the Frost Monarch, shooting forth as fast as a bullet. The Frost Monarch was startled when Jinwoo appeared right in front of him in the blink of an eye. Jinwoo swung his daggers, aiming for the creature's face with skin as rough as the bark of an old tree.

Klang!

Before Kamish's Wrath could cut anything, something hard intercepted the dagger. The Fang Monarch had blocked the strike with his wrist.

"Do you really think this useless piece of metal can so much as scratch me?" The Fang Monarch chortled, revealing his wickedly sharp teeth covered with flesh and blood.

But Jinwoo also chuckled.

You dare to laugh at me?

A black aura surrounded Kamish's Wrath before the beast could pick up that something was wrong.

Shunk!

The dagger sliced right through the beast's sturdy wrist. The surprised Fang Monarch narrowly avoided the blade plunging into his chest by bending backward at his waist, but it still left a gash on his chest.

Jinwoo sensed power close by and looked up.

......!

The Queen of Insects was aiming a punch packed with magic power right at him.

Whoosh!

Jinwoo landed on the ground and immediately tried to repel the Queen's fist with Ruler's Authority, but he underestimated her and barely managed to block it.

Pow!

The Queen's fist struck the force field created by Ruler's Authority, generating a shock wave that swept away the human spiders near them. But more human spiders took their place and skittered after him.

Jinwoo stepped on one of their heads and bounded into the air. He gathered his magic power on Kamish's Wrath.

Zzzzt!

The black aura concentrating on the dagger's vibrating blade distorted the space around it.

"Raaaah!" With a roar, Jinwoo swung his dagger with all his might.

Shhhk, shhhk, shhhk, shhhk, shhhk, shhhk, shhhk, shhhk!

His magic power spread out in dozens of directions and swept away his enemies below.

Dragon's Claw!

The attack eliminated half of the golems and spiders, but......

Fwip!

As Jinwoo looked to the side to see a giant palm about to hit him, the shadow of the palm covered his face.

Crap.

The attack was from an angle he couldn't avoid, so the only thing he could do was put his guard up. The Queen of Insects swatted Jinwoo into the side of a building as if he were a mere bug.

Thud!

The impact was so great, the buildings across the street shook as well. Jinwoo made his way out of the debris, but he fell to the ground, breathing heavily.

"Gah......"

He felt dizzy, and his ears were ringing. His vision got a bit blurry, but he didn't have time to catch his breath. When he looked up, he saw several thousand ice arrows trained on him floating over his head, courtesy of the Frost Monarch.

Jinwoo got up and held his breath as he deflected the ice arrows raining over him. He moved so fast, he looked like a blur.

But how long can he withstand our pincer attacks?

The Frost Monarch smiled wickedly while continuing to summon arrows. He was waiting for when Jinwoo inevitably slowed down.

Shunk!

"......?" The Frost Monarch stared uncomprehendingly at the dagger suddenly sticking out of his chest. His own blood was smudged on his hand. When he looked up, the insolent human was staring at him. Jinwoo had managed to throw one of his daggers even as he deflected arrows.

The Frost Monarch's blood boiled. "How dare a miserable human harm me, a Monarch?!"

Shhhk!

Jinwoo quickly summoned back the dagger from the Monarch's chest. It had pierced his heart. It would've been a fatal injury for an ordinary human, but the Monarch barely seemed to register it. At least the rain of arrows had stopped.

Jinwoo growled as he held up Kamish's Wrath. "Like I said, you're going to die today."

"Graaaaah!"

The golems controlled by the outraged Frost Monarch, the human spiders manipulated by the Plague Monarch, and the Fang Monarch whose arm had fully regenerated and now was armed with a sword he'd

pulled out from a pocket dimension similar to Jinwoo's inventory—
Jinwoo was able to track all their movements as they resumed their
attacks. He gripped the two Kamish's Wrath daggers in hand, taking
deep breaths.

Kriiiiiik!

Just then, a loud crack sounded over his shoulder, accompanied by a
voice he was ecstatic to hear.

"My kiiiiiiing!"

* * *

A few minutes ago......

As one of Jinwoo's most loyal subjects, he felt utterly helpless while
held captive in the Frost Monarch's ice prison. Was he truly this weak?
What had he continuously leveled up for?

Beru was miserable that there was nothing he could do as his king
was surrounded by the enemy right in front of him, but he couldn't
do anything about it. The Frost Monarch's existence was on a different
plane than his, and Beru had no counter for his magic spell. All he could
do was pray that his king would make it out safe. Fortunately, Jinwoo
seemed to be holding his own against his mystical enemies.

*My king is as phenomenal as I expected...... This lowly servant is once
again in awe!*

Beru was so moved by his master's display that it brought him to
tears. However, being outnumbered was starting to weigh heavily on
Jinwoo. Beru struggled to break free as he watched the opposition corner Jinwoo.

My king! My king!

Seeing the Plague Monarch send Jinwoo crashing into a building was
the last straw.

His king was in danger. His king was in danger. His king was in danger. Beru needed to protect his king.

Snap!

Beru lost his mind. He went into emergency mode, losing all rationality and operating solely on the instinct to protect his king.

"Skraaaaaaaah!" Beru roared, his face grotesquely distorted. His arms, shoulders, neck, chest, thighs, calves, and ankles! Every part of Beru's body expanded at once, pushing at the block of ice that was imprisoning him.

Krik, kriiiik!

Hairpin cracks started to form in the seemingly impenetrable cage. Beru thrashed his whole body.

Kriiiiik!

Unable to withstand the insanely agitated ant soldier, the surface of the ice prison began to give. The only thought in Beru's head was to save his king.

"Skraaaaah!"

Twisting his body with all his might, Beru finally broke through the ice.

Kra-koooom!

Beru ripped wide an opening with his bare hands and flew straight toward Jinwoo. *My kiiiiiing!*

"Beru!"

Although his master welcomed him, Beru didn't have time to be happy. Instead, he noticed the small scratches and cuts on his master that had come from the insect woman swatting him into the building earlier. How dare that insect woman lay a hand on Jinwoo? How dare she touch his king?!

"Skraaaaaaaaaah!" Incensed, Beru shot toward the Queen of Insects.

The Frost Monarch was thunderstruck as Beru's cry rang through the downtown area of Seoul. "A mere shadow soldier broke free of my binding spell?"

That should've been impossible. The Frost Monarch inspected Beru's power level and couldn't help but gasp. It was not a mere shadow soldier.

"How did that human give rise to a marshal?!"

Marshals acted as extensions of the Shadow Monarch, and each one was an incarnation of destruction.

While the Frost Monarch was taken aback at this news, the Queen of Insects advanced.

"This impertinent child doesn't even recognize who his mother is. He must be punished."

"Skraaaaah! You crazy hag!"

"What did you call me?" The Plague Monarch, the master of all bugs in the World of Chaos, was angered by the ant king's insolence.

Whoosh!

Beru dodged her and aimed a roar of magic power at her midsection, where bugs were swarming. "Graaaaah!"

The ant king's screech tore away the bugs, revealing the true form of the Plague Monarch for a moment: a woman with rotting flesh and hollow eye sockets filled with maggots. The Plague Monarch was enraged by the ant king defying his one true master.

"Gyaaaaah!" The Queen of Insects retaliated with her own roar that ripped through the air and pushed Beru backward. The ant king eventually regained his balance after skidding back a distance.

"Skree...... Gah...... Ugh..." Out of breath, Beru shook his head to clear it.

The Queen of Insects summoned back the insects to re-form her giant body.

Okay.

Jinwoo observed their fight and nodded. The enemies were too strong, so Beru wouldn't last long. However, he could keep at least one of them preoccupied. The other monarchs were also watching Beru fight the Queen. Jinwoo detected how alarmed they were.

Beru could only buy him so much time, so Jinwoo bolted toward the Frost Monarch at full speed, faster than anyone expected.

Zooooom!

With each step, the asphalt split under his foot. The Frost Monarch generated an ice spear as he kept an eye on Jinwoo charging fiercely toward him. But then, Jinwoo abruptly changed direction just before he reached the Frost Monarch and leaped at the Fang Monarch.

"......!"

The Fang Monarch had been planning a counterattack for when Jinwoo attacked the Frost Monarch, so he flinched at the sudden change in course. He barely blocked Jinwoo's dagger, his animalistic reflexes kicking in.

Jinwoo sucked his teeth in disappointment.

Tsk!

He'd hoped to deliver a fatal blow to the Fang Monarch with a surprise attack, but the Fang Monarch had reacted a little quicker than Jinwoo was anticipating. Fortunately, it wasn't a total loss. After all, he'd managed to startle the Fang Monarch.

Let's keep pushing.

He spun Kamish's Wrath into a reverse grip and unleashed a continuous attack. The sound of the sharp blades ripping through the air echoed, leaving cuts on everything around them.

Klank! Klang! Klank! Klang! Klank! Klank!

The King of Beasts struggled to keep up, grimacing as he was forced back. Suddenly sensing hostility behind him, Jinwoo quickly twisted his torso, and the Frost Monarch narrowly missed Jinwoo's midsection with his ice spear. It was now two against one. For a split second, Jinwoo made eye contact with the Frost Monarch and picked up on his animosity.

Jinwoo audibly gritted his teeth together as he struck the ice spear with one dagger. The impact on the spear caused the Frost Monarch to double over. Jinwoo quickly took advantage of that.

Shhhk!

Jinwoo aimed for the Monarch's arrogant eyes, but he was only able to deliver a shallow wound in that area of his face when the Frost Monarch quickly turned his head to avoid it.

So close......

Jinwoo anticipated an attack from the King of Beasts next and whirled around.

Klang!

It was a close call, but Jinwoo didn't even have time to be relieved. The Frost Monarch gripped his spear tightly and resumed his attacks. The Frost Monarch in front of him. The Fang Monarch behind him. The two overpowered monsters swung at him relentlessly.

Klang! Klaaang! Klang! Klang! Klang! Klaaang! Klaaang! Klang! Klaaang! Klang!

Kamish's Wrath whipped around at lightning speed, blocking and repelling their strikes. Jinwoo and the Monarchs were moving so quickly that humans could see only a blurry string of afterimages. In fact, it was impossible for Jinwoo himself to physically see the Monarchs' movements.

Instead, Jinwoo was able to read the flow of the attacks. Their actions, line of sight, breathing, muscles, the movement of magic power...... With his outstanding perception, he didn't miss a thing.

......I can see it all.

If Jinwoo moved a little faster, he could surpass his enemies. Just a little faster.

Faster, faster, faster!

The Monarchs were flabbergasted as Jinwoo's speed continued to increase.

How......? How is that possible......?

He shouldn't be able to use the full power of the Shadow Monarch yet, but he's still......!

Their opponent was evolving past his species' limitations right before their eyes. The two Monarchs couldn't help but recall their fear of one of the most powerful kings in the World of Chaos.

Bam!

With his daggers crossed, Jinwoo blocked the two Monarchs' weapons and sent them hurtling backward.

"......!"

"……!"

The two Monarchs couldn't hide their astonishment.

* * *

Lennart was sure that he was the only one here able to follow the fight with his own eyes, as Thomas was currently surrounded by healers tending to his serious wounds. But he was unable to make things out clearly.

"……"

He was amazed. Despite facing off against the beast that had subdued a national-level tank and the monster who had frozen the entire area with a single breath, Jinwoo never relented.

Soon, Hunter Sung sped up, moving too fast for the naked eye. It was like a tornado was hitting the area, complete with loud explosions of sound.

"What……?" Thomas couldn't help asking at the sudden loud noises. "What's going on?"

Lennart couldn't take his eyes off Jinwoo and answered incredulously. "It's like……"

Was this what it looked like when beings capable of destroying the planet battled it out?

"It's like I'm watching the end of the world." Lennart shook his head as he answered honestly. The one comforting thing was that at least one of the fighters was on their side.

* * *

"Skraaaaah!"

Jinwoo turned at Beru's scream. The Queen of Insects had trapped Beru under her foot, and no amount of struggling could break him free. Jinwoo's eyes widened as he felt magic power leaving Beru's body, the ant soldier's very existence fading.

Is this how they got rid of the soldier attached to Thomas?

Jinwoo first repelled the attacks of the two remaining Monarchs and then called Beru back into his shadow.

[You cannot call back the designated target.]
[You cannot call back the designated target.]

The system repeated the message like a parrot.

Jinwoo's expression grew dark. He couldn't lose Beru this way. Beru was a valued soldier and the best weapon in his shadow army arsenal.

Without Beru, the precarious balance of power will shift.

The result of the fight would be decided.

Jinwoo shook off the spear and the sword coming at him and charged at the Queen. She was preoccupied with sending the shadow soldier back to the void, so she belatedly noticed his approach.

"Human!"

Jinwoo expelled magic power from his throat just like Beru had done earlier. "Raaaaah!"

The bugs covering the Queen fell off by his magically charged roar.

Her true form revealed, the Queen could not hide her alarm. She quickly spat green goo at Jinwoo's face, which he easily blocked using Ruler's Authority. The leftover poisonous fumes were cleared away by a passive skill.

[The remnants of Skill: Deadly Poison have been detected in the air.]
[Buff: Detoxing has been activated.]
[3, 2, 1...... Detoxing is complete.]

Not only was the Plague Monarch not a threat to Jinwoo, but she was also within his reach now. Jinwoo's eyes gleamed.

The Frost Monarch survived a stab to the heart earlier.

It was highly likely that the Plague Monarch would as well. Jinwoo would have to attack until he found a weak spot. He gripped his daggers tightly.

Mutilation!

Shhhk, shhhk, shhhk, shhhk, shhhk, shhhk!

Jinwoo's daggers dotted the Queen's body with holes like a Gatling gun, ripping her to shreds.

"Arghhh!"

But the maggots inside her twisted and bound together to instantly regenerate her body.

Regeneration?

Not a problem. If the Queen had the ability to regenerate, Jinwoo simply needed to pour on the attack and push things beyond her healing abilities. He followed her as she was knocked back, continually using the Mutilation skill.

Shhhk, shhhk, shhhk, shhhk, shhhk! Shhhk, shhhk, shhhk, shhhk, shhhk!

Surrounded by a black aura, Kamish's Wrath bit into her nonstop.

"Ahhhhhh!"

Jinwoo stripped the Queen of Insects of every inch of flesh by relentlessly using Mutilation until finally......

[You have defeated one of the Nine Monarchs, Queresha the Plague Monarch.]

[You have leveled up!]

[You have leveled up!]

[You have leveled up!]

......

A medley of messages popped up.

Nice!

But he didn't have time to enjoy the victory because there were still two more enemies who wanted his neck. Jinwoo hurriedly spun to defend against the murderous energy coming for him, but the opponents were a little faster than he was this time. While he had been preoccupied with the Plague Monarch, the enemy reached for him with one hand. Jinwoo felt five wisps of wind at his back.

Shunk!

Five claws burst out of his chest.

......

The Fang Monarch had now fully transformed into a werewolf and dug his claws in the dead center of Jinwoo's back, penetrating critical areas. Jinwoo's body froze.

Klink.

Klang.

Kamish's Wrath fell from his hands.

The Frost Monarch stood in front of him. The Monarch formed an ice dagger in his hand.

"This is the end." He thrust it into Jinwoo's stomach.

Shunk!

Having regained consciousness, Beru screamed. "M-my king!"

Jinwoo shook his head at Beru as the ant soldier attempted to stand on shaky legs, but Beru disregarded the order, extending his claws and limping toward the Frost Monarch.

"Skreeeee!"

Beru's sorrow and despair flowed into Jinwoo. The hunter didn't want Beru to be sent back to the void by the hands of the Monarchs. Realizing what Jinwoo was about to do, the ant king shook his head as tears welled up in his eyes. Despite the ant king's protests, Jinwoo forced Beru back into his shadow.

The ancient ice elf grinned, sure that victory was at hand.

"Is that all you've got, human?" He put his mouth close to Jinwoo's ear and whispered, "Then I suppose you won't live to see the day our armies descend on this plane. Nor the mountains of human corpses and rivers of blood they will leave in their wake."

The Frost Monarch moved back and snickered. "However, your homeland will suffer a different fate. I shall personally torture the people of this nation simply because they come from the same wretched place as you do. They will be made to live the rest of eternity in a state between life and death."

The cold emanating from the dagger piercing Jinwoo's stomach spread throughout his whole body, freezing him. Even as his face frosted over, Jinwoo's eyes blazed with anger.

The Frost Monarch laughed at him. "Continue to hate me even in death, for that will also bring me great pleasure."

The King of the Snow Folk pulled the dagger out from Jinwoo's stomach and stabbed it into Jinwoo's heart. The dagger shone with a cold white light as it crushed through Jinwoo's rib cage and burrowed into his heart.

Shunk!

Once the Frost Monarch was sure the hunter's heart had been destroyed, he pulled out his dagger. Jinwoo helplessly fell to the ground and hit his head on the asphalt. He felt dizzy, but he could still sense his enemies getting farther and farther away from him.

No...... I can still......

He tried to move his body, but he didn't have the energy to bend a finger. He quickly lost his senses and consciousness. Soon, he was floating in darkness as his human heart stopped.

Notifications began popping up one by one.

[The Player's HP is now 0.]

[The Player has died.]

[The Player possesses the Black Heart.]

[All the requirements for Passive skill: (Unknown) have been met.]

[Passive skill: (Unknown) has been activated.]

The skill information window opened unprompted. The list of Passive Skills blinked and updated.

[SKILLS]

Passive skill: (Unknown) Lv.Max, Willpower Lv.1, Dagger Master Lv.Max

*   *   *

Shf......

**Passive skill: Evolution Lv.Max, Willpower Lv.1, Dagger Master
Lv.Max**

* * *

"Are you awake?"

Jinwoo heard a familiar voice as soon as he opened his eyes, the white
ceiling above him and the smell of disinfectant stimulating his nose, plus
the uncomfortably hard bed. He knew exactly where he was: the hospital.

Jinwoo was sure the cold dagger had stabbed him in the heart.

But......I'm alive?

Jinwoo sat up to see two anxious people who looked as if they had
been waiting a long time for him to wake up. Jinwoo knew one of them
very well.

"President Woo. The Monarchs...... I mean, those monsters? What
happened to those monsters? How did I survive?"

Jinchul exchanged a surprised look with the Surveillance Team member next to him and took off his sunglasses.

"I have three things to tell you." He scooted his chair closer to the
bed, his subordinate standing right behind him.

"Firstly, I am not the president of the Hunter's Association. I'm
the manager of the Surveillance Team. Secondly, I was rather hoping
you could tell *me* about the moving stone statues, Hunter Sung. And
thirdly......" Jinchul looked sternly at Jinwoo. "How do you know me?
Have we met before?"

"H-hold on. What do you mean, 'moving stone statues'?"

"Taking survivors' reports into account, the Surveillance Team
brought along members of the White Tiger Guild, but when they
arrived at the room, everything—"

"No, that's not what I meant......" Flooded with unexplainable feelings, Jinwoo cut Jinchul off and shook his head at this absurd situation.

Could it be? Jinwoo looked back up at the ceiling. He'd thought it looked familiar, but he hadn't expected it to be the same place.

Of course I would recognize this place......

Jinwoo had spent two straight weeks in this VIP hospital room provided by the Hunter's Association after narrowly coming out alive from the double dungeon. Now he was back in that exact room, and based on what Jinchul had just said, the room wasn't the only blast from the past.

How......?

As Jinwoo sat speechless, Jinchul worriedly asked, "......Are you okay?"

Jinwoo kept his head down, rubbing his throbbing temples. He waved off Jinchul's concerns.

"I'd like a moment alone with my thoughts, if you please. Why don't you finish evaluating my magic power?"

How did this E-rank hunter know that they suspected he might have been reawakened? Jinchul stared at Jinwoo, then shook his head and got back to business.

"First, we would like to hear what happened in there. If you saw anything before you passed out......"

"I already told you, I don't remember anything."

Had Jinchul already talked to Jinwoo? No, he was sure he'd never spoken with Jinwoo before. As a member of the Surveillance Team, Jinchul never forgot any hunter he had ever met, but he had no memory of Jinwoo Sung.

His trauma must be rather severe.

Jinchul came to this conclusion and decided to wrap things up quickly. "Bring it over."

The subordinate approached with a small mana meter.

"Ha......"

Jinwoo barked a laugh as everything played out as he had remembered.

"All you have to do is place your hand on this essence stone."

"Right."

With his cooperation, the process was finished quickly, but after looking at the results, Jinchul frowned. He fiddled with the device a few times before finally turning to his subordinate.

"Why isn't this working? Didn't I tell you to check it before we left?"

"Sir?" The panicked subordinate hurriedly checked the mana meter, but he couldn't get it operational. It had been working fine until a few minutes ago when Jinwoo placed his hand on it.

Tsk.

Jinchul clicked his tongue and apologized to Jinwoo. "It looks like there was a mistake on our end. We'll find a new mana meter as soon as possible, so could you please wait for us? This procedure is a necessary part of the investigation......"

Jinwoo nodded before Jinchul could explain further, so the association employees hurriedly started to leave the room. However, something made Jinchul stop and come back.

What's up with him?

This was different from his memories. Jinwoo looked up as the Surveillance Team director leaned in.

"By the way...... You do know what happens to false rankers, correct?"

"......"

"I've met many high-ranking hunters in my time, but I've never met one with eyes like yours. If you're hiding anything, you should tell me n—"

"No, I'm not."

Jinchul gazed at Jinwoo for a beat longer, then gave a polite bow. "Apologies if I've offended you."

As he watched Jinchul leave the room, Jinwoo couldn't help but think that the man was definitely better suited to being the manager of the Surveillance Team than the president of the association.

But never mind that.

"Stat window." Jinwoo ignored the notice of unread messages and immediately called up his stats.

〖Name: Jinwoo Sung〗 〖Level: 146〗
[Job: Shadow Monarch]
[Title: Demon Hunter
(and 2 others)]

[HP: 93,300] [MP: 155,720]
[Fatigue: 0]

〖Stats〗

Strength: Stamina: Agility: Intelligence: Perception:
324 320 340 340 321

(Available ability points: 0)
Physical damage reduced by: 65 percent
Magic damage reduced by: 44 percent

〖Skills〗

Passive skill: Willpower Lv.1, Dagger Master Lv.Max
Active skill: Flash Lv.Max, Murderous Intent Lv.2, Mutilation
Lv.Max, Dagger Barrage Lv.Max, Stealth Lv.Max, Ruler's
Authority Lv.Max

〖Job-Exclusive Skills〗

Active skill: Shadow Extraction Lv.2, Shadow Storage Lv.2,
Monarch's Domain Lv.2, Shadow Exchange Lv.2

Is the increase in levels from killing the Plague Monarch?
That wasn't all. Everything Jinwoo had stashed in his inventory was

still there. Seeing the two Kamish's Wrath daggers in the very first slot of his inventory, it felt like the wind had been knocked out of his sails. He'd returned to the very beginning with all his prizes in his possession.

I don't have any shadow soldiers left, though......

He'd have to collect them again. With his abilities and memories intact, he was confident that he could do everything better than before.

But what had happened? Why had he gone back in time? This may have been a second chance for him, but he couldn't bring himself to be happy. He racked his brain for anything that might have slipped his mind.

Soon......

Sure enough, Jinah burst into the room. "Jinwoo!"

Ever since the orc incident at her school, Jinah'd had a gloom about her even when she smiled, but the Jinah in front of him didn't have those memories haunting her. The brightness of her expression brought tears to his eyes, and he drew her into a hug.

"J-Jinwoo?" Jinah had been ready to nag Jinwoo about quitting hunting, but she was flustered by his sudden gesture. "What? What's wrong with you? Did you hit your head or something?"

Jinwoo eventually let go of her and beamed at her. Her anger having abated, Jinah looked at him suspiciously. She couldn't place her finger on it, but there was something different about her brother. Perhaps he'd grown taller in the few days she hadn't seen him.

Jinah may have been perplexed, but Jinwoo's mind was now clear. He'd finished drawing up a step-by-step plan of what he needed to do. He kicked his sister out of the room to change. His clothes from the past barely fit and were an absolute mess, but there was nothing he could do about it. He couldn't very well walk around town in a hospital gown.

As he left the room and sped past his sister, she yelled after him. "Where're you going?"

"To the Hunter's Association."

"What for?"

"I'm going to quit being a hunter."

"Really?

Jinwoo looked back at Jinah, whose surprised eyes were as large as dinner plates. "You should get back to school. I know you only have permission to be off campus to check on me."

"What?" Jinah was more confused than ever, but her brother was already out of sight.

* * *

The employee of the association rubbed his eyes several times while verifying the reevaluation results. The last time this had happened was with Haein Cha two years ago, wasn't it? He paled as he gazed upon the tenth Korean hunter to get an unmeasurable reading. To think this man dressed in rags would be an S-rank hunter.

"H-Hunter Sung, it's not possible to measure your magic power—"

"I know. Would it be possible to meet with the president of the Hunter's Association before redoing the reevaluation?"

"Th-the president of the association?"

"Yes." Jinwoo was quite familiar with the reevaluation process.

Dazed, the employee picked up the phone receiver without a second thought. "Yes, yes. Yes, sir. That's right, unmeasurable. Understood. Yes, I will tell him that."

The president of the Hunter's Association had actually agreed to meet Hunter Sung.

"Allow me to escort you to the president's office—"

"I know where it is. No need to take me."

The flustered employee stared as Jinwoo walked to the elevator after shutting down their conversation quickly.

How does someone outside the association know where the president's office is?

The employee worried as he watched the numbers go up on the elevator. Against his expectations, the elevator carrying Jinwoo stopped on the correct floor.

"Oh……!"

Ding!

As Jinwoo exited the elevator, a familiar face brushed past him.

Jinwoo turned. "Hey, you."

The man pressed the button to keep the elevator doors open. "Are you talking to me?"

"You're not on the watch list of high-rank hunters, which means you haven't reported to the association that you can use Stealth."

It was Taesik Kang, a member of the Surveillance Team. He froze. "How do you know......?"

"Someone will ask you to avenge his daughter. I don't care what you do with the criminals, but if you harm any innocent hunters, I'll kill you."

Taesik flinched at the antagonism coming from Jinwoo and reached for the knife he kept at his waist, but it was gone.

"Are you looking for this?" Jinwoo tossed the knife in the air a few times before returning it to Taesik.

Realizing this man was completely different from the other hunters he had previously faced, Taesik took the knife back quietly.

"You only get one warning."

Knowing very well Jinwoo could take him down if he so desired, Taesik nodded as he holstered his knife. He called after Jinwoo as the other man walked away.

"Wait...... Who are you? Have we met before?"

Jinwoo entered the president's office at the end of the hallway without replying.

Once Jinwoo was out of sight, Taesik looked at his clammy hand and finally released the open-doors button. "......I feel like I just saw a ghost."

* * *

President Go......

Jinwoo came to a halt. There was President Go, alive and well as he went over documents. Jinwoo stood in the doorway, his heart aching at the sight.

President Go let out a chuckle. "You opened the door with such confidence, but you don't seem to have the courage to enter. Please come in, Hunter Sung." He moved himself to the couch in the room and gestured. "Why don't you have a seat?"

Jinwoo's face fell as he realized that this President Go was meeting him for the first time. He stood with a blank face for a moment before taking a seat. "Thank you."

President Go addressed Jinwoo. "Seeing as you came straight here after the reevaluation, it appears as though you're familiar with the process."

"That's right."

"Then allow me to cut to the chase."

"Before you begin, I have a proposal for you."

"A proposal?" President Go was caught off guard at this young man who seemed to already be aware that he'd been reawakened as an S-rank hunter. On the other hand, spunk was a great weapon for a youngster's arsenal. He found that he rather liked this man sitting across from him.

Maybe that was why he didn't bother hiding his smile and let him continue. "What is it you're asking for, Hunter Sung?"

"Please change the rules so that a hunter's minions can be counted as strike squad members."

"Change the rules......? That's quite a big ask. I expect you have something to offer in exchange that I won't be able to refuse."

Jinwoo paused for a beat. "I'll kill the ants on Jeju Island."

Jinwoo's priority was to replenish his army, and plenty of quality magic beasts awaited him on Jeju Island. If President Go accepted this deal, he would be able to replenish his soldiers and progress with plans without worry about minimum requirements for raid members. Jinwoo wanted to finish this step before waking up his mother with the Elixir of Life.

But to President Go, it sounded like Jinwoo was out to get himself killed. "Stop talking nonsense!"

Jinwoo had expected that reaction. Instead of faltering, he calmly released the entirety of his magic power for a split second. Infinite power spilled out of Jinwoo. Only powerful individuals could recognize another powerful individual like this, and President Go, the man known as a god among gods, could not believe the sheer power he was witnessing.

"How......how could this......? What *is* this?"

He trembled with excitement. President Go had never felt this much magic power from anyone anywhere until now. Jinwoo seemed to be well beyond even the national-level hunters. President Go's jaw hung open in surprise.

"I can take care of the ants on Jeju Island."

That was President Go's lifelong wish. He'd been about to lecture Jinwoo about being too reckless, but he changed his mind.

"Are you......serious?"

Jinwoo nodded. "I'm the only one who can do this. Please leave it to me."

* * *

Jinwoo looked at the remains of the ant-type magic beasts scattered as far as the eye could see. And right beneath his feet lay the corpse of the Ant King. It hadn't been that long since he last saw him, but Jinwoo already missed Beru.

He called out, "Arise!"

Jinwoo watched as shadow soldiers emerged from all the dead ants, including Beru.

"My king......"

Jinwoo slowly nodded as he gazed at the thousands of ants kneeling to him. His new army was swearing their allegiance to Jinwoo. However, after talking to his soldiers, he became sure of something.

"......Let's stop this."

Assembling his army wouldn't fill the hole in his heart. Beru looked up in concern, but Jinwoo could tell that both the worried expression and the distress the ant felt weren't real. Facing him made Jinwoo's heart ache more.

He shouted at the top of his lungs. "I know this is all fake. Quit it and reveal yourself!"

The illusion felt very real, so he'd tried to pretend for a while that it was. But the longer he stayed, the more the emptiness kept growing, and he was now no longer able to hide it.

Jinwoo yelled at the artificial energy swirling around him. "Hurry up!"

He abruptly quieted down as he noticed something change. Time had stopped. The lifeless stares of the ant soldiers gave him goose bumps.

At that moment, Monarch's Domain quickly spread out from Jinwoo's feet. Everything touched by the shadow vanished: Beru, the other shadow soldiers, the corpses, the land, the sea, and lastly the sky. Soon, the whole world was covered in shadow.

A deep voice rang out from the darkness. "You may stay in this world forever if you wish. It would be like never waking from a happy dream."

Jinwoo searched for the source of the voice. "Are you inviting me to stay trapped in this fantasy you've created?"

"No, I didn't create this world. This is of *your* making."

"Excuse me?"

What nonsense.

His argument died in his throat as he sensed something approaching from behind. Jinwoo whirled around.

A figure advanced toward him from the other end of the deep darkness. He wore sophisticated-looking armor that was incomparable to that of the regular shadow soldiers. In his formidable presence, Jinwoo could barely part his lips.

"This world was created by your desire to make up for all the mistakes you've made, coupled with my power. This is the world of death. In other words, this is *my* domain."

Jinwoo suddenly realized that this darkness he was standing in felt more inviting and cozier than any place he'd ever been.

Eternal rest......

Death. That meant that the man who had just claimed this, the other side of consciousness, as his domain had to be......

Jinwoo wanted to hear the answer for himself. "And you are......?"

The man drew closer. "I've been watching you for much longer than you think. You've been closer to death than anyone, but you've also fought death more desperately than anyone."

He'd......been watching Jinwoo?

Eventually, the man came to a stop in front of Jinwoo and looked down on him with eyes that seemed to absorb everything in sight.

"I am the history of your struggle, the evidence of your resistance, and the reward of your pain. I am death, rest, and fear all at once."

The man's every word reverberated deep inside the hunter. Jinwoo's heart pounded as it brought to mind all the times he'd desperately clung to life.

The man then grabbed Jinwoo's hand and placed it on his own chest. Jinwoo's eyes widened. He could feel it even through the thick armor. How could he not? It was the familiar heartbeat he could always hear when he concentrated on it. It was the sound of a second heart that beat from parts unknown.

It was the Black Heart, beating strongly in this man's chest.

"I......," the man murmured, "......am you."

5

MEMORIES OF THE SHADOW MONARCH

5

MEMORIES OF THE SHADOW MONARCH

"I am you."

As the bearer of the Black Heart, Jinwoo understood what those words meant.

He turned to his right, and a tree as tall as dozens of skyscrapers combined rose into the sky. He turned to his left, and a Maglev train shot past him in the blink of an eye. The items instantly appeared as soon as he thought of them. Something had been created from nothing.

"That is right," the Shadow Monarch confirmed. "In my domain, you can do anything you wish."

"Because you and I have the same power?"

The Shadow Monarch nodded. He turned his gaze to the giant tree, and it immediately shrank down into a small, common flower.

Despite it being limited to this domain, the Shadow Monarch's ability to create, unmake, and transform this world was marvelous. And now that omnipotence was in Jinwoo's hands as well.

Jinwoo blinked, and the same kind of flowers began spreading out from under his feet.

Perhaps it was due to Jinwoo's keen perception or because they were connected, but the hunter could sense the satisfaction the Shadow Monarch felt as he watched the flowers bloom.

The Shadow Monarch returned his attention to Jinwoo.

"I've been waiting to meet you for a long time." He officially introduced himself. "I am the Shadow Monarch, the King of the Dead who wields the power of death itself. I am the overseer of the deepest reaches of darkness."

Despite being before Death himself in the entirety of his majestic glory, Jinwoo wasn't frightened at all. They were one and the same, after all. Jinwoo was overcome with emotion at meeting his second half. At last, he was able to ask the question that had weighed on his mind ever since he'd first encountered the system.

"But......why me?"

Why had the system chosen Jinwoo as the Player? Was it just because Jinwoo had survived the double dungeon? No, there had to be another reason. It was finally the moment of truth.

"I shall show you." The Shadow Monarch slowly stretched his hand toward Jinwoo. When his index finger touched Jinwoo's forehead, what he could see in front of him changed. "I shall show you our beginning and our end, as well as your beginning."

* * *

In all of human history, had this many people the world over cried out at once? Screams tore through the air as the monster's dagger plunged into Hunter Jinwoo Sung's chest.

Silence then fell like a block of steel, broken only by mourning gasps as everyone watched Jinwoo collapse limply to the ground.

"Ah......"

First the national-level hunter Thomas Andre and now Jinwoo. There was nobody left. People were literally petrified knowing full well there was no one left to defend them.

"What? What's going on? Huh? Huh?"

The last thing broadcast before the live transmission cut out was the reporter's flustered cry.

The monolithic gate floating in the sky of Seoul. The sudden emergence of monsters that were killing off the top hunters one by one. Viewers everywhere could not help but think it was the end of the world. Yet amid their shock and awe, they could not bring themselves to pull away from their screens even after the broadcast was cut off.

* * *

The helicopter that had been filming the scene was now frozen solid and falling out of the sky, leaving a trail of smoke.

The Frost Monarch lowered his hand and looked back down at Jinwoo's body. His icy lips announced, "He has breathed his last breath."

The Fang Monarch confirmed the death with his wolflike vision and hearing. There was no trace of life in Jinwoo at all.

The Monarchs were thrilled by their victory. They had succeeded in killing one of the Rulers' allies before he could be much of a variable. But there was still some business to take care of. The two Monarchs' eyes snapped to where Thomas Andre had managed to escape.

Sensing their eyes trained on their location, Lennart shuddered. "Dammit......!"

He had managed to muster up the resolve to die defending against the bestial man, but now there was an ice elf to contend with as well.

How did Hunter Sung deal with them for as long as he did......?

Lennart's heart stuttered. He was now the only hunter who could buy some time against those two enemies. He took a deep breath.

"Hey...... I can't sense Hunter Sung anymore. What happened?" Thomas asked, not even halfway recovered.

Lennart struggled to reply. "He was......"

Just then, the two approaching Monarchs spun around at the same time.

"......!"

"......!"

The impossible had happened. The human's heart had been destroyed without a doubt, but a powerful heartbeat was coming from his body once more. But how?

The two Monarchs exchanged looks of disbelief as the worst-case scenario popped into their heads. They had overlooked one possibility.

"Don't tell me……"

They had thought that if they killed the human vessel, the Shadow Monarch would die as well, just like them. However, their opponent was the King of the Dead. Death came for everyone, but there was no guarantee it would be the same for him. The end for one could be the beginning for another.

"No…… This cannot be!"

They had to stop the advent of the true Monarch through the vessel's death. Instinctively, the two alarmed Monarchs advanced on Jinwoo, aiming their sharp claws and ice spear at him. They focused all their magic power in their weapons in an attempt to stop Jinwoo's body from becoming the avatar for the rise of the Shadow Monarch.

However, their weapons were blocked by the daggers of a mysterious stranger who had noiselessly appeared on the scene. The Shadow Monarch was still unconscious, so who could it be?

"……?" The two Monarchs could not hide their shock as their attacks were blocked.

An individual wielding two daggers deactivated Stealth and revealed himself. He glared from under a shimmering golden robe.

"Keep your hands off this child."

* * *

In the beginning of another world, there was only light and darkness. The Supreme Being divided the light to create Envoys of the Light and divided the darkness to create the Monarchs.

The prime directive for the Monarchs was to destroy the world, while the Envoys were directed to protect the world. Thus, they continued to kill each other's armies in a never-ending stalemate.

Eventually, the brightest Fragment of Luminosity approached the Supreme Being, tired of the ceaseless conflict.

* * *

O Divine Ruler,
Why do you not help your loyal subjects who fight in your name?
Why do you ignore our suffering?
Have you not heard the cries of the soldiers who have died for you?
Please help us.
Please lend us the strength to vanquish our enemies. We will cut off their *heads and offer them up to you.*

However, there was no response from the Supreme Being. At that moment, the Fragment of Luminosity realized something. The war between the Envoys and the Monarchs had merely been a source of ongoing entertainment for the Supreme Being, and so the Supreme Being had no desire for the war to end.

The Fragment fell into deep despair at this revelation. The war would never end as long as the Supreme Being was alive. The despair turned into rage, and the rage turned into hatred. In an act of rebellion, the Envoys drew their swords to try to end the meaningless war.

Jinwoo witnessed the march of countless soldiers that seemed to span the whole universe. "Oh my God……"

However, another group of soldiers appeared in the distance to stop the rebels. The Shadow Monarch stretched his hand out and pointed at the six-winged Fragments of Luminosity standing at the front.

"Behold, me in the past."

He was the only Envoy of the Light who opposed the rebellion against the Supreme Being. His pitiful band of soldiers fell helplessly to the allied armies of the other Envoys. Loyal to the end, the brightest Fragment of Luminosity died watching his brave subordinates overwhelmed by countless adversaries.

He assumed it was over. That is, until he opened his eyes in the darkness and realized that the Supreme Being had hidden a special power within him, his most faithful servant. A sinister power, a fail-safe to be used if everything went wrong.

Within the dark abyss, the King of the Dead was finally awakened to this power. He tore off his own wings, which had been burned in battle, and used the very darkness around him to fashion himself new armor.

"Arise!"

He then woke up the souls that were asleep in the abyss and returned to the world with his new legion of soldiers.

But it was all over by the time he arrived. The other Fragments of Luminosity, those so-called Envoys of the Light, had killed the Supreme Being and established themselves as the gods of this new order, the Rulers. Using the power of the Supreme Being, they began to hunt down the Monarchs.

The capture of Regia, the Monarch of the Beginning, the King of Giants, shifted the balance of power, and the other Monarchs realized just how dire the situation was. It was then that the Shadow Monarch offered his hand to the Monarchs. They took his hand to counter their common enemy, the Rulers.

Just like that, the war between the Seven Rulers and the Nine Monarchs raged on. However, as things dragged on, the shadow army grew larger and larger. Time was on the Shadow Monarch's side. Thanks to his brilliant performance, it appeared as though victory would go to the Monarchs.

However, as the shadow army became as powerful as the destructive army led by the King of Wild Dragons, the Rulers weren't the only ones who came to fear them. As the war drew to a close, the Monarch of White Lightning and the Fang Monarch decided to backstab the Shadow Monarch.

The scene shown in the data unfolded. Together, the demon army and the beast army advanced on the shadow army, bringing them to the brink of annihilation. The Fang Monarch, the King of Beasts, abandoned his own soldiers early on, leaving the Monarch of White Lightning, the King of Demons, to pay the price for their betrayal.

Jinwoo's eyes widened as he finally got to hear Balan's dying words, which had been redacted from the data previously. After that, a quartet of six-winged angels slowly descended from the skies, marking the end of the footage the data had presented to him back then.

Surrounded by four of the Rulers, the weary Shadow Monarch didn't have the strength to manipulate the shadow army. He threw his sword on the ground in surrender.

But if they killed the Shadow Monarch here, then how did the Shadow Monarch in front of Jinwoo come to be? Jinwoo swallowed hard as he watched what appeared to be the demise of the Shadow Monarch.

However, at that very moment, the Rulers dropped to their knees before the Shadow Monarch.

The Ruler in the front of the group spoke. "Please forgive us, O Greatest Fragment of Luminosity."

The Rulers were asking for the Shadow Monarch's forgiveness even though they clearly had the upper hand? If they wanted to, they could send the Shadow Monarch to the void, but they wanted to reconcile with him instead.

They used to be comrades who had been born from the same light. This was a show of respect to the greatest warrior, who had led the Envoys' armies on the front lines against that of the Monarchs. Although the Shadow Monarch hadn't been their leader, they nonetheless had the utmost respect for him. That was why they ignored the command from their own leader, the brightest Fragment of Luminosity, to kill the Shadow Monarch and knelt before him instead.

"We no longer have a reason to fight."

The Shadow Monarch thundered, "How dare you say we have no reason?!"

He grabbed the collar of the Ruler who had asked for his forgiveness and forced him to his feet.

"Did you not betray my master with your swords and spears?"

"He was our master as well."

"Which makes your sin all the more abominable!"

Despite the Shadow Monarch's anger, the Rulers maintained their decorum. "You know better than anyone how we felt about taking up arms against our master, don't you?"

The Shadow Monarch looked up to see that his soldiers had gathered and were now looking on with concern. His devoted soldiers. How could he not know the feeling of watching them fall at the hands of the enemy? He had been the one to lead them in battle in the name of their master, after all.

"We simply wish to end this war."

The Shadow Monarch loosened his grip on the collar of the Ruler.

"And we finally have a chance to do so."

"Yes, you can end this." The Shadow Monarch picked up his sword and put it in the Ruler's hand. "Strike me down with this sword."

He looked around at the other Rulers and declared, "Pierce my heart with your spears! That will bring the end you speak of! You will be the victors of this war!"

But the sword fell out of the Ruler's hand. None of the other Rulers raised their weapons, either. Instead came a desperate plea.

"Please, won't you forgive us now?"

Their desperation pained the Shadow Monarch more than any weapon ever could. After losing his men, after losing his master, and after plunging into the eternal darkness himself, the one thought that brought him back was revenge. The desire for revenge was what had taken him this far. His determination to make them pay was what led him to command the army of the dead.

But how could he hate these Rulers who were begging for forgiveness and trying to end this fighting? He who had fought to protect his master and they who had fought for the lives of their soldiers were all victims of destiny. He realized that the beings kneeling in front of him weren't horrible enemies but his allies in life and death.

With his reason for living gone, the Shadow Monarch screamed, "Kill me!"

He would end it all right now. He would rather return to the void and be at peace, able to forget everything.

"Do it now!"

But the Rulers didn't budge a millimeter, staying on their knees with their heads bowed. The Shadow Monarch looked up at the sky. The Rulers' soldiers placed their fists on their chests in remembrance of the greatest soldier they had ever fought with.

"......"

Although they had been on opposing sides because of their different ideals, they hadn't lost their respect for him. There were so many soldiers that they blocked out the sky. As the last soldier bowed to him, the Shadow Monarch quietly turned his back on them. And with that, he simply vanished.

Because of the infighting between the Shadow, Fang, and White Lightning Monarchs, the Monarchs eventually lost to the Rulers and retreated with the remnants of their armies through the gap between dimensions.

Jinwoo was rendered speechless by the sight of the Monarchs' soldiers passing through a humongous gate.

The losing army still has that many soldiers left......?

He couldn't even imagine how many soldiers had sacrificed their lives for the so-called Supreme Being's entertainment. He understood why the Rulers had decided to rebel against their master.

But then the Shadow Monarch resurfaced. The other Monarchs grew nervous at the possible confrontation between him and the Fang Monarch, but the Dragon King intervened before it came to that.

"Now is the time to rebuild our diminished armies, and I will not allow you two to fight despite what has occurred before."

The Dragon King then welcomed the Shadow Monarch back into their fold.

The sight of the Dragon King in his humanoid form made Jinwoo nervous despite knowing that he was watching a memory.

It's the King of Wild Dragons, the Monarch of Destruction......

Jinwoo could tell just by his eyes that the Dragon King held incredible amounts of power.

The Monarchs had fled through gaps in the dimensions and were searching for a new world where they could rebuild their army out of the Rulers' sight. Various planets and galaxies flashed before Jinwoo's eyes before stopping on one planet.

Jinwoo couldn't help but gasp. "Oh......"

Shining in the middle of a dark expanse was a beautiful blue planet: Earth. The Monarchs had found a passage to Earth after much effort. Annihilation was inevitable for humankind at the sudden appearance of such creatures. Jinwoo was startled to see cities in ashes just as he had seen on each floor of the Demon's Castle dungeon.

"Is this the future?"

"It is what has happened in the past."

Jinwoo stared bewildered at the unexpected answer.

The Shadow Monarch calmly explained. "The Rulers belatedly caught wind of the Monarchs' movements and sent in their soldiers, but by that time, it was all over."

If the purpose of the Monarchs was to destroy, the purpose of the Rulers was to protect. That was how they maintained the balance of the universe. So it infuriated the Rulers to see the Monarchs and their armies elude them and destroy another world. To right this wrong, they then used a forbidden tool.

Before rebelling against the Supreme Being, they had made it a priority to steal the Cup of Reincarnation from him. It was an incredible item that could reverse ten years of time.

Ten years!

Was it a coincidence that gates and hunters had first begun to appear in his world ten years ago?

"It is as you suspect."

The Rulers had done their best to protect Earth, but it was too weak to endure a war between them and the Monarchs. Earth did not contain the magic power it needed to survive such a struggle. No matter who won, whether it be the Rulers or Monarchs, the planet was doomed.

After repeating the same battle over and over again, the Rulers came to a decision. If they couldn't save everyone, they would find a way to at least save enough of this world to allow it to continue on.

"So you mean......?"

"They came up with a process to create humans capable of surviving the clash between Rulers and Monarchs. The Rulers meant to protect you in this way."

Finally, it hit Jinwoo. He realized why the Rulers had worked in secrecy, avoiding direct contact with humans, despite knowing that this disaster was to come.

The only people who would survive in this new world......

Would society have functioned normally had it known that everyone, save an extremely small, exclusive group of people known as hunters, was doomed to die? Absolutely not.

Jinwoo mentally shook his head. At long last, he had finally been told the purpose of gates and hunters, but his biggest question was still unanswered.

The Shadow Monarch seemed to have read Jinwoo's mind, and he transformed their surroundings with a wave of his hand.

"Higher beings such as Rulers or Monarchs are able to recognize time altered by the Cup of Reincarnation."

The Shadow Monarch added that they were, however, unable to control time in any way. As the Rulers corrected their mistakes, the Monarchs altered their plans. This would continue until the forbidden tool no longer functioned.

"Hang on...... The Cup of Reincarnation has limitations?"

"No power lasts forever. Every power has its limits, just as the Supreme Being met his end at the hand of his own creations." The bitterness in the Shadow Monarch's voice compelled Jinwoo to turn and look at him.

"Now that you mention it, how were the creations able to kill their creator?"

"It is not that different from your kind meeting your end by your own inventions."

That made sense. Machines created to help humans could cause harm, depending on how they were used. This was the reason why humans feared artificial intelligence despite it being created by humans.

"We were given life in order to fight, and we were imbued with power enough to kill our own master."

Jinwoo nodded in understanding.

Jinwoo recognized a few of the Monarchs whose images popped up next.

"Observing the Rulers' methods, the Monarchs were struck with an idea."

Much like how the Rulers had loaned their power to humans so that they could spread magic power over the planet by killing magic beasts, the Monarchs decided to borrow the bodies of humans, and once they were acclimated to Earth, they would bring over their armies earlier than the Rulers anticipated.

"The Monarchs' plan was to make Earth itself into a huge trap by using the magic power the Rulers had released on the planet."

"That way, they could devour the Rulers' armies who came to help humankind......"

"That is correct."

The Monarchs possessed great power, so they needed human vessels in order to come to this world. One by one, each of the Monarchs found human bodies capable of hosting them, except for the Monarch of Destruction and the Shadow Monarch. Their powers were too great, so they were unable to find humans capable of withstanding their power.

"It was then that a powerful mage who worked for the Monarch of Transformation offered to find the right human for me."

That mage had been the Architect. He had aided the Shadow Monarch in this endeavor in exchange for immortality. Keenly interested in the human world, the Shadow Monarch agreed to the deal, but unfortunately, no human had been able to withstand the power of death.

"One human was highly sensitive to magic power. Another human had an incredible physical strength. Still another had extraordinary intelligence. Yet none of them could handle my power and were either driven insane or died."

No living being had been able to contain death itself. A contract with a Monarch was no ordinary promise, and as time passed, the Architect grew more and more anxious. But as the Architect searched in vain for other candidates, one human caught the Shadow Monarch's eye.

"......" Jinwoo looked up to see hundreds of monitors airing various images of him.

"I witnessed you escape from the brink of death a number of times."

The four years when Jinwoo had worked as the weakest of E-rank hunters. He had constantly risked his life by entering dungeons, but he kept entering them anyway for the sake of his mother and sister. Jinwoo repeatedly threw himself into the lion's den and clawed his way out.

Those four years of struggling were recorded in the Shadow Monarch's memories.

"I chose you against the Architect's wishes."

Jinwoo's heart pounded as the Shadow Monarch pointed at him.

"I am the history of your struggle, the trace of your resistance, and the reward of your pain."

He hadn't been referring to Jinwoo after the hunter had become the Player, but rather, his life before. Each word the Monarch spoke reverberated in his heart anew.

"The anxious Architect did as I asked and reached out to you."

The double dungeon. The tests of survival. The Player. Everything had been part of the Architect's plan to prepare a new vessel for the Shadow Monarch.

"The Architect had ample time to study humans during the different time loops. From this, he gleaned that he could create a system based on a beloved pastime to help them adapt to my mighty power."

"A beloved pastime." In other words, video games. That explained why the system had been designed as such.

Jinwoo had been the only success to come from this experiment.

"The Architect borrowed my power to create the system, and the system gradually transformed your body to suit my needs."

"But you betrayed the Architect, right?"

Jinwoo recalled the angel statue from the double dungeon that had thrown a fit about how the Shadow Monarch had apparently deceived the other Monarchs. The Shadow Monarch had broken his contract with the Architect and chosen Jinwoo instead.

"Why did you do that?" asked Jinwoo.

"……"

For the first time, the Shadow Monarch hesitated to answer. He looked to be deep in thought, so Jinwoo didn't rush him.

"I merely wanted to."

It was rather simple for how long the Monarch had deliberated, but Jinwoo also found himself chuckling.

"I suppose I didn't want to lose you because I enjoyed our time together."

The Shadow Monarch had chosen to assimilate with Jinwoo's personality instead of overwriting it and stealing his body. The Monarch had chosen to coexist, and this was the result. The Shadow Monarch slowly took hold of the helmet covering his face and pulled it off. Jinwoo was startled at the face underneath.

……!

Jinwoo's own face stared back at him. But that wasn't all. When Jinwoo looked down, he realized that he also had been cloaked in armor as black as night, just like what the Shadow Monarch was wearing. The two were mirror images.

"I have become you and you have become me." The Shadow Monarch meant that quite literally. "It matters not which of us controls your body."

The two were already the same being.

"So I will give you a choice. You get to decide." When the Shadow Monarch raised his left hand, people Jinwoo missed dearly appeared. "You can enjoy the eternal rest with the beautiful dream you've made in this domain of death."

There was President Gunhee Go guffawing, Jinwoo's mother before she contracted the Eternal Sleep Disease, and even a younger version of himself.

"If not......" When the Shadow Monarch raised his right hand, the people disappeared, and an insanely huge dragon flew toward him. An army of dragons followed close behind and began burning down the city. "You will have to go back to reality and fight."

Jinwoo grimly watched the Dragon King and his army wreak havoc. He then asked a question.

"Why did you run away to another world with the other Monarchs when you gave up on fighting the Rulers?"

"Because there was no place for me there."

The Shadow Monarch had been both a Ruler and a Monarch in his time, but he did not fit in with either group. And so he'd gone searching for a place of his own in another world.

Jinwoo made his decision. "My answer is the same as yours."

The Shadow Monarch wore a small smile even before he heard Jinwoo's answer.

"This isn't where I belong."

"......Very well." This was why the Shadow Monarch had chosen Jinwoo.

"I won't see you again, will I?"

"I shall return to the eternal rest. And as the Shadow Monarch, you shall be immortal. We'll more than likely never cross paths again."

The Shadow Monarch looked content. After all this time, he could rest. Jinwoo bid his final good-bye to the joyful Monarch.

"Thank you for giving me this opportunity."

"......" For a fleeting moment, the Monarch looked wistful. "With your death, your power is complete. The way back is—"

"I know the way." Because Jinwoo *was* the Shadow Monarch.

The Shadow Monarch smiled. After wandering for so long, he had finally found his place. "This is farewell."

He retreated one step and quietly stared at the hunter, who nodded in reply.

Jinwoo then uttered the word that would trigger his rebirth as the one true Shadow Monarch. "Arise."

The female voice of the system responded as if it had been waiting for this moment.

["Arise."]
[The delete code for the Player development system has been entered.]
[The system will be deleted.]

Now that Jinwoo had been bestowed with the ultimate power of the Shadow Monarch, the obsolete system began deleting itself. It felt like saying good-bye to a teacher who had helped raise him.

"By the way, where did you get the female voice for the system?"

"......That's the Architect's voice." The Shadow Monarch made it sound like the reveal was common knowledge. "The Architect belongs to a race of intersex beings, members of which possess the ability to produce both feminine- and masculine-sounding voices."

"......"

Jinwoo had often wondered who the clear and pleasant voice of the system had originated from. To think it was the asshole Architect. Embarrassed, Jinwoo avoided making eye contact with the Shadow Monarch, who muffled his laugh.

Heh-heh!

Every little thing about Jinwoo delighted the Shadow Monarch.

Jinwoo had been worth breaking his promise with the Architect for, despite how important trust was to the Shadow Monarch. But there was also a fleeting moment of sorrow in the Shadow Monarch's eyes.

[The restrictions on the Player's power have been removed.]
[All shadow soldiers who have been awarded authority by the Monarch as leaders of the shadow army will have their powers restored.]
[Marshal Igris will have his powers restored.]
[Marshal Beru will have his powers increased greatly.]
[The previous Shadow Monarch Ashborn will return to the endless void.]

Jinwoo had been silently listening to the notifications. He now looked up to see the Shadow Monarch watching him.

In this domain of death, Jinwoo had fully come to understand the Monarch's agony through the memories he shared. He sent him a heartfelt good-bye.

Farewell, my king. May you rest in peace in your promised land.

The system gave its final notification.

[Are you sure you want to delete the system?]

The options for "Yes" and "No" blinked in front of him.

Jinwoo turned toward the Shadow Monarch. The King of the Dead didn't drop his smile, as this would be the last image they would have of each other.

Jinwoo smiled back as he gave his final order to the system. "Yes."

* * *

Whoooosh!

A great gust of wind accompanied by a blinding flash pushed the Fang Monarch and Frost Monarch back.

The Fang Monarch quickly recovered, his eyebrows twitching. "A Fragment of Luminosity......?"

The man in front of them wore a robe and radiated a gold light, a hallmark of the Rulers. It was a human borrowing the power of the Rulers. But why was this person protecting one of the most powerful Monarchs?

The Frost Monarch yelled at him. "The human you are protecting is the harbinger of tragedy! Are you planning to bring the end of all things by your own hands?"

"......" Instead of answering, the man raised his hands up to his chin, each wielding a dagger in a reverse grip. He refused to step aside.

The Frost Monarch scowled at the show of determination. The strange man was attempting to borrow a Ruler's power while still in his human body, but human bodies were incapable of withstanding a god's power. Without the Ruler taking total possession of the human body as the Monarchs did, this vessel would crumble to dust.

And yet......he's risking his life to help the Shadow Monarch's resurrection? What in blazes do the Rulers think they're doing......?

The Frost Monarch exchanged looks with the Fang Monarch. Time was running out. The King of Beasts nodded, and the two Monarchs charged at the man, one from the right and the other from the left.

But the man skillfully blocked the relentless claws and spear while getting in some jabs of his own. He moved like a warrior who had seen his fair share of battles. Though he was facing certain death, he proved to be a tough opponent with his excellent skills and strength.

Boom!

The man in the robe blocked his opponents' mana-charged weapons and pushed them back. The two Monarchs landed at a distance as they realized how difficult it would be to end this fight if they continued to battle in this manner.

Tak. Tak.

The man stood his ground instead of chasing after the two Monarchs, as if his only purpose was to protect the Shadow Monarch's vessel.

"......Who are you?" The Frost Monarch demanded to know the man's identity, but he said nothing.

It was then that the Fang Monarch transformed out of his werewolf form. "I shall retreat."

His sharp fangs regressed, and his long, pointy claws turned into the fingernails of a human.

The Frost Monarch called after him. "You're running away after we have come this far? Are you out of your mind?"

"Can you not feel it?" The Fang Monarch raised his head. His exceptional perception sensed a change in the air that made his body tremble. "The mana in the air is crying out. The Shadow Monarch is coming." The Fang Monarch turned his eyes from the sky to the Frost Monarch again. "I am leaving."

"Y-you promised to help me battle the Shadow Monarch!" the Frost Monarch sputtered.

But the Fang Monarch shrugged. "I promised to help with the Shadow Monarch in a human state, not his true form. I have no reason to stay."

"So you run away with your tail between your legs? And you call yourself the King of Beasts?!"

Affronted, the Fang Monarch snatched the Frost Monarch by the collar. "You do not understand because you have never faced the true power of the Shadow Monarch!"

The Fang Monarch had witnessed the Shadow Monarch survive an assault from six armies simultaneously: his own army of beasts, the army of the Monarch of White Lightning, the armies of four Rulers. Such a monster was en route, so what did pride matter? Even if it meant being ridiculed for hiding behind the Dragon King, survival was the most important matter.

It had been the right call to abandon the Monarch of White Lightning, the King of Demons, on the battlefield. And the King of Beasts was not willing to now destroy all his hard work by risking an encounter with the true Shadow Monarch.

As the King of Beasts, the Fang Monarch's power came from the vitality of living creatures. Because of this, nothing frightened him more than death.

The Fang Monarch didn't have time to argue with the Frost Monarch. He sensed death approaching quickly. He let go of the Frost Monarch's collar and generated a gate for himself.

"I wish you luck." With that, the King of Beasts stepped through to the other side.

The Frost Monarch glared at the closing gate. "Fool."

How could someone who abandoned prey ripe for the taking be considered the best hunter in the World of Chaos? The Frost Monarch was ready to do whatever it took to kill the Shadow Monarch, outside interference be damned. He had already cornered his prey at the edge of a cliff, so he certainly didn't need help from that coward.

The determined Frost Monarch transformed into a spiritual body. Because he was not of this world, maintaining this form consumed a lot of his stamina. He needed to end this as quickly as possible before the Shadow Monarch awakened.

"Taste the terror of frost, puny human!" The Frost Monarch transformed into a raging snowstorm. The living storm thundered as it looked down at the man in the robe.

"Face my true power!"

Mana crystals in the air merged to create tens of thousands of icicles. They blew violently through the air like spears made of ice, each packed with enough power to instantly kill any human. The attack swept cars off the road like mere toys, and gales ripped buildings apart.

Despite this, the man in the robe stood his ground and protected Jinwoo to the best of his ability, enduring scars from the countless ice spears.

The Frost Monarch did not relent. "My soldiers!"

Thousands of soldiers made of ice emerged from the snow that had piled up knee-high.

"Charge!"

The ice soldiers leaped at the man in the robe. He fought desperately to shake off the hunks of ice coming at him from all sides.

Shhhk!

The man stumbled as he was stabbed in the shoulder by an ice spear.

"……"

He gritted his teeth and straightened back up, holding his own against the oncoming wave of soldiers.

Seeing the man in the robe persist, the Frost Monarch joined the attack. He transformed into a crystalline manifestation of cold energy, and white vapor rose from his body as he approached.

"Move!"

His icy lackeys scattered out of his way.

Standing in front of the man in the robe, the Frost Monarch opened his mouth wide. Bone-chilling cold began gathering in his mouth. The air itself began to freeze, and frost formed on the man's exposed chin from under the robe.

The man in the robe knew he couldn't take too much more of this, but he also knew that if he dodged, Jinwoo would get hit. And so the man in the robe continued to stand his ground.

The Monarch's face twisted in fury. This human was merely borrowing the power of a higher being, so how dare he look arrogantly upon the face of his mighty power?

A frightening burst of cold energy shot out of the furious Monarch's mouth.

Hwoooosh!

The man crossed his arms in front of his chest to block the icy energy. His two arms froze from the blast, rendering him unable to move them. He could no longer defend himself from the following barrage of attacks.

Pow! Pow! Pow! Pow!

With each punch, the man's upper body teetered, but his feet remained planted firmly on the ground. He endured the attacks even as blood pooled at his feet.

"The gall of this mere human!" The Frost Monarch raised his right arm behind him. Cold energy coated his arm, forming a massive column of ice. Would the man be able to withstand this? The Frost Monarch dropped the ice column, aiming to not only take down the human but also crush the Shadow Monarch's vessel.

Whoom!

As the ice column descended upon him, the man raised his frozen arms above his head. He would protect Jinwoo to the last, even if it meant breaking his arms or being completely crushed. His body shone as he mustered every ounce of the Ruler's power within him.

Boom!

A collision. But he felt no impact.

What's going on......?

The man peeked up to see someone standing in front of him.

......!

Pitch-black armor. A long red mane atop a black helmet. It was Igris, a loyal subject of the Shadow Monarch. To the Frost Monarch's disbelief, Igris had caught the column of ice with both hands and shoved it out of the way, perfectly blocking his attack.

"Igris the Bloodred?"

The appearance of a marshal could mean only one thing. The startled Frost Monarch hurried to look behind the human. Sure enough, the vessel of the Shadow Monarch had vanished from sight.

The Frost Monarch now understood what the Fang Monarch had been saying earlier. The mana in the air was practically vibrating as a reaction to the appearance of a transcendent being.

Igris turned around, respectfully dropped down on one knee, and bowed his head.

"Skraaaaaah!"

Beru had appeared at the same time as Igris. He roared to announce the return of their master and went down on one knee.

Jinwoo walked out between the two soldiers. He scanned the terrible destruction before turning to the Frost Monarch.

"Did the beast run away?"

"......"

It wasn't until he was finally facing the true Shadow Monarch that the Frost Monarch realized why the Fang Monarch was so frightened. Despite being the king of all things frozen and being the embodiment of the shivering cold itself, the Frost Monarch couldn't stop quivering.

Jinwoo frowned. "......I did not allow this."

Puzzled, the Frost Monarch asked, "What?"

"I did not allow him to leave."

"What are you talking about......?"

Jinwoo ignored the bewildered Frost Monarch and closed his eyes, expanding his perception beyond South Korea to locate the Fang Monarch's unique magic-power signature. He was confident he could find the Fang Monarch as long as he was hiding somewhere on earth and not between dimensions. He eventually hit the jackpot as he detected the Fang Monarch in his hideout.

Jinwoo opened his eyes and smiled. "Found you."

As Jinwoo focused all his attention on locating the beast, the Frost Monarch saw an opening. This was his one and only shot. Despite the gap in their powers, Jinwoo was letting his guard down in front of his opponent. If he let this opportunity slip through his fingers, all that awaited him would be death. It was a last-ditch effort to avoid the encroaching shadow of death.

I must finish him with one strike.

He wound his right arm all the way back as mana gathered around it, and he generated the most powerful ice spear he could create. The Monarch poured every drop of his power into this spear, so much so that the ground he stood on froze and began to crack.

Then, when the ice spear in his right hand was impossibly huge, he sent it ripping through the air like a missile.

Whiiiiish!

At the same time, his ice soldiers went after Jinwoo like a pack of angry dogs.

Whish!

Right before the spear of ice pierced Jinwoo's face, he opened his eyes.

"Found you."

Time seemed to stand still, as if someone had pressed Pause on a video. Well, it was more like time slowed down to the point that it looked like it had stopped. The spear of ice was moving slowly but surely. Behind the spear, Jinwoo could see the Frost Monarch glaring angrily at him. He was also able to clearly see each movement of the ice soldiers surrounding him.

This was how the Shadow Monarch saw things when he was in a battle. His cognitive ability was beyond human comprehension, so living objects appeared to be frozen in time. Jinwoo casually surveyed his surroundings as the entire world seemingly held its breath.

I've felt this before......

When had that been? Jinwoo slowly recalled the moment he had been about to die at the hands of the stone statues. Time had drastically slowed for him back then as well.

The Shadow Monarch was already with me at that time.

Jinwoo was coming to understand just how long the Shadow Monarch had been watching him after unlocking the full extent of his powers.

As he looked around, he saw the backs of his two marshals.

Oh?

Although everyone else seemed to be frozen in time, Beru and Igris were slowly responding to the enemies' attacks. It was evidence of their unparalleled agility. As he looked upon them with pride, Jinwoo then remembered the spear coming at him.

Oh yeah.

The spear inched closer like a bug crawling in midair. Jinwoo used his power to stop the spear's advance.

Ruler's Authority.

Of all the Shadow Monarch's abilities, this was the one he had put into practice the most. As soon as Ruler's Authority was activated, mana wrapped around the ice spear and stopped it on the spot. Jinwoo gasped in amazement as he saw the inner workings of Ruler's Authority for the first time.

So it wasn't some invisible hand.

Instead, it was mana that couldn't be seen by the naked eye carried out by the will of the user.

Awesome.

When he increased his perception to the max, he could sense every single flow of mana around him. His eyes sparkled with delight. This was what the Rulers had given the world to strengthen it. Though this world hadn't had a single ounce of mana before, it now overflowed with it. And with the Shadow Monarch's power, Jinwoo had free rein over it all.

Ba-dump, ba-dump!

His heart leaped as he felt the ebb and flow of the mana around him.

......Let's give it a try.

Jinwoo approached his two marshals and put his hands on their shoulders.

You two don't need to do anything.

Beru and Igris immediately paused at Jinwoo's instruction.

He walked past them. He had practiced Ruler's Authority whenever he'd had the chance. Now he could maximize his control of the mana. Jinwoo took a deep breath as he looked around at the ice soldiers. He was filled with appreciation for the Shadow Monarch and how much he had taught him through the system. He concentrated and took control of the mana around him. The entire area seemed to shake.

Woooom!

It literally took only a second for the powerful wave of mana Jinwoo had emitted to sweep away the massive number of ice soldiers. The Frost Monarch felt the mighty mana storm coming toward him as well.

"......!"

He rushed to create an ice barrier to protect himself. When the Frost Monarch deactivated the shield, he saw the remains of his ice soldiers strewn throughout the area. The powerful mana had swept away everything, including the blizzards he had conjured up.

This was the power of the Shadow Monarch, also known as the greatest Fragment of Luminosity and one of the two mightiest kings.

"H-how......?!"

The Frost Monarch was left trembling in fear. The Shadow Monarch was like a wall the Frost Monarch could never overcome.

Satisfied by the results, Jinwoo nodded as he made eye contact with the frightened Frost Monarch. Even at this distance, Jinwoo was able to feel the Frost Monarch trembling.

He still had a debt to settle with the ice elf. Jinwoo's expression turned cold as he remembered the late President Go, and he decided on his plan. He'd kill this one last and give him time to wallow in fear about his imminent death.

"You'll go last," Jinwoo said as he slowly sank into the shadow beneath his feet. "Wait here while I go after that beast."

* * *

President Jinchul Woo slammed his fist down on the desk when the live broadcast cut out.

Bam!

The last thing they'd shown was Jinwoo's body falling to the ground in defeat. He was devastated. If this desk hadn't belonged to the late President Go, Jinchul would've smashed it to pieces.

Jinchul's tightly clenched fists shook. The subordinates who were watching with him in the president's office kept their mouths shut tight. A heavy silence fell on the room.

However, Jinchul knew better than anyone that they didn't have time to just sit there and do nothing. "Has any guild reached the area?"

"Yes, all five large guilds have arrived at the scene."

Jinchul quickly rose from his seat. "The Surveillance Team must also head there. Myself included."

"It's too dangerous, sir!"

"What does that matter in this case?"

The subordinates trying to stop him were at a loss for words as he glared at them. Korea had lost Jinwoo Sung, their strongest line of defense. That meant there was nowhere to retreat. Every hunter had to work together to stop those monsters or there would be no tomorrow.

As Jinchul hastily put on his jacket, he glanced at a monitor broadcasting another live feed. This particular camera was fixed on the sky, constantly filming the monolithic gate above Seoul. It gave Jinchul pause.

Maybe......

Maybe Korea was already finished. His heart sank.

Even if they got lucky and killed the monsters, the damage would be too great. Would the remaining hunters be able to handle a gate of that scale without Jinwoo? Thinking of both the monsters in the downtown area and the monolithic gate hit him with an overwhelming sense of despair.

But Jinchul managed to shake his head. Even if every citizen of Korea thought the same thing, that wouldn't change the fact that someone had to fight on the front lines. This was the reason why hunters had been bestowed their powers. Jinchul bit his lip hard and banished the negative thoughts from his head.

He was about to leave when one of his staffers hurriedly called out, "President Woo, sir!"

Jinchul whipped around toward the large TV screen from which the voice of a reporter came with breaking news.

"Our camera on location is back up!"

Based on the wide angle of the scene, it looked like the camera was shooting from the top of a faraway skyscraper, but that was good enough. The snowstorm that had been blanketing the area was being dispersed by an unknown force.

Jinchul excitedly pushed past the employees who had jumped to their feet in order to get closer to the monitor. As the fog lifted, they were able to see five people. No, make that four people and one insect. Jinchul knew exactly who the man standing in front of the insect was.

"Hunter Jinwoo Sung!" Jinchul blurted out as everyone cheered at the sight of the crushed remains of the ice soldiers.

"Yeaaaaah!"

They'd thought he was gone, but not only was Jinwoo alive, he had put the enemy on the ropes. How could they contain their emotions? Tears welled up in Jinchul's eyes.

There seemed to be one enemy left. The monster that used ice seemed immobilized by fear, like his feet had been nailed to the ground. The viewers had no idea what had happened inside the blizzard, but the tables had turned.

Jinchul could tell that everyone around the world was watching this scene unfold. How would Jinwoo crush the monster? Jinchul stared expectantly at the screen.

Strangely, it looked like Jinwoo merely said something to the monster before Jinwoo began to sink into the ground.

......?

The employees who had been hugging one another and cheering froze as Jinwoo completely disappeared from view. The flustered cameraman swung the camera around in search of Jinwoo but was unable to find hide or hair of him.

"Huh......?!" Equally confused, Jinchul rubbed his chin as another heavy silence filled the president's office.

* * *

The Fang Monarch was trembling inside his hideout in the jungle. It felt like a noose was tightening around his neck. He should've retreated earlier. Arguing with the Frost Monarch had taken too much time.

Back when he'd gone after that Brazilian hunter, the earth had been full of easy prey for him. It had been exciting to be freed from the gaps between dimensions on these new hunting grounds.

He never would have imagined the Shadow Monarch had descended on this world with such a malicious scheme. A human pretending to be the Shadow Monarch was one thing, but he refused to fight the actual Shadow Monarch. The power of the Monarch of Destruction was needed to take on the Shadow Monarch.

There's nothing for it. I'll have to hunker down until the Dragon King arrives......

The beast lay on a bed made of leaves and tree branches. Denizens of chaos, known by the humans as magic beasts, lay at his feet. These powerful creatures were his royal guard, but they purred like pets and nuzzled his hand as the king stroked them.

His hand froze as he sensed something strange.

Hmm......?

The beasts' fur stood on end as their instincts kicked in. The Fang Monarch got goose bumps on the back of his neck, and they all fixed their gazes on the same spot. The Monarch's eyes narrowed until they were slivers.

The shadow of a nearby tree appeared to be moving.

The Fang Monarch picked up on the scent of death inside his hideout. He nervously muttered, "Is that......?"

Something was slowly rising from the tree's wiggling shadow.

The human......?

No, the Shadow Monarch? The beast was unable to identify his opponent, but every single one of his senses was telling him that the man's presence felt identical to the one who almost did him in those many moons ago. Whoever it was, this trespasser possessed ultimate power in his hands.

He chased me here?

The King of Beasts shuddered as the terror of death permeated his bones as Jinwoo rose from the ground.

Grrrrr!

In an attempt to protect their master, the beasts bared their fangs to intimidate Jinwoo. One of them dashed toward him. It was a magic beast that resembled a wildcat with three red eyes, and it was one of the most savage beasts from the World of Chaos.

Rowr!

Dozens of sharp fangs gleamed inside its mouth. Unfazed, Jinwoo stared as the savage S-rank magic beast grew closer. The Jinwoo of the past would have readied himself to fight it, but it posed no threat to him now.

Bam!

Before Jinwoo could bother to deal with the savage beast, the Fang Monarch leaped at it and crushed its head into the ground. He pulled his fist out of the ground as the wildcat's limbs went limp.

Why did he just kill his own soldier......?

The Fang Monarch lowered his body and head subserviently as Jinwoo watched him curiously. He shakily pleaded, "O Shadow Monarch, I, the King of Beasts, do not wish to fight you. Please forgive my transgressions and accept me as your ally."

His beastly instincts had kicked in. If you cannot fight or flee, submit. The Fang Monarch was an animal by nature, so he cast aside his pride.

"The Dragon King will soon descend upon this land with his soldiers. When that time comes, my army of beasts and I will be by your side."

He lowered his body as much as he could.

Whimper!

The savage creatures behind the Monarch wet themselves as they remained paralyzed in complete terror. Survival was everything to these creatures, so they feared nothing more than the approach of death.

Jinwoo looked down at the King of Beasts with his tail between his legs.

"Fine."

A smile spread across the Fang Monarch's lowered face. What a fool! *That can't be the true Shadow Monarch.*

If it were, he wouldn't have made the mistake of forgiving the one who had not only betrayed him once before but also attempted to destroy the vessel of his rebirth. The King of Beasts had bought some time thanks to the human's soft heart and ignorance. How could he bring himself to obey the Shadow Monarch while he had the scent of prey mixed in? He would pretend to work with him until the arrival of the Monarch of Destruction.

When the time comes, I will rip your body apart with my own hands and devour you.

It was no wonder he couldn't hold back a grin.

"I swear my loyalty to y—" The King of Beasts recoiled in fear after meeting Jinwoo's frigid gaze, putting a considerable distance between himself and the Shadow Monarch in a flash.

The beast's face paled as Jinwoo noted, "First, we need to settle the debt between us."

The King of Beasts forced out, "Debt? You mean what happened back then......?"

Having inherited the Shadow Monarch's memories, Jinwoo was well aware of how the Fang Monarch and the Monarch of White Lightning had attempted to betray the King of the Dead in the past. But it had nothing to do with Jinwoo. He took out one of the Kamish's Wrath daggers from the other dimension the system had referred to as his inventory.

Vwoooom.

With the index finger of his free hand, he indicated five spots on his own chest. "These are the five spots where your claws penetrated my chest."

He vividly remembered the awful pain.

"If you can withstand five of my attacks, I will forgive you."

In other words, the Fang Monarch would have to survive five fatal wounds. The King of Beasts let out a roar fitting of a beast as he realized that the Shadow Monarch had never had any intention of forgiving him.

"How dare you trick me! Me, the King of Beasts......!"

The Fang Monarch triggered his true form and transformed into a humongous wolf. It was smaller than pictured in the Shadow Monarch's memories, though it was because this wasn't the wolf's home dimension. Whatever his size, the King of Beasts possessed enough power to destroy all of earth.

The furious Fang Monarch bellowed, "This may be the end of the line for me, but I'm going to take you down with me!"

Shunk!

At that moment, a cold breeze blew past the wolf's face. He turned to try to follow Jinwoo's movements as the human vanished from in front of him. Jinwoo had stopped behind the wolf and was slowly turning toward him.

"That's one."

The wolf noticed the awfully powerful black aura around Jinwoo's entire body and swallowed hard. There was no doubt that the man in front of him was the true Shadow Monarch. His movements were identical.

Plop!

Something hit the ground. The wolf couldn't help himself. He glanced down to see a huge ear on the ground. A wolf's ear had been placed at his feet. Soon, the Fang Monarch felt extreme pain as blood gushed from his wound.

Gnashing his teeth, the wolf looked up and saw a second dagger in Jinwoo's other hand. Jinwoo gripped both Kamish's Wrath daggers as he delivered his final verdict to the wolf.

"That leaves four."

* * *

The Frost Monarch was surrounded. Jinwoo had left him in a tough spot. Fleeing would be the best option, since he had no chance of winning here, but he eyed the two marshals of the shadow army.

Never mind the bastard ant who's healing a Ruler's vessel......

The remaining shadow was the problem. Igris the Bloodred, one of the two wings of the shadow army, kept his eyes on the Frost Monarch. The soldier's nickname was the Death Knight, and he was a powerful warrior who had fought on countless battlefields and killed countless enemies under the command of the Shadow Monarch. This was the opponent the Frost Monarch needed to be most wary of.

With that being said......

The ancient ice elf was a Monarch, not some common foot soldier. At his best, the Frost Monarch should have been able to defeat both marshals without a problem. The issue was that the marshals possessed the power of regeneration. They would keep coming back for more until the Shadow Monarch ran out of mana. This did not bode well for the Frost Monarch, who lost much stamina after utilizing his true form.

Additionally, attacking them was the same as informing their master of his moves, as every shadow soldier was connected to the Shadow Monarch. Even if the Frost Monarch succeeded in defeating the major generals, it would call the Shadow Monarch back to this location. The Frost Monarch needed to prevent that at all costs.

Then......

He turned his body to create a gate to escape.

Fwip.

Igris blocked the Monarch's path. The soldier shook his head and tapped the hilt of his sword at his waist as a clear warning to not do anything stupid.

Fwip.

The Frost Monarch turned and was met by the ant's mandibles.

"Skraaaaaah!"

The ant had been healing the arm of the interloper. If he was here, then...... The Monarch spotted the fully healed interloper walking toward him.

"You bastards......!" The Frost Monarch was trembling with rage at the enemies surrounding him. "You worms dare to......!"

The furious king's screech shook the land. The air began to turn frosty, and dark clouds gathered overhead once more.

"How long do you think you can last against me?"

Igris pulled out his sword, Beru flashed his sharp claws, and the man in the robe brandished a dagger in his hand. But before they could clash, the Frost Monarch sensed a disturbance in the air.

"......!"

The other three followed his gaze to see a shadow quivering.

The Frost Monarch bit his lower lip. He needed to buy some time.

"Shadow Monarch!"

Jinwoo rose up from the nearby shadow.

Love that the cooldown period is gone.

Any restrictions to his power had been lifted with the deletion of the system. Jinwoo was able to return in a snap to where he had been earlier. He looked at the Frost Monarch and tossed over the object in his hand.

The Frost Monarch caught it and stared. "Is this......?"

It was a wolf's ear. There could be only one wolf with an ear that large.

"You mean to say that you killed the Fang Monarch in the few minutes you were away?!" the surprised monarch bellowed.

Instead of responding, Jinwoo summoned his two daggers just as he had done with the King of Beasts. The Fang Monarch's blood that dripped from them was still warm.

The Frost Monarch trembled as the powerful man before him chose his next target. The two marshals and the man in the robe retreated when they spotted the black aura rising from Jinwoo's shoulders.

Jinwoo tightened his grip on the daggers. He had held the enemy on ice for long enough. It was time for payback. The Plague Monarch, the Fang Monarch, and the Frost Monarch. Their deaths would be a warning to the rest of the Monarchs.

When Jinwoo smoothly rushed at him, the ancient ice elf quickly generated ice arrows to fire at him.

"You bastard!"

Despite being hastily made, the magic arrows had been created by a higher being, so they were deadly, powerful enough to fell an S-rank hunter with one shot. Countless arrows rained down on Jinwoo.

Fwiiiiiiiiish!

The Frost Monarch made a concerted effort to stop Jinwoo's approach. "Graaaaah!"

But Jinwoo's hands were faster than the arrows. He didn't slow down as he swatted away the ice arrows coming at him.

"Graaaaaaaaaah!"

Fwiiiiiiiish!

Despite the barrage of arrows, Jinwoo repelled every one of them and reached the Frost Monarch.

Shunk!

Jinwoo thrust Kamish's Wrath into the Frost Monarch's shoulder where Jinwoo had stabbed a dagger once before. He did this to remind the Frost Monarch of the late President Go.

"Arghhh!"

The Frost Monarch looked up and screamed from the intense pain. The Monarch quickly spat cold energy from his mouth before Jinwoo could stab him with the second dagger, but Jinwoo fully covered his mouth with a hand.

Mmmph!

As the Frost Monarch thrashed at the cold energy trapped in his mouth, Jinwoo stabbed the Monarch in the chest with his dagger.

Crack!

The Frost Monarch's ribs shattered as his heart was penetrated. It mirrored the attack Jinwoo had received earlier.

"Arghhhh!"

Having already disposed of two other Monarchs, Jinwoo was confident that this attack would kill the Frost Monarch.

"The beast died on my fourth attack." Jinwoo's eyes gleamed. "How many attacks can you take?"

The terrified Frost Monarch looked into the eyes of the King of the Dead, the greatest warrior who had taken down their enemies on countless battlefields! The Frost Monarch finally realized whom he had offended, and he quaked in fear.

Then the dagger stuck in the Monarch's heart was dragged downward, slicing his body in two.

"Gyaaaaah!"

6

THE KING'S FURY

6

THE KING'S FURY

Had there ever been a time when the entire world cheered with one voice? When Jinwoo reappeared and stabbed the Frost Monarch in the chest, everyone pumped their fists and screamed with joy.

"Whoo-hoooooo!"

It was the best gift they could've asked for after the despair of witnessing the death of the most powerful hunter in human history at the hands of monsters. People passionately called out his name. Some were in tears, while others tried to comfort them. And every one of them watched as the Asian hunter killed the monster that had threatened the whole human race.

When national-level hunter Thomas Andre fell and top hunter Lennart Neirmann stepped up to help, the monsters had stopped being just South Korea's problem. It became about the survival of all humankind.

The horrifying memory of Kamish the dragon devouring city after city in the United States was still fresh in their minds. No one wanted to see a tragedy like that happen again. Viewers across the US, Germany, and around the world lost their minds over Jinwoo's victory. It was as if they were trying to wash away the defeat and fright that had overcome them when they saw the greatest hunters fall.

"Yeaaaaaah!"

The cheers continued each time Jinwoo attacked the Frost Monarch until finally the tenacious monster fell, his ashes scattering in the wind to a deafening roar.

"Whoooooooooo!"

The triumphant cries of the people echoed throughout different cities. Even news anchors currently on air joined in the celebrations.

"We've just received word that Thomas Andre, who appeared to sustain severe injuries, is currently in stable condition......"

"Ambulances have arrived on the scene and are transferring the injured to a nearby hospital."

"The monster that slaughtered citizens has stopped moving. It is now nothing but ashes!"

Confirmations that the fight was over continued to pour in, and the people's excitement could not be stopped. "Jinwoo Sung! Jinwoo Sung! Jinwoo Sung!"

But the most elated person in the world was most likely Jinchul Woo, president of the Hunter's Association. His eyes remained fixed on the TV screen while his subordinates cheered and hugged one another. He spotted something that made him raise an eyebrow.

Wait......

With a shaky hand, Jinchul urgently pulled out his cell to play a video he had saved. He had replayed the surveillance camera footage of President Go being murdered in this very office so many times. He pressed Play.

The man in the video. It wasn't easy to make him out because he appeared for only a moment and the video was blurry, but the man resembled the monster Jinwoo had defeated a moment ago. In addition, the speed with which the icy ground melted away was the same.

That means......!

It finally hit Jinchul exactly who Jinwoo had been up against: President

Go's killer. When he recalled his conversation with Jinwoo after learning of President Go's death, chills spread across his body.

"Thank you for being with President Go at the end."
"I'm going to kill him with my own hands."
"Huh?"
"I'm going to kill the magic beast who took President Go's life, whatever it takes. So please save your thanks for later."

Jinwoo had made good on his promise. The tip of Jinchul's nose grew red and his eyes filled with tears as he watched the TV.

The camera zoomed in on Jinwoo's face. Jinchul felt like he could somewhat sympathize with Jinwoo's rather tired expression.

Jinchul's heart felt like it was about to overflow with emotion. President Go could finally rest in peace. As memories of the mentor he'd admired came to mind, he looked at Jinwoo with gratitude.

...... *Thank you, Hunter Sung.*

* * *

The human form of the Frost Monarch slowly disintegrated into dust. Jinwoo had avenged the late President Go as well as himself. He glared at the vanishing Frost Monarch and turned around.

The marshals had been waiting from a distance for Jinwoo to finish punishing the Frost Monarch, and they now approached their master.

"......"

Igris kept his respectful and calm demeanor even after getting his full power back. On the other hand, Beru expressed with everything he had how happy he was to see his master again.

"My kiiiiiing!" Beru's eyes were wet with unshed tears.

Jinwoo patted him on the shoulder and looked around. The other man. He could no longer see the man in the ragged robe.

"Who was that man earlier?"

Igris answered instead of the emotional Beru. "He was determined to protect you with all his might while you were unconscious."

Jinwoo was slightly shocked to hear Igris's rumbling voice speaking for the first time, but the novelty of it quickly passed. He raised an eyebrow. "He protected me?"

"Yes, sire."

Unlike Beru, Igris spoke the language of magic beasts, since he wasn't used to speaking human languages. Jinwoo had no problem communicating with him.

Why had the man protected him? Jinwoo had never met him before. As he continued discussing things with Igris, Jinwoo spotted something on the floor.

This is......

Jinwoo picked up the object, and his eyes widened imperceptibly.

* * *

The man in the robe walked behind a building that was half-demolished and took off his hood. His hair was messy, and his beard was unkempt. Ilhwan Sung leaned on the wall to catch his breath.

"Haah, haah......"

He raised his left hand, which he'd lost all feeling in. Sure enough, it had gone gray, and the fingertips were slowly turning to ash. It was the consequences of using a higher being's power in a human body.

But despite his extreme pain, Ilhwan looked pleased with himself. "I did it......"

He'd been able to use that power to protect his son. And now that Jinwoo had taken on the mantle of the Shadow Monarch, he would be a great help to humankind. It was all worth it in the end.

He looked away from his disintegrating hand, let his head hit the wall, and closed his eyes.

The Rulers had loaned their power to Ilhwan and asked him to stop the Shadow Monarch. Not that he had a choice when he had been stuck in the gap between dimensions after the gate closed. He'd returned to earth as an avatar of the Rulers with a very important mission.

However, he was unable to fulfill his duty. How could a parent kill their own child even if that child housed the worst disaster of humankind?

Ilhwan could do nothing but observe Jinwoo from a distance. While he was putting off his mission, the Rulers' objective changed, and the brightest Fragment of Luminosity gave Ilhwan a new order.

"Protect the Shadow Monarch."

The Rulers had realized that they needed the Shadow Monarch at full power to stop the other Monarchs' plans. The Dragon King and his army of destruction would arrive here before the soldiers of the sky, and the only one strong enough to stop him was the Shadow Monarch. The Rulers were not sure whether the Shadow Monarch would side with the humans, so it was a big gamble on their part.

The answer was now clear. Jinwoo had chosen to stay with the humans, and his decision aligned with that of the Shadow Monarch. The Shadow Monarch had been reborn as Jinwoo himself. It had been worth it to protect Jinwoo at the risk of his own life.

"......"

Ilhwan regretted that he had to leave like this without saying goodbye to his son, whom he hadn't seen in ten years. But no one had the right to take a parent away from a child twice, even the parent themselves. It would be better for Jinwoo if Ilhwan just disappeared quietly. Ilhwan comforted himself with this thought as he watched his body turn to ash.

Just then, he felt a familiar presence nearby. Using his right hand, which was still functional, Ilhwan quickly put his hood back over his head and stood up. Someone was standing in front of him, and Ilhwan knew exactly who it was without having to check.

It was Jinwoo.

Ilhwan walked past the son he desperately wanted to call out to.

Jinwoo turned toward him. "Did you think I wouldn't know who you are if you covered your face?"

Ilhwan stopped dead in his tracks. How......?

As Ilhwan turned back to face his son, Jinwoo tossed something at him. Ilhwan caught the object, which turned out to be the dagger he had dropped as his left hand went numb. Ilhwan looked up from the weapon to his son's resentful gaze.

Jinwoo could recall his father's daggers from his childhood. He remembered getting in trouble for playing with those daggers when he was younger.

It suddenly hit Jinwoo why daggers were his weapon of choice as opposed to the Shadow Monarch, who typically wielded a sword on the battlefield. It was because of the memories of his father. The system had been affected by parts of Jinwoo's memories and continuously provided daggers for him.

"Were you planning to leave without a word again, Dad?" Jinwoo asked in a low voice.

Dad.

Ilhwan removed his hood as the word burrowed into his chest. His right hand was also gradually turning to ash now. Jinwoo was startled as he caught sight of his father's hands.

"I didn't want you to see me like this," Ilhwan said with a wry smile.

Jinwoo knew that nothing could be done once someone's body lost its vitality and began to turn to ash. He made to run to his father, but Ilhwan raised his right hand to stop him. His left arm had already turned to ash up to his shoulder.

Jinwoo unwillingly stopped in his tracks. "Then what about you, Dad?"

"......?"

"Did you not want to see me?"

Ilhwan's right hand dropped to his side. "I did want to see you... This whole time."

Ilhwan was thankful that he had been able to observe Jinwoo from afar, even though Jinwoo couldn't see him. When Jinwoo stepped in front of him, Ilhwan touched his face with his remaining hand, and Jinwoo's tears dripped onto it.

Despite his absence, Jinwoo had......

"You grew up to be so strong."

"Did the Rulers do this to you? Did they abandon you after using you?"

There was a burning rage in Jinwoo's voice, but Ilhwan shook his head.

"They gave me a choice. I chose to protect you, and that was the correct choice." Ilhwan's right hand was turning to ash and scattering in the air now. "I'd like to talk to you more, but......"

He had wanted more time with his son. What a cruel thing he'd done, forcing his child to erase his father from his heart for a second time.

Ilhwan couldn't hold back his tears. "I'm so sorry that I wasn't a good father."

With those words......

Fwiiiiish......

Having consumed all his energy in the fight against the Monarchs, Ilhwan's entire body disintegrated. Jinwoo attempted to hug his father, but all that remained was ash.

Something shattered in Jinwoo's heart. Unable to hold it in any longer, he let out a roar toward the sky.

"AHHHHHHHH!"

The mana in the air vibrated. The sky, the air, and the land cried out.

A voice like that of the Monarchs' came out of Jinwoo's mouth. "Mark my words, Monarchs!"

Everything had been because the Monarchs had targeted Earth, and Jinwoo was going to make them pay by any means necessary.

His mana-infused voice spread throughout the entire world.

"I swear to make you pay for what has happened today!"

The Shadow Monarch's rage shook the heavens and the earth.

"Are you listening, Monarchs?"

That day, a human who had acquired a peculiar power decided on how to use it. That was the day the war truly began.

* * *

Perhaps it was a good thing that Jinwoo had made his proclamation in the language of the World of Chaos. His voice was heard throughout the earth, and most people brushed it off as thunder rumbling in the sky. Opinions differed on why they'd heard the same sound, but discussion didn't last long, since everyone was celebrating Jinwoo's victory.

The scene was the same at ground zero. Hunters who were nervously awaiting their turn to join the fight cheered when they heard the monster had been killed. The guild masters of the two best guilds in Korea, Jongin Choi and Yoonho Baek, breathed out sighs of relief and grinned at each other.

"President Baek, you didn't look so good earlier. You feeling better now?"

"Wipe the sweat off your forehead before you speak, President Choi."

"Surely it's not heart palpitations, right? I've got an herbal remedy that can help you."

"My goodness, look at all that sweat. Here, please take my handkerchief."

The two engaged in a bout of banter, but they were able to make fun of each other only because the crisis had been averted. They'd barely been able to breathe properly due to anxiety just a few minutes ago. After all, a national-level hunter had been tossed around like a rag doll. That put not only the two guild masters' lives in danger but the lives of their guild members as well.

Every single hunter who had gathered there was keenly aware that if not for Jinwoo, they would've lost their lives.

The two guild masters were now relieving some of the pressure that had been weighing them down by poking fun at each other. In between gibes, Yoonho's gaze fixed on something over Jongin's shoulder.

"Oh......"

Jongin followed Yoonho's gaze to see a man was emerging from the ruins of the downtown area. Jinwoo was silently making his way toward them. The cheering and excitement died down as the other hunters also spotted Jinwoo. The only sounds they could hear were the ambulance sirens echoing in the distance.

It's Hunter Jinwoo Sung.

That's the man who……

Although the battle was over, Jinwoo's aura still overwhelmed the entire area. Seeing Jinwoo like that rendered everyone speechless. Steam rose from his shoulders, a sign that he had just fought an epic battle.

When their eyes met, President Baek respectfully bowed his head at Jinwoo. And that was the start. One by one, the other hunters also bowed to Jinwoo as a salute to a soldier returning from the battlefield. It was a sign of respect and admiration to the hunter who had fought so spectacularly.

Jinwoo took in the sight.

……

He then walked past the hunters, who cleared a path for him, and approached a familiar-looking van parked nearby.

Thomas was about to board an ambulance with Lennart by his side when they spotted Jinwoo from behind. Lennart looked concerned.

"Hunter Sung doesn't look happy."

Thomas was in a much better state after emergency treatment from some healers. He nodded in agreement. "You're right."

"Why do you think that is? He defeated such powerful monsters."

Hunters understood one another best. They understood the unexplainable exhilaration of breathing fresh air after clearing a high-level dungeon. So why did Jinwoo look so glum?

Thomas had a theory. "Hunter Sung probably didn't like how he fought against those creatures."

"……!" Lennart hadn't expected that.

Jinwoo had displayed superhuman abilities, but he was upset by the way he had fought? Did that even make sense?

Thomas continued, as if he'd read Lennart's mind. "It's hard for me to believe as well...... But he was probably disappointed by a few missteps he made during the battle."

Oh, that. Lennart hissed as he remembered the moment the beast's claws penetrated Jinwoo's chest. Lennart had also felt like his world was collapsing when the ancient ice elf stabbed Jinwoo. But those things had happened because the enemies were too powerful, right? How many people in this world could stand up to just one of them, much less both?

Lennart shook his head at that thought.

No......

Only an ordinary hunter like Lennart would think that getting hurt was inevitable. But victory was assured for someone on Jinwoo's level. The question would be how? Chills ran up Lennart's spine as he considered that.

Thomas concluded, "Hunter Jinwoo Sung is one scary man."

"......I agree."

During the ride to the hospital, Thomas nodded to himself.

I was right not to raise a fuss in his guild office that day......

On his end, Lennart resolved to never get on Jinwoo's bad side.

Screeeek!

Boonggo, also known as the Ahjin Guild's van, came to a stop, and a young man got out of the driver's side. Jinho had rushed to the site immediately, as soon as he saw Jinwoo being brutally attacked. Although he didn't possess the perception of a high-rank hunter, he was able to track down Jinwoo in the crowd of hunters immediately. Jinho ran toward him with tears in his eyes.

"Bossssss!"

The anger in Jinwoo's eyes waned a bit when he saw Jinho running toward him. Jinho tackled him in a hug, and though Jinwoo would normally dodge it, he stayed put and accepted the hug. Today was different.

As Jinho clung to him and bawled, Jinwoo gently patted him on the back. Knowing that someone was so genuinely concerned about him slowly melted Jinwoo's frozen heart. Maybe Jinwoo did need some consolation.

Jinwoo cracked a small smile as Jinho managed to calm himself enough to lift his snotty, teary face off Jinwoo's chest.

"Are you okay, boss?"

"No, I'm not."

"What?" Jinho's eyes widened in surprise at the unexpected answer.

In response, Jinwoo pointed at his snot- and tear-stained shirt.

"Oh!" Jinho hurriedly wiped his eyes and his nose with his sleeve and hung his head. "I'm sorry, boss. It's just that I was so happy that you were okay......"

Jinwoo chuckled. Jinho had always been a little eccentric, but he'd also always been quick to clue in on what Jinwoo needed.

Jinho's face brightened. "Boss, I went ahead and brought you a change of clothes."

"Clothes?" Jinwoo looked down at himself. He was a complete mess after his battle with the Monarchs.

"If you show up at home like this......your mother will get worried again, won't she? So I brought you some fresh clothes."

Well, well......

Jinho beamed as Jinwoo looked at him proudly. "Let's go, boss. I'll drive you home."

Jinwoo nodded.

Mom and Jinah probably saw it all on TV, so first things first. I should go and reassure them that I'm okay.

As Jinho got in the driver's seat, Jinwoo looked back at the downtown area. Many people had rushed to the location to help and were getting the job done.

Jinwoo had gained a thing or two in this battle.

The biggest priority is finding a communication device that I can use in that forest.

He couldn't make the same mistake twice. But the biggest thing he'd gained were the daggers his father had left behind. He could still feel his father's warmth coming from the handles.

Dad......

When Jinwoo made no move to leave, Jinho cautiously called to him. "Boss?"

Jinwoo gently kissed the hilt of each dagger before storing them in his inventory. He then slid into the passenger's seat.

"Let's go."

"Yes, boss!"

With that, the long day finally came to an end.

* * *

The Hunter's Association of Korea eventually announced that the monsters that had appeared in Seoul were unidentified magic beasts. The destruction had been catastrophic. Many people had been injured or killed, and innumerable vehicles and buildings had been damaged beyond repair.

However, all was not lost. Perhaps this could be considered a blessing in disguise, but people had learned how to respond to a crisis. Additionally, the impressive strength Jinwoo had displayed promptly changed the mindset of people around the world. This change motivated action, even from the most unexpected places.

That evening, Jinchul visited the Blue House to discuss how to handle the aftermath of the magic beasts as well as the monolithic gate over Seoul. Considering the importance of these matters, the president of South Korea welcomed him. They exchanged brief greetings before getting down to business.

"Shouldn't you relocate outside Seoul?" asked Jinchul.

President Kim hesitated, then sighed. "I apologize for my rude behavior during our last meeting. But please don't think I have neglected my duties as the president of this country."

His expression was that of someone who was fearful but trying to push past it. "What would the people of Korea think if I ran away without a word? I do not want to go down in history as a failure."

President Kim had long since given Jinchul the impression that he was a typical politician scrambling to get more votes, so Jinchul snorted at the unexpected explanation. The president might have considered his reaction rude, but he let it slide as he, too, had said regrettable things in the past.

"I see." Jinchul took out some documents he had prepared for presentation.

Before he could start, a government employee rushed in and whispered something to the president.

"What? Is this true?" President Kim jumped out of his seat in disbelief.

The employee nodded with a serious expression. "It's true, Mr. President. What would you like to do, sir?"

"Put the call through. I'll talk to them."

They handed President Kim a cell phone, and a voice every South Korean would recognize came through the receiver.

"I've been deliberating for quite some time now...... And I've decided that it would be beneficial to help the people of South Korea with this matter."

It was the voice of the leader of North Korea.

President Kim cocked his head. "Help us with......what?"

"There's a gate above Seoul, no? We will send some of our hunters to help. Let us combine the forces of the north and south and take care of this."

".......!"

North Korea was sending signals. Though the gate was unusually large, there had been little to no offers of cooperation from surrounding countries. After the fight against the monsters, however, their attitudes had changed.

South Korea or, rather, Jinwoo Sung must not fall in battle.

*   *   *

That was the conclusion reached by the leaders of the world. A tragedy in South Korea would not end there. If Jinwoo couldn't stop the disaster, would any hunter from any other country be able to? Hunters from both neighboring countries like North Korea, Japan, China, and Russia and faraway nations such as the United States of America, Germany, England, and France all made their way to Seoul.

They had but one goal.

We need to help Hunter Sung block the monolithic gate.

Thanks to Jinwoo's performance, they believed that South Korea would be their last stand. Hunters from around the world joined the South Korean hunters in Seoul.

* * *

At dawn, when everyone was still asleep, Jinwoo returned to the forest in Japan that had been designated as a restricted area since the dungeon break with the giants. His visit this time wasn't to level up or go stargazing but because of the night before.

When he looked up at the night sky, he thought of Haein. After a stop at home to assure his family that he was fine, Jinwoo had hastily returned to the hotel. She understood why he'd had to excuse himself before they had dinner. She knew more than anyone what could've happened if Jinwoo hadn't gone back to Seoul.

Strangely enough, Jinwoo kept recalling how Haein had tried to hide how worried she was.

...... *Time to get started.*

He looked at his surroundings. The empty forest welcomed him as usual with its silence. There was something he needed to do in this place. Jinwoo found a nice open area and summoned some of his soldiers.

Come on out.

His shadow spread wide as shadow soldiers emerged. They were the most recently added soldiers to his army.

Jinwoo had mixed feelings as he looked at them. Yesterday, he had broken his own rule for the first time and made soldiers from ordinary humans. They were the victims of the Monarchs. These soldiers were a mix of average humans who had died unjustly and the hunters who had died trying to save them. Hundreds of them stood before their new master.

Jinwoo had broken his vow not to turn any innocent souls into his soldiers. And so he wanted to ask them for their cooperation.

Please lend me your powers until this war is over.

To protect their families, friends, and nation.

I will return you back to the eternal rest once it's all over.

Although the dead were compelled to be loyal to Jinwoo because of the Shadow Monarch's power, their individual personalities were still intact. Jinwoo's sincerity and determination reached them.

Beneath their helmets, their eyes were filled with hatred and rage toward the magic beasts that had made them this way. They knew that this was their chance to exact revenge with their own hands. The Shadow Monarch was the one giving them this opportunity. They would fight along with their master! They would protect their families and their homeland from the magic beasts! Determination swelled within them.

As the Shadow Monarch leveled up, so too did the abilities of his shadow soldiers. Unlike the soldiers who had spawned when Jinwoo was borrowing the Shadow Monarch's power through the system, these shadow soldiers brought forth by the true Monarch were not to be underestimated.

Jinwoo asked again.

Please lend me your strength.

The shadow soldiers immediately responded by raising their hands toward the sky and letting out a terrifyingly loud yell that echoed throughout the entire area.

"Raaaaaaaaaah!"

The yell spread as more and more soldiers joined in.

"Raaaah!"

The spiteful roar shook the land. The army of the dead was ready and complete.

Jinwoo's eyes gleamed as he watched the soldiers. He would do whatever it took to take revenge on the Monarchs for what they'd done. The soldiers' yells went on for quite some time.

* * *

It was the day before the projected dungeon break from the monolithic gate. Two days had passed since the system's deletion. Jinwoo was getting used to his life without the daily quest. Without the limitations of the system, he'd run into plenty of both conveniences and inconveniences.

One such inconvenience was the loss of the system's shop. Jinwoo took out a bottle of healing potion from the inventory and stared at it as if trying to shoot lasers out of his eyes.

......

The items in the shop were originally conjured up by the Shadow Monarch by manipulating mana. Theoretically, Jinwoo should have been able to create the same items at will. He closed his eyes and pictured the healing potion in his mind. As he did, he could sense the mana moving around him.

Focus...... Focus......

However, the mana failed to coalesce and scattered every which way instead. It was a failure.

Jinwoo opened his eyes and let out a sigh. Crafting by himself would be difficult to master.

I guess I need to practice more.

At that moment, his cell phone vibrated.

"Hunter Sung. It's Jinchul Woo."

"Yes, President Woo." Jinwoo sat down on the edge of his bed as he answered his phone.

President Woo's voice sounded a bit hoarse. He had most likely been working around the clock due to various incidents.

"Hunter Sung, um...... If it's not too much to ask, could you please stop by the association today?"

The estimated moment of the dungeon break was imminent, and the association needed some advice from Jinwoo as the one who would play a pivotal role in this raid.

Since he didn't have any plans, Jinwoo agreed. "I'll see you at the association."

Click.

Jinwoo was getting ready to leave when Igris piped up.

"Master."

Yeah?

Jinwoo still found it a little awkward to hear Igris's uniquely deep tone and deferential way of speaking.

"There is something I would like to discuss with you."

* * *

The following day, every TV station in the world interrupted their regularly scheduled programming to report on what was happening in Seoul. Some channels broadcast live footage from ground zero and went with a standard news format, while others brought in a panel of experts for commentary.

One of the latter was the Hunter Channel, a popular American network. As the program got underway, the footage showed the area packed with hunters.

An expert on the panel got emotional as they asked, "Do you know the last time this many hunters from different nations gathered in the same place?"

The host laughed. "I'm not sure...... But I'm guessing it hasn't been as long as we think, since guilds from different countries sometimes work together."

The expert shook his head. "It's been eight years. Eight years! It's actually closer to nine years at this point."

Eight years. Everyone watching the program immediately recalled the massive magic beast that had terrorized humankind at that time.

"Eight years...... You're talking about the Kamish raid?"

"Yes, exactly. This is the first time since Kamish that more than five different nations of hunters have come together like this."

Out of the record number of hunters that came to the aid of the United States, all but five had perished. Those five survivors eventually came to be known as national-level hunters. For the countries that had lost their best hunters, it had been a terrible loss to bear.

"Since then, countries have been hesitant to involve themselves in the affairs of other nations."

That much was to be expected. No nation wanted hunters to lay down their lives for another country. Guilds from different countries sometimes worked together for the guilds' benefit, but very rarely did hunters assemble like this for a single country's sake.

"So, Professor, you mean to say that South Korea's Hunter Sung brought hunters together again after Kamish tore them apart?"

"That's correct." The professor took a breath in order to continue his lengthy explanation. "It all began with Hunter Sung resolving the dungeon break in Japan."

Prior to then, Japan had mobilized to help Korea with Jeju Island, but the result of that had been a bust. Had the story ended there, public opinion would have been strongly against interfering with another country's affairs. But everything changed when Jinwoo stepped up to defeat the giants invading Japan.

Historically, South Korea and Japan didn't have the best relationship. Additionally, Japan had recently tried to cheat Korea as well. Yet a Korean hunter had stepped in to help Japan in spite of everything.

"It's probably difficult to put into words just how thankful and touched the people of Japan were."

When Jinwoo came to Japan's rescue, the unwritten rule of minding your own business and not interfering with another country's problems had been broken. This gave other hunters the confidence to follow Jinwoo's lead.

"Besides, it became clear when Thomas Andre fell a few days ago."

Who, then, could stop those monsters?

"Hunter Jinwoo Sung himself showed us the answer to that."

The question now was tougher to answer. What would they do if Hunter Sung fell?

"If Hunter Sung falls, then it's all over. There's no one else. He's our last line of defense."

Other countries had realized that the moment Jinwoo went down, the monolithic gate in the sky would no longer be Korea's problem alone. After South Korea would be North Korea, then China or Russia, and eventually the rest of the world. The monolithic gate had become the common enemy of the entire world, and a single hunter from Asia had been the one to open everyone's eyes.

Just as the expert was about to elaborate on how this affair would need to be safely dealt with in order to cement this notion in people's minds......

"L-look!" The host jumped out of his seat after a producer gestured to him urgently.

All the experts on the panel turned to a monitor. The live feed showed the extremely large gate opening like a gaping maw.

"Oh my God......"

Everyone in the studio was rendered speechless at the unbelievable sight.

* * *

The air itself seemed to be vibrating as tens of thousands of hunters surrounded the area under the gate and anticipated the dungeon break with bated breath. The moment they had been waiting for was here. The hunters who specialized in close-quarter combat readied themselves. The hunters who specialized in ranged attacks prepared for a preemptive strike. Arrows containing magic power and magic spells were pointed toward the sky.

The tension in the area could be cut with a knife.

The hunters kept their eyes on one of two things: the sky and Jinwoo's back. The Korean hunter stood at the forefront, his eyes fixed on the gate above.

The dungeon break crept closer with each passing minute. He could sense it coming.

Ba-dump, ba-dump, ba-dump!

The Black Heart, which now beat in place of his destroyed human heart, pounded in his chest. The other hunters' hearts were racing out of apprehension, but Jinwoo's raced for an entirely different reason. He tried to keep his cool while he awaited the big moment.

Haein stood next to him and peeked at his expression. "This is the first time I've seen you this nervous."

"Really?" Jinwoo grinned at her.

She smiled back tenderly, then drew her sword and looked at the gate. She sensed that a life-and-death battle was just around the corner.

Soon......

But Haein had been mistaken. Jinwoo placed his hand over his heart and closed his eyes. His heart was beating not out of fear or anxiety but excitement.

"Th-they're coming!"

"The gate is opening!"

Finally, the gate began to open. The black layer between the gate and this world disappeared, and the creatures inside were unleashed. The mass of magic beasts instantly eclipsed the sky.

The hunters were aghast at the swarm, which easily numbered more than a hundred thousand.

"How......? How could that many magic beasts come out at once?"

"Th-there's way too many!"

Gasps and screams of despair rang out.

The creatures descended slowly, as if they were using a gravity-altering spell.

"Attack! Attack!"

"Everyone, attack!"

In an attempt to cull their enemy's numbers before the creatures could fight back, hunters took the chance to get in the first attack. Magic twinkled on fingertips. Bowstrings were pulled tightly as arrows were aimed at the sky. Tankers raised their shields up to their chins in preparation for the clash.

But before anyone could make a move, Jinwoo bellowed to them. "Stop!"

The force of the mana behind Jinwoo's command got his meaning across even to those who did not know Korean. It stopped them all dead in their tracks.

Why?

Why did Hunter Sung stop us?

Tens of thousands of incredulous hunters stared at Jinwoo as he repeated himself.

"Stand down, everybody!"

Jinchul wiped sweat off his brow as he watched from a distance. If they didn't attack now, the enemy would land safely. If that happened, the hunters on the front lines might get in the way of the hunters in the back. They were already outnumbered by the magic beasts. They didn't need the additional concern of trying not to hit one another.

A subordinate uneasily approached Jinchul. "President Woo......"

It was time to make a decision. Logic dictated that Jinchul should give the order to attack, but he decided to trust Jinwoo.

"Do not attack!"

"Do not attack!"

When even their commander gave the order to halt, the hunters could only stand around in a daze.

What in the world are they thinking?

They want to fight those magic beasts head-on without dealing some ranged attacks first? Against that many of them?

Confusion and terror swept across the battlefield as the creatures finally landed. The hunters were about to lose their minds at the sea of black creatures.

One of the beasts split from the horde and walked in front of the group. Jinwoo made his way toward him.

What was going on? The hunters held their breaths as they watched Jinwoo.

....

...

They stopped in front of each other. Then the magic beast knelt before Jinwoo. The soldiers behind it followed suit.

Thud!

Hundreds of thousands of soldiers bowing to Jinwoo was an incredible sight to see. After a short silence, the first magic beast raised its head.

"Grand Marshal Bellion and the shadow army reporting for duty, sir."

7

THE INHERITANCE

7

THE INHERITANCE

The fifty thousand or so hunters from around the globe who had gathered to deal with the monolithic gate were flabbergasted to see the black magic beasts kneeling before Jinwoo.

"Damn......"

The countless kneeling soldiers were either clad in black armor or cloaked in black smoke. Each possessed incredibly high magic power. But that wasn't what had the hunters in stunned disbelief.

"A-are those......?"

"Back there...... You see what I'm seeing, right?"

"......I definitely am."

Blood drained from the hunters' faces as they pointed to the three dragons at the rear of the magic-beast army. The dragons had also obediently lowered their heads like pets heeling before their master. The hunters were rendered speechless at the sight.

Kamish was the one and only dragon to have appeared through a gate in human history, and it had killed numerous high-rank hunters and nearly bathed the entire planet in fire. There was a good reason people referred to it as the Undying Flame. Being faced with three such creatures was enough to drain the fight out of the hunters. What would've happened if the hunters had clashed with those magic beasts? Chills ran up the hunters' spines as they imagined how things could have played out.

That further called into question the identity of Jinwoo, who was standing there in front of the magic beasts as if it were a perfectly natural thing.

Jinwoo looked out at Bellion and the kneeling soldiers.

So this is the real shadow army......

Igris was right. He had notified Jinwoo of this a couple of days ago.

"My lord, the shadow army has completed all of its preparations."

Jinwoo had needed some time to process that shocking announcement.

He then found himself in a dilemma. Was there any way to explain to others the unbelievable tale of conflict between the Monarchs and the Rulers, as well as the truth about gates? There was no way he could convince this many people who had traveled from all over the world for the sole purpose of keeping the gate from turning into the greatest disaster ever. And in the one-in-a-million chance that Igris was wrong, what then?

So Jinwoo had decided to wait for the gate to open and confirm things with his own eyes. And now here they were.

Jinwoo swallowed hard as he scanned the soldiers. Although he hadn't created these soldiers, he could feel his connection to each of them. It was a complex network, much like a spiderweb. Through it, he could feel how overjoyed they were to be reunited with their master.

This is my inheritance from the previous Shadow Monarch......

The soldiers silently swore their devotion to their new master. Jinwoo's heart overflowed with as much emotion as theirs did.

His gaze moved from the dragons bringing up the rear to Grand Marshal Bellion in the front of the army. Bellion possessed a commanding presence and strength well suited for his rank, and on his back were the scars of wings that had been torn off.

Four wings......

Ordinary foot soldiers had two wings, while the Rulers had six. If that was any measure, he had a good idea of what an intrepid soldier Bellion was. He focused his perception and detected the grand marshal's extraordinary levels of mana that he had kept hidden out of deference for Jinwoo.

I knew it......

Bellion was able to lead an army that included dragons in its ranks precisely because he was this powerful.

The shadow army. The king itching for war had been reunited with his soldiers.

Ba-dump, ba-dump, ba-dump!

But this wasn't the extent of his army. In addition to those who had served under the previous Shadow Monarch Ashborn, Jinwoo had his own soldiers as well.

Come out.

His original shadow army silently materialized behind him at his call. Their numbers were nearly two thousand strong. Beru, Igris, Greed, No. 6, Fang, Iron, Jima, Tank, and the rest appeared behind Jinwoo.

Thump!

They, too, bent at the knee and bowed their heads. Every single shadow soldier silently swore their allegiance to him. Jinwoo nodded in satisfaction. The once-divided shadow army was complete. He finally had a force that was strong enough to go up against the Monarchs' armies.

Everything was going smoothly. Well, almost everything. Jinwoo looked over his shoulder.

......

......

Tens of thousands of hunters and hundreds of reporters who had come to record the historic battle stared back at him. Everyone looked puzzled, unable to comprehend what was going on.

Okay......

Jinwoo smiled awkwardly as he took in their blank expressions.

......How do I explain this?

* * *

The world was turned upside down. The scene of the magic beasts pouring out from the massive gate and then dropping to their knees in front of Jinwoo had been broadcasted live across the globe. Viewers were still reeling from the shock, and online communities exploded with heated discussions.

> └WTF? What the hell is with those magic beasts? Anyone know what's going on?
> └Could all those magic beasts be Hunter Sung's minions?
> > └Damn...... I heard that at least 100k magic beasts came out of the gate.
> > └No way. How could minions come out of a gate? Stop trolling.
> > └Then feel free to explain what just happened.
> > └They look exactly the same as Hunter Sung's minions for sure. But how are minions coming out of a gate?

Disbelief was the most common reaction, but there were other perspectives as well.

> └Still, thank goodness they're not coming after us.
> > └Oh, for sure.
> > └If they did, we'd all be dead by now. I saw in an interview that three of the magic beasts were dragons.
> > └Three dragons. LMAO. Absolutely insane. LMAO.
> > └LOL. Kamish would've taken one look and gone back inside its gate.

└Huh? What do you mean? Kamish has been dead for almost nine years.
└Dang, ruining the punch line......
└I feel like I'm going insane...... Really wish Hunter Sung would explain what's going on......

TV networks replayed the footage again and again as they tried to analyze the situation, but no one could adequately explain how minions, which somehow included dragons, had come out of a gate instead of magic beasts.

"Hmm......"

"I'm not sure how......"

"Um......"

They could only silently shake their heads. Some experts were especially taken aback by the sight of more than one hundred thousand minions kneeling before Jinwoo. No matter how you looked at it, these subjects were bowing to their master.

Some people suggested "Demon Lord" as a nickname for Jinwoo, which was fitting for someone so majestic that he was surrounded by soldiers in black.

Other experts considered the incident to be nothing short of a miracle.

"It's been shocking to say the least, but this is a fortunate situation for us."

"Fortunate, you say?"

"Look at the number of magic beasts—or rather, minions."

The expert pointed to the countless bowed heads of the shadow army pictured on a monitor. The host gulped when he tried to estimate their numbers and found them impossible to count. Even without the three dragons, their numbers were excessive.

"If the hunters had to fight those minions, it wouldn't just be a matter of winning or losing. It would be a countdown to the complete and utter annihilation of humanity as they swept across the planet."

The host unconsciously nodded, engrossed.

"That's why it's fortunate that they're Hunter Sung's minions and that he can control them."

But that was just that expert's theory.

"Of course, only Hunter Jinwoo Sung knows the truth," the expert concluded.

As if on cue, the monitor played the most shocking moment of the entire length of footage.

"Right here, this part."

After scanning the hunters, Jinwoo sank into his own shadow and disappeared.

The host shook his head and adjusted his glasses as he spoke. "Hunter Sung is at the heart of all this confusion. But where is he now?"

The Hunter's Association of Korea was bombarded with nonstop calls asking for details, but their official response was that they had no knowledge of Jinwoo's whereabouts. Jinwoo was a hot topic, and the association's response was inevitably fanning those flames.

The host excitedly turned to the camera. "We can only hope he comes back soon and answers some of these questions for us."

* * *

Jinwoo returned to the deserted forest in Japan, leaving the prying eyes behind. This large swath of land that seemed to go on for days was the best place to test his control of his shadow army.

Jinwoo stood at a distance from the 130,000 soldiers he had divided into two groups.

Go.

At Jinwoo's telepathic order, the two units charged at each other.

Thud, thud, thud, thud, thud!

The sound of the soldiers stomping shook the land as the gap between the two units shrank in an instant and the soldiers clashed.

Jinwoo repositioned the soldiers who had strayed behind, making them sweep around to surround their opponents. He then sent other soldiers to places that needed reinforcements by recalling and then summoning them in the appropriate spot. The flow of the army was as fluid as the flow of water. He applied his own combat experience to this army of more than a hundred thousand soldiers with expert precision.

"Stop," he murmured.

The shadow soldiers immediately paused.

Jinwoo addressed the being next to him, who was also observing the mock battle. "What do you think?"

Grand Marshal Bellion was impressed. "I had never thought of maneuvering soldiers in this way. That was quite amazing, my lord."

Bellion had stood on countless battlefields alongside the previous Shadow Monarch, but he had never seen an army commanded in such a manner. He was most awestruck by Jinwoo's strategy of recalling and summoning soldiers.

Igris straightened up proudly, accustomed to this style of battle, since he had been by Jinwoo's side for some time. Jinwoo couldn't help but chuckle at the knight.

Just then, his phone vibrated.

"Boss, it's me, Jinho."

"Oh, hey."

According to Jinho, the Ahjin Guild had been inundated with as many calls as the association following Jinwoo's vanishing act, making it impossible to use the company phones.

"......Sorry about that. I just need some time to gather my thoughts."

"No need to apologize, boss. The Ahjin Guild's whole purpose has been to allow you to focus on raids without dealing with this kind of thing, right?"

As Jinho laughed, Jinwoo smiled in return.

"Oh, right, have you contacted your family yet?"

"I told them that I'd come home after I've had a chance to clear my head."

"That should be some relief to them. That's good, boss."

Jinwoo let out a heavy sigh as he tucked away his phone. He knew he couldn't avoid things for too long, but if he talked about the shadow soldiers and the gate, he'd have to explain Rulers and Monarchs. How should he go about telling everyone that Earth was soon to be the battleground for the armies of the warring Rulers and Monarchs, and armies were going to spill out of the eight remaining gates?

Jinwoo had to flee to get a chance to think things through. This was the best he could do. He wanted to let them enjoy their blissful ignorance for just a bit longer.

I'm sure it'll be okay to put it off for a few days.

As soon as he came to this conclusion, Beru approached. He had been uncharacteristically quiet this whole time.

"My king......"

"Yeah?"

Jinwoo turned to see Beru on his knees with his head bowed.

"Please allow me to be tested for the rank of grand marshal."

"Grand marshal?"

Didn't Jinwoo already have a grand marshal? Jinwoo suddenly remembered what the system had said about the marshal rank.

Does he mean......?

Sure enough, Beru looked up and declared, "I, Marshal Beru, would like to challenge Grand Marshal Bellion."

Beru was referring to something the system had mentioned before its deletion. There could be only one leader of the army. If more than one soldier reached the marshal rank, a hierarchy had to be decided among them. Since Beru had recently become a marshal, Jinwoo assumed that he had the right to challenge the grand marshal. Just like it was with ant-type magic beasts, Beru wanted to make the hierarchy of the colony clear.

A fight between marshals......

Jinwoo raised an eyebrow at the other marshal, Igris, but Igris politely declined to get involved. The knight wasn't interested in jockeying for position among the marshals.

When Igris stepped back, Jinwoo's gaze fell on Bellion, who had been standing next to him. As the commander of 130,000 shadow soldiers, the only one who could overrule Bellion was Jinwoo himself. Bellion met Jinwoo's eyes and lowered his head, but even like that, he was still a good head taller than Thomas Andre.

Bellion softly replied, "As you wish, master."

As he wished, huh? Jinwoo snorted with laughter at his response. Bellion's answer had been worded politely, but what that meant was that he would accept any challenge as long as his master approved.

Jinwoo glanced over his shoulder to see Beru with claws out, raring to go at Bellion's acceptance.

"Skraaaaaaaah!"

Unlike Bellion, who was concealing his magic power as best as he could, Beru didn't bother holding back.

Hmm......

Jinwoo considered it. "Fine."

Jinwoo knew Beru well, but he had no information regarding Bellion. Any insight into Bellion's combat power would help him better command the shadow army. There was no reason to disallow the showdown.

"However, the fight will end when I say it does."

With permission granted, Beru's eyes sparkled. He passionately cried, "You have the eternal gratitude of this humble ser—"

"Don't. Just don't."

"......Thank you, my king."

In the meantime, Bellion calmly prepared for the fight.

First, there was something Jinwoo had to check on before letting them run wild. He summoned one of the Kamish's Wrath daggers, poured some of his aura into it, and gently swung it toward the forest.

Kraaaaaaack!

Black energy was sent hurtling through the forest, wiping out a section of trees. However, the damage wasn't as much as Jinwoo had expected. He nodded and returned the dagger.

This should do......

The fight between the two marshals wouldn't cause any unnecessary damage to the area. The land had been strengthened with concentrated mana and was suitable as a battlefield.

......

Jinwoo briefly frowned at that fact. Then he looked back up at the two combatants. He had high hopes for this match.

"All right, then......"

The grand marshal and the new marshal both nodded at him and waited for his signal.

"Give us your command."

"I humbly await your order, my king!"

Jinwoo grinned. "Take your places."

* * *

Though the actual emergency was resolved, the emergency response meeting room of the Hunter's Association of Korea was even busier now.

"The foreign press is demanding an official statement!"

"The Hunter Command Center in the United States is asking us to share Hunter Sung's location."

"Seoul Metropolitan Fire and Disaster headquarters want to know when the evacuees can return."

"*The Jimmy Show* from the Hunter Channel wants to interview Hunter Sung......"

"Tell Timmy or Jimmy or whoever to try and reach Hunter Sung himself!"

Fortunately, despite the flood of calls, the phone lines were still operational.

President Woo sighed heavily as the tower of paperwork on his desk continued to grow, even though he'd been giving out orders all day.

"Whew......"

He had a mountain of things to do. Or by this point, it was more like a mountain range. It was enough to send an A-rank hunter's head spinning.

As he shook his head to try and rouse his tired body, he overheard one of his subordinates say something he just couldn't let slide.

"Ugh, did Hunter Sung's minions have to use that gate......?"

The subordinate's grousing snapped him to attention.

"Would you prefer that they were magic beasts instead, Sungwon?"

"Pardon, sir? Um, that's not what I......" Sungwon was too flustered to reply.

Jinchul chided him. "What if all these calls you had to answer were coming from the families of deceased hunters instead of the media? Would you be able to grumble about work then?"

Sungwon could not look Jinchul in the eye. Only those employees with field experience could fully understand what hunters went through in emergency situations. They had no idea what kinds of things happened within the depths of the dungeons away from prying eyes.

Considering the many different ways the raid on the monolithic gate could have gone south, yesterday's outcome was much more preferable. More than a hundred thousand magic beasts had emerged with no injuries or destruction. And the magic beasts had been absorbed into Jinwoo's army. Who could've predicted that? It was beyond anyone's wildest dreams.

But it was thanks to the peaceful outcome that Jinchul was able to cope with all the work he had to do around the clock these past few days with a smile. So for a Hunter's Association employee to be complaining just because he felt tired was utterly ridiculous. If Jinwoo was around, Jinchul might even have hit Sungwon over the head before Jinwoo had a chance to get mad, because he understood where Jinwoo was coming from.

Jinchul stopped his employees for a minute. "I understand very well that you may be freaking out because Hunter Sung has disappeared."

But for a hunter who took his responsibilities seriously to up and vanish meant that he had his reasons.

"Hunter Sung is probably more shocked than the rest of us."

With great power comes great responsibility, or so Jinchul had once heard in a movie. It was an apt way to describe the weight of the burden on Jinwoo's shoulders.

I've known Hunter Sung for some time now, but I've never seen him this stressed out before.

It looked like Jinwoo wasn't sure what to expect next. He'd been prepared to sacrifice his life to defend a dungeon break, but instead, the magic beasts had pledged their allegiance to him. Who could blame him for being so confused?

The Hunter's Association's duty at this time was to empathize and endure this hardship with him until he returned and explained everything to them. The association was first and foremost a dependable bulwark for their hunters.

"If we at the Hunter's Association can't understand what Hunter Sung is going through, then who can?"

As they listened to the president's impassioned speech, the employees forgot how tired they were, their eyes stinging with unshed tears.

Sungwon hung his head. "I'm sorry, sir. I wasn't thinking straight. I'm so sorry."

Jinchul gently patted his employee on the shoulder and let him return to work. Jinchul sat back down with a heavy sigh.

"Phew......"

The pile of documents on his desk seemed to have doubled in the short time he'd been talking.

......

Though he stared at the mountain of paperwork, his thoughts were with Jinwoo.

What is Hunter Sung doing now?

* * *

Jinwoo looked delighted as he put some distance between him and the two marshals. Igris took a place next to him, and the other shadow soldiers spread out to form a huge circle with enough room for the two fighters to move around.

"Skraaaaaah!"

From opposite ends of the circle, Beru fully extended his claws and let out a screech as Bellion quietly unsheathed his sword from his waist. At first glance, Bellion appeared to be a swordsman like Igris.

Oh......?

Jinwoo's eyes fixed on Bellion's unique sword.

Can you even call that a sword?

The blade was made up of dozens of joints, not unlike a centipede.

The marshals finished their preparations and turned to Jinwoo at the same time.

"Begin!"

On Jinwoo's command, Beru immediately charged at his opponent.

"Skreeee!"

Beru approached Bellion at an incredible clip and swiped at him. Bellion dodged the attack and spun around to face Beru's back as the ant shot past him.

......!

Jinwoo could only stare as Bellion's sword began to stretch like a snake and aimed for Beru.

Swoooooosh!

As Beru hurriedly changed directions, he reflexively batted the sword away.

Clang!

And so the battle began in earnest. Bellion used his sword like a whip and launched a veritable storm of slashes. The concentrated mana in the sword swirled freely through the air, razing the land around Beru.

Hwp! Hwp! Hwp!

Merely blocking Bellion's attacks kept Beru busy.

"Skraaaah!"

Jinwoo watched Bellion's innovative use of the sword and imagined himself facing Bellion as an opponent. Time slowed down for him, but even in this mode, Bellion's sword was quick enough to present a danger.

Jinwoo narrowed his eyes as he tracked the movements of the

unpredictable sword. Upper left, right side, upper left again, then lower left and upper right. In his mind's eye, he dodged all the attacks and got in front of Bellion. He then lopped off Bellion's head. He could've accomplished all that in the blink of an eye.

A chill ran up Bellion's spine, and he hurriedly looked over his shoulder.

Whoops......

Jinwoo had been focused too intensely on the never-before-seen weapon. He met the eyes of the flustered Bellion and shot him an apologetic look.

Beru did not pass up the opportunity. He knocked away Bellion's sword and streaked toward him like a bolt of lightning.

"Skreeeeeee!"

Shhhk!

However, it was Bellion who thrust his weapon into his opponent's stomach, to Jinwoo's surprise. Bellion's reflexes were well beyond Jinwoo's expectations. In addition, he possessed an awesome destructive power that could split the ground with a single strike. Bellion was, without a doubt, a soldier worthy of the grand marshal rank.

......Still, he shouldn't let his guard down.

An insect's greatest attribute was its tenacity, and sure enough, Beru expanded his body with the sword still stuck in his stomach. He swung down his enlarged fist on his opponent's head.

Wham!

The impact was so great that part of Bellion's helmet broke off, releasing black smoke into the air.

"Skreeee!"

Beru slammed his fist down a second time, or at least he tried to. Bellion managed to grab Beru's wrist. Beru attempted to shake off Bellion's grip, but Bellion wouldn't budge.

Meanwhile, the knight pulled back his other arm and focused a large amount of mana on it. Then......

Whack!

Bellion punched Beru in the chest, sending the ant flying backward. The resulting shock wave ripped the surrounding trees out from their roots. The forest that was once thick with trees now had a clear path through it.

"Skraaaaaaah!"

Beru came to a halt by spreading his wings, but he could do little else before Bellion appeared right in front of him. Bellion hammered him from above and sent him hurtling toward the ground.

Whud!

Beru crashed into the ground like a meteor. Bellion followed close behind, and despite the impact, Beru jumped to his feet and fought back. Any other enemy would've been ripped apart by this point.

Shhhk!

Beru swung his claws at Bellion, who deflected them with a backhand and struck Beru in the head.

Bam!

What followed was a total slugfest.

Pow! Ka-pow! Pow! Pow!

Beru's strikes were only able to make Bellion lose his balance momentarily.

Ka-boom!

On the other hand, Bellion's attacks contained enough power to kill any other person.

Kriiiik, krak!

Beru's exoskeleton cracked as if it would soon come apart.

"Skraaaaah!"

Beru fought tooth and nail to the end. When he attempted to bite Bellion on the shoulder, Bellion grabbed him by the neck.

Crack!

Immobilized, Beru thrashed in Bellion's grip. Bellion concentrated a tremendous amount of mana in his other arm for his ultimate attack.

It would be enough to crush a dragon's head with one blow, and it distorted the air around them.

The victor was clear. Bellion's fist flew toward Beru's face.

Not wanting to see Beru lose his head, Jinwoo took hold of Bellion's fist.

"Enough."

Bellion instantly withdrew, then dropped to one knee and bowed his head. "My king."

...... *Well done.*

Jinwoo's eyes twinkled with praise for Bellion for the display of his abilities that held nothing back. He then approached Beru splayed on the ground.

"Skree...... My king, I— Skrah! I can still fight......"

"......"

Jinwoo looked down at the pitiable ant struggling to stand. "Beru, why are you so determined to become grand marshal?"

"Urgh...... I...... I wish to stay by your side forever......," Beru sorrowfully explained.

Jinwoo scratched his head. "The grand marshal will be my right hand, and you can be my left."

"......!" Beru's eyes widened at Jinwoo's declaration. "My liege—"

"Don't." Jinwoo sighed at the emotional Ant King, then looked up as another soldier approached.

It was Igris, who had been listening in on their conversation. "My king, please allow me the opportunity to also issue a chall—"

Jinwoo interrupted him as if he had been expecting this. "And you can have my back."

"......!" Igris had nothing else to say at his master's foresight.

* * *

"I see...... So the Shadow Monarch has become our enemy." The Dragon King, currently in human form, calmly received the report from the Monarchs already on Earth. In this darkness, the only thing he could hear were their voices.

"I understand. I will take care of him. Do not do anything. We must not sustain any more losses."

The Dragon King ended the connection after fully understanding the situation. Silence fell. The gap between dimensions was a world in which nothing existed. Filled with emptiness, it was hell to the Monarchs, since there was nothing to destroy.

Born for the purpose of destroying everything in existence, the Monarch of Destruction had been making every effort to escape this place. And finally, his efforts would bear fruit.

The Dragon King turned and relayed an order to the creatures in the darkness. "Prepare for war, my soldiers."

Dozens of ancient dragons, hundreds of dragon soldiers, and tens of thousands of dragon folk hiding in the darkness roared, their eyes glittering.

Raaaaaaah!

* * *

Late at night, Jinwoo sat comfortably atop a high hill. Under the bright moonlight, he could see the forest clear as day. He had given his shadow soldiers some free time, so they had spread out in the area below him.

The large frame of Fang and the dragons caught his eye. After talking with Fang, the dragons appeared to be engrossed in a serious conversation. Eventually, the largest of the dragons approached Fang.

What are those guys up to?

The other soldiers around them ran to get some distance from the four figures. Soon after, the big dragon shot fire into the sky.

Fwoooom!

Seeing the size of his flames, Fang sneered and took a step forward.

Fwooooooooom!

An incredibly huge pillar of fire shot out of Fang's mouth and lit up the night sky. The high orcs cheered and whistled triumphantly, and the big dragon hung his head. It seemed they had made a bet about whose fire power was the greatest. But......

Isn't it cheating to use the Sphere of Avarice?

Fang had been surreptitiously tucking the sphere away inside his clothes but froze and smiled awkwardly when he made eye contact with Jinwoo. Jinwoo burst out laughing at Fang's gall but waved his hand to let him know it was fine. Fang grinned and bowed several times in gratitude.

It was peaceful. But although Jinwoo wore a tranquil expression, his mind was in turmoil.

......

He looked up at the sky. Jinwoo could faintly sense the life-forms from a different world growing ever closer. Their maliciousness and power prickled Jinwoo's mind, though they felt like trying to make out a blurry object through heavy fog.

Who knows when they'll make their move?

Jinwoo's heart was heavy with the fact that there was no way to avoid the coming confrontation. He was lost in his thoughts for a while before he looked up again.

He spotted something strange and peered closer to see ant soldiers diligently carrying off lumber and stones.

......*What are they doing now?*

Before Jinwoo could summon Beru to ask, a voice came from behind him. "It appears they wish to build a small shelter for you to rest comfortably while we are here, my liege."

It was a soft voice that didn't suit the large frame of Grand Master Bellion.

Jinwoo nodded as he watched the ants at work. "I'm guessing this is Beru's doing."

The only marshal who quickly and passionately set out to do something Jinwoo hadn't requested of him was Beru. On the other hand, Igris was the type to flawlessly carry out everything Jinwoo asked of him. And Bellion......

Bellion was still a mystery, as Jinwoo didn't know that much about him yet. The strong bond connecting Jinwoo to Bellion had been forged with the previous Shadow Monarch. Jinwoo wanted to get to know his grand marshal.

Bellion seemed to have read his mind. The knight drew closer and stood right behind him.

"My king, why do you not call back your shadow soldiers?"

Jinwoo continued to watch the soldiers. "I don't want them to feel imprisoned. They were stuck in the gap between dimensions before arriving here, after all."

"......" Not expecting that response, Bellion didn't say anything for a time.

Jinwoo asked him something in turn. "Aren't you sad that you can no longer see Ashborn? The previous Shadow Monarch?"

Having lost his father, Jinwoo knew the pain of losing someone important. He assumed Bellion would feel the same way.

"I stood by his side when he tried to stop the Rulers in the rebellion against the Supreme Being. When he acquired power over the dead, I was the first to volunteer to be his soldier." Bellion's voice was steady. "I assisted him for nearly an eternity, and I never once questioned his decision."

"That doesn't answer my question, though." Jinwoo repeated his initial question.

However, Bellion didn't know how to answer him. "I......have never thought about my feelings."

"That's why I've given you an opportunity to think about them."

"......"

There was a long and heavy silence, and in it, Jinwoo felt Bellion's sincerity. Words hadn't been spoken, but they'd still been communicated.

Jinwoo finally turned to look at him. "I'd like to hear the story of you and Ashborn, if that's okay with you."

"It is a long story."

"Good. I need a story long enough to listen to until I fall asleep."

As Jinwoo looked straight ahead again, Bellion took a seat next to him. "The story begins when I was still but a fruit in the World Tree."

"A fruit? You used to be a fruit?"

"Every soldier of the sky is born as a fruit on a branch of the World Tree. The tree is enormous, and its branches cover the entire sky."

"You don't say......"

The night wore on as Jinwoo listened to Bellion recount the epic story of the Shadow Monarch.

* * *

The sun hadn't risen yet as Jinwoo slowly ran through the forest. He'd gotten in the habit of running ten kilometers a day, so even though he no longer had any daily quests, it came naturally to him. While breathing in the fresh morning air, Jinwoo had almost finished working everything out in his mind.

......*It's time I head back.*

He needed to inform people about the eight approaching armies that would arrive in the near future. He needed to let everyone know that war was coming.

Jinwoo could not promise everyone's safety or that the world would ever be the same. The Dragon King that he'd seen in the Shadow Monarch's memories was just that powerful. The Monarch of Destruction and the army he commanded turned everything before them to ash.

And their next target was Earth. That was why Jinwoo needed to give everyone, including himself, time to prepare.

He stopped running after exactly ten kilometers, even without the system to prompt him. Since he had done the daily quest almost every day without fail, he had maintained that muscle memory.

Of course, good habits weren't the only thing that his body had memorized. He had learned through many fights and gained much power as a result. The previous Shadow Monarch had wanted to rest, and the last gift he had given Jinwoo was a fighting chance against the oncoming disaster.

Jinwoo changed direction and headed toward the sun rising over the ridge of a far-off mountain.

* * *

Now able to use Shadow Exchange freely, Jinwoo teleported to the Ahjin Guild headquarters. He materialized outside the office because he didn't want to give anyone a heart attack, but he ended up running into a woman he didn't recognize anyway. Although he didn't know her, she did look somewhat familiar.

The woman must have also had the same thought about him, as she spun toward him and called out, "Um, excuse me……!"

"……?" Jinwoo wordlessly waited for her to continue.

However, she seemed startled by something, and she muttered that it was nothing and quickly sped away.

How weird.

Jinwoo entered the office.

"Huh?"

"What?"

The office workers froze in their tracks with disbelief on their faces.

Should I have said hi while walking in?

If people were going to react like this anyway, there had been no point in appearing outside the office. Even before he could pointedly ask if that was how guild employees should be greeting their president, Jinho saw him and gleefully darted toward him.

"Boss!"

Jinwoo immediately asked about the strange woman. "Who's that person who just left the office?"

"Oh, that was my older sister. She showed up here because I've been ignoring her phone calls. Wait, was she rude to you or something……?"

"No, not at all."

Well, that explained it. She had looked familiar because she was related to Jinho.

He glanced at the door and nodded. "So what did she want?"

"Oh......" Jinho hesitated and then peeked at Jinwoo's reaction. "You know how I was with you before the massive gate opened?"

"Yeah."

"Apparently I was caught on tape, boss."

Jinwoo understood the gist of what he was about to say.

"My family wants me to turn in my hunter's license and stop going to dangerous places now that I'm the vice president of the Ahjin Guild."

Since Jinwoo, the guild master, was a hunter, Jinho, the vice guild master, didn't necessarily need to be a hunter. His worried family members certainly had a point. Regardless, Jinwoo didn't try to persuade Jinho either way, because he knew the younger man very well.

Jinho probably wants to accompany me as a hunter until the very end.

Although Jinwoo did all the heavy lifting, the two of them had been through life-and-death situations together. Feeling proud of Jinho, he reached out and ruffled his hair.

"B-boss?"

Jinwoo left Jinho flustered and went into the president's office. He took off the clothes he had been wearing for a few days now, changed into new ones, and walked back out.

"I'm going to use the van."

"Huh? Do you want me to drive, boss?"

"No, I'll be right back."

"Where are you going?"

"To the Hunter's Association."

As Jinwoo took the key and headed out, Jinho hurried to stop him.

"Wait, boss! There are reporters—"

But before he could tell Jinwoo about the journalists camped outside, the S-rank hunter was already gone. Sure enough, outside the building, reporters hoping for a big scoop were waiting for Jinwoo. Not having slept or eaten in days, they looked like zombies. Their response to seeing Jinwoo in person was explosive.

"Hunter Sung! It's Hunter Sung!"

"Hunter Sung is here!"

"You're filming this, right?"

Their voices died down quickly.

"Huh?"

"Wh-what?"

The perplexed reporters couldn't believe what was happening. They looked down and realized that they and everything around them were floating about ten centimeters off the ground.

"How is this—?"

Fortunately, this strange phenomenon passed quickly.

"Oh!"

By the time the reporters returned to the ground, Jinwoo was already gone. They exchanged looks of panic, then burst out laughing.

"Ha-ha......"

"Well......"

They had nothing else to say. This was just one more thing to add in their articles about Hunter Sung.

* * *

Jinwoo drove Boonggo directly to the Hunter's Association. Having already called ahead, he was met by President Woo and his entourage. However......

......*What's going on?*

The association employees had ominous looks on their faces.

President Woo hurriedly approached Jinwoo as he got out of the van. His voice was shaky, but he tried to sound calm. "Hunter Sung...... have you heard the news?"

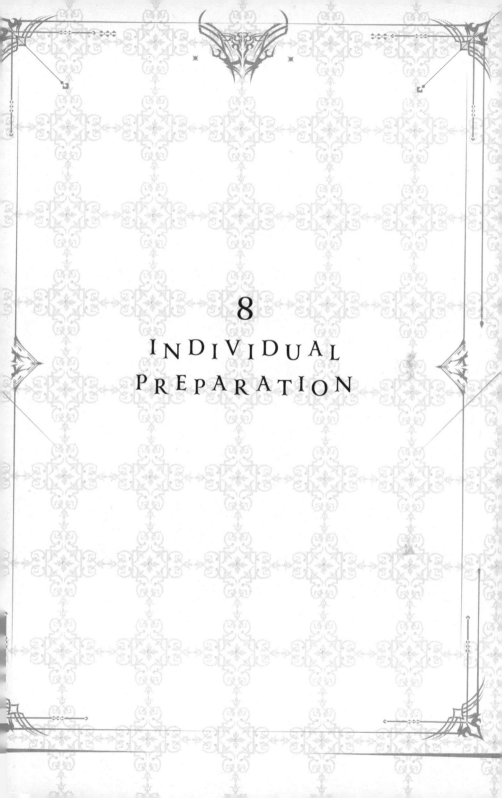

8

INDIVIDUAL PREPARATION

8

INDIVIDUAL
PREPARATION

......Strange.

Due to her brother's stubbornness, Jinho's older sister, Jinhee, was returning home alone. She carefully pulled her car over to the side of the road.

The man she had walked past as she left the Ahjin Guild......

Hunter Jinwoo Sung......

Everyone in Korea knew his face. No wonder she'd thought he looked familiar. A regular person would have shrugged and left it there, but Jinhee was the daughter of Chairman Yoo, a man well-known for never forgetting a face after just one meeting. Though she wasn't as good, she had inherited her father's talent for facial recognition. She was certain she had seen him at that exact angle where he'd brushed past her.

When was that......?

Her eyes widened as soon as she remembered.

Was it......?

It was at the hospital. When her father had been admitted for the Eternal Sleep Disease, she had passed someone at the hospital entrance with a similar frame. Why hadn't she recognized Jinwoo back then? Though it was understandable, because she had been a little out of sorts with her father in a coma.

Yeah, that was definitely him.

Jinwoo had been the person she had passed that day. And right after that, Jinhee had been told that her father had come to, even though the doctors had been saying he'd never wake up again. Could it have been a mere coincidence?

Goose bumps covered Jinhee's entire body, and she took out her phone to call her father.

Beep, beep, beep!

But she hesitated before she finished dialing.

What am I doing......?

Why did she think Jinwoo had anything to do with her father's recovery just because he happened to be there that day? She was being delusional. She let out a sigh and wondered where her mind had gone before she started the car again.

Then her phone rang. Right on cue.

Mr. Secretary

Jinhee smiled at the caller ID. Her father's assistant was probably calling her about the visit to the Ahjin Guild on his behalf.

I see that he still can't communicate honestly with his own children.

Jinhee tried not to laugh as she answered the phone. "Hello?"

"Yes, Miss Yoo. This is Secretary Kim."

The conversation went exactly as she had expected. Before she hung up, Jinhee took the opportunity to ask Secretary Kim something.

"By the way, how well does my father know Hunter Sung?"

"Pardon?"

Secretary Kim sounded surprised.

"Why the sudden question?"

Although flustered by the serious tone in Secretary Kim's voice, Jinhee continued. "It's nothing...... It's just that I saw Hunter Sung leaving the hospital that day. So I was wondering if he had visited my father."

"Are you saying Hunter Sung was at the hospital on the day Chairman Yoo collapsed?"

"Yes, we passed each other in the lobby right before I got the call about my father waking up."

"Are you sure it wasn't someone else? Or could it have happened on a different day, perhaps?"

"I'm sure. I was a mess at the time, so it took me a while to remember...... But why do you sound a little strange?"

"N-no, it's nothing. I'll call you back later, miss."

Instead of simply saying good-bye, Secretary Kim planned to call her back.

Was it something I said?

Jinhee cocked her head, but before she could put away her phone, it rang again. She was surprised by the caller ID on the screen.

Dad's calling me personally?

Calls from the one and only Chairman Yoo were rather rare. Maybe she was right, and Jinwoo had something to do with her father's recovery?

Jinhee cautiously answered her phone. "Dad?"

* * *

Beijing International Airport, the biggest and busiest airport in China, was crowded with so many people, there was no room to maneuver. They were there because the Chinese hunters were scheduled to return today from helping Korea.

Like in many other countries, the top Chinese hunters were practically celebrities chased by mobs of fans everywhere they went. The most popular among them by far was Zhigang Liu, leader of the Korean support team and a seven-star-ranked hunter.

One of the journalists reporting on the scene spotted Zhigang. "Oh! There's Hunter Liu!"

Ahhhhhh!

Zhigang's fans screamed as he held his two trademark swords in one hand and waved at them with the other.

Eeeek!

Zhigang may have been a middle-aged man, but his solemn demeanor appealed to young women. A special task force of hunters followed him.

Ahhhh!

At the sight of hunters they usually saw only on TV, the fans' passionate screams filled the airport.

The reporter addressed the camera. "The hunters, the pride and joy of our nation, have returned from Korea."

The cheeriness on her face reflected how China felt about the successful mission. Because the elite Chinese hunters had bravely offered to help with the monolithic gate in the sky over Seoul, the country would be able to boast that they didn't turn their back on their neighbors in their time of need. Additionally, none of the hunters had gotten hurt thanks to the way events had unfolded. This was truly the best-case scenario for them.

Zhigang had convinced the best hunters in China to help him form this team, and many Chinese people applauded him for it.

However, there were also many who criticized him and Korea online.

ᒪThe government dumped loads of cash on Zhigang Liu to protect China, so why's he running off to Korea?

ᒪAnyone know where Liu's ancestors are from?

ᒪSomeone check Liu's bank account to see if the Koreans paid him off.

ᒪWhy does a great country like ours need to help some small, ungrateful hunk of land? Never again.

ᒪHear, hear!

ᒪOur hunters didn't even have to go, but since they went anyway, they should've been paid! For a group with that net worth to do charity work? Calculate each hunter's daily fee and invoice Korea!

ᒪSince Jinwoo Sung supposedly made so much money from the giant incident, make him pay for it!

* * *

As the toxic commentary scrawled across the bottom of the screen, the reporter interviewed Zhigang live on air.

"Many people have applauded your brave decision, Hunter Liu. On the other hand, quite a lot of other people are criticizing your decision to help South Korea. What do you have to say to them?"

Zhigang took off his sunglasses and glared at the reporter. "What idiot is saying things like that?"

"I beg your pardon?" The reporter looked like a deer caught in headlights.

Zhigang angrily continued. "Are their brains just for decoration or do they really not know how to read a map? Do they seriously not know what country is just a little ways north from South Korea?"

"Oh......"

"If you'll recall, a giant-type magic beast from Japan crossed the ocean and almost reached Chinese soil. I'm guessing you've seen that footage at least once, since I've been told that broke all the viewer rating records."

Zhigang glared directly into the camera. "The same thing could have happened on an even bigger scale this time. My colleagues and I were of the same mind and wanted to prevent that."

The harsh online criticisms promptly stopped.

Zhigang leveled his gaze at the camera and raised his voice to directly address his critics. "Tell all these damn people talking nonsense that I, Zhigang Liu, went to Korea to help Hunter Sung because I didn't think I could prevent any disaster that he couldn't handle. Anyone out there who has a problem with that can go hunt magic beasts on their—"

Zhigang's heated comments were making his supporters very happy, but he abruptly stopped. It wasn't that he suddenly realized he was live on air. Zhigang was just about the only person in China who could get away with such antics on TV.

He stopped talking because of something he'd spotted outside the airport. What could he be looking at?

The reporter was the first to follow his gaze. Then the other hunters behind Zhigang, the staff assisting the hunters, and eventually the civilians in the airport—everyone stared outside with shock on their faces.

Hardly anything fazed Zhigang, but even he let out a low gasp. "Oh my God......"

Darkness was slowly blanketing the sky over Beijing.

* * *

"Hunter Sung......have you heard the news?"

Jinwoo shook his head. He had been in Japan since the raid of the monolithic gate and headed straight to the Hunter's Association when he returned to Korea. He hadn't had a chance to check the news just yet. Besides, Jinho would've told him if any problems had occurred while he was away.

Seeing the grim looks on everyone's faces caught Jinwoo off guard. "What's going on?"

Jinchul took out his cell phone and showed Jinwoo several videos that had gone viral.

"Damn! Do you see that?"
"Whoa!"
"It looks bigger than the gate that appeared in Korea, doesn't it?"

Eight extremely large gates had appeared in the sky in various places around the world. People were simultaneously scared and awed by the phenomenon and were sharing videos on social media.

Jinwoo coolly watched the videos as Jinchul audibly swallowed. "Hunter Sung......could these also be—?"

"They're not." Jinwoo quickly cut him off, making it clear that he had nothing to do with these gates.

Jinchul had hoped that these, too, would pose no threat, but his expression darkened as his hopes were dashed. What if hundreds of thousands of magic beasts came out of each gate like they had over

Seoul? Would that signal the end of humanity? Jinchul shuddered at the thought.

After watching all the clips, Jinwoo spoke to him. "Let's go somewhere private."

"Right."

The two men quickly went up to the president's office and sat down on couches facing each other.

"You said you had something to tell me......?" Jinchul asked carefully.

Jinwoo posed a question in response. "Do you trust me, President Woo?"

Jinchul nodded. "Yes, I do."

"Then please believe everything I'm about to show you."

"Excuse me?"

Jinwoo touched his index finger to Jinchul's forehead just like the previous Shadow Monarch had done to him. At that precise moment, darkness clouded Jinchul's vision, followed by a barrage of images.

"Oh!"

Jinwoo shared only what he thought Jinchul needed to know: the Rulers' plan, the Monarchs, and their encroaching armies.

"Huff, huff, huff......" Jinchul was shown the power of the Monarchs. He panted heavily as soon as the images stopped. "This is insane...... How could this be......?"

All this time, Jinchul had believed that God had gifted special powers to a small number of individuals in order to defend humanity, which was why they did so. But if what Jinwoo had shown him was true, he had been too arrogant. Everything he'd believed was wrong.

Awakened beings were merely the results of the process of transforming humans so that they could survive a coming war. And it wasn't a war between humans and the Monarchs but the Monarchs versus the Rulers.

However, a human had become an unexpected variable and inserted himself into the war. Since the armies of the Monarchs had arrived much earlier than expected, that variable was the last hope for humankind.

"No way......" Jinchul's hands trembled as he looked up with teary eyes. "Hunter Sung......are you actually planning to fight them? By yourself?"

Jinwoo wasn't about to give up before the battle had even begun just because the enemy was strong. That wasn't how he'd lived his life up until now.

And so he wordlessly nodded. "Yes."

Jinchul wanted to help Jinwoo in any way he could. "Then how can we......no, how can *I* help you?"

Jinwoo had expected this question, so he knew exactly what to say. "Please call a meeting of the leaders of the world."

* * *

David Brannon, the director of the Hunter Command Center, was frustrated out of his wits. "What did the Hunter's Association of Korea say?"

"No official word yet, sir."

"Then what are you doing here?"

"......Excuse me?"

The director hadn't called this subordinate up to his office to stand there and blink at him. Brannon blew up at him. "Get me an answer, even if you have to squeeze it out of the president of the association! Do your job!"

"S-sorry, sir!"

"Figure out what's going on—now!"

The director continued to huff and puff even after kicking out the head of his intelligence department. An extremely large gate even bigger than the one in Seoul had appeared in the sky over Canada. The United States and Canada were allies, and they shared a border. It wouldn't take long for a fire that started in Canada to reach the United States. The best result would be for this gate to turn out harmless like the one in Seoul. It would be great if more of Hunter Sung's magic fell out of the gate.

But the problem is......

Jinwoo and the Hunter's Association of Korea were the only ones who knew what was going on, but they were keeping silent. It had been three hours since the new set of gates had appeared all over the world. The United States government was already pressing the Hunter Command Center for a plan.

Our Hunter Command Center is one of the best intelligence organizations in the United States...... Yet here we are, waiting on the Hunter's Association of Korea.

David had never been in such a situation before. He couldn't help his anxiety.

Beep.

As he took deep breaths, Brannon spotted the blinking light of an incoming call on his office phone and picked up the receiver.

"What?"

"The president is asking for you, Mr. Brannon."

"Tell him I'm not in."

"M-Mr. Brannon?"

Klak!

The director slammed the receiver down. As he stared at the ceiling in a daze, the chief of intelligence returned, out of breath.

"Mr. Brannon!"

"Why did you come crawling back?"

The director was about to chuck the phone at the man, but the chief of intelligence quickly raised his hand.

"Th-the Hunter's Association of Korea has replied!"

A smile blossomed on David's face.

"See? There you go!" He put down the phone and approached the other man. "So what did they say?"

"Well, the thing is......they said if we want any information about the massive gates, we need to go to Korea."

"......"

Both men stared unblinkingly at each other until David snapped back to his senses.

"Who? Who did they ask for?"

"They said any government-appointed representative was fine."

"......"

At that moment......

Beep.

The light on his phone turned back on.

"Mr. Brannon, the president said if you keep avoiding his call—"

Click.

Brannon hurriedly hung up the phone and spoke determinedly. "Tell them I'm going."

"Pardon me?"

The director exaggerated each word to make sure the confused chief understood him. "I. Will. Go. To. Korea!"

* * *

Representatives from the countries who had received the call from the Hunter's Association of Korea boarded their planes.

It was a great reversal. A mere two years earlier, a South Korean S-rank hunter had defected to the United States due to the subpar reputation of South Korea's hunters. But now they were calling over the leaders of the world.

Even as recently as a year ago, Japan had sneered at Korea for being incapable of handling the Jeju Island dungeon break.

Then a single hunter—who surpassed such labels as "elite," "the epitome," and "the apex"—had changed everything. This man had tamed the magic beasts that poured out from the monolithic gate, so he might be the one who could explain the existence of the gates dotting the skies around the world. And hopefully, that would put what he had been through in the past few days into perspective.

The key to everything was in this man's hand. The problem was that the man was too powerful to take the keys by force or persuasion. Even if one of the national-level hunters managed to knock him out by going at full strength, he had a hundred thousand minions behind him now. It was an impossible task.

For this reason, presidents, prime ministers, premiers, and directors of hunter organizations responded to his summons.

"Have you heard from any more attendees?"

"No, sir. So far, one hundred and fifty-two countries have checked in since this morning."

"Got it."

Inside the emergency response room that had been established for the raid of the monolithic gate, President Woo was overseeing each step of the process.

"The Hungarian representative has just arrived at the airport."

"Who is the Hungarian representative?"

"Anor Yadeshi, the Hungarian president."

"Oh boy……"

When a VIP from a country visited, the protocol called for a reception fitting of their title. However, the Hunter's Association didn't have the bandwidth for pomp and circumstance at this time. For a brief moment, there was regret on President Woo's expression.

"Please escort him to his hotel."

"Yes, sir."

Jinchul sensed the man hesitating to leave, so he looked up from the document he was reading.

"Hmm? Is there anything else?"

"Oh……" The employee built up his courage. "Sir, if I may ask, what did Hunter Sung say to you yesterday in your office? I've never seen your face that pale."

In fact, before seeing Jinchul yesterday, he hadn't realized a person's face could get that pale. Just what had they talked about in his office? The employee hadn't been able to shake Jinchul's face from his mind all night, so he risked being rude and getting in trouble for prying.

Sure enough, Jinchul's face hardened like stone.

"I'm sorry, sir. I shouldn't have asked……"

"No, I'm not upset at your question."

Jinchul was recalling the images that had come from Jinwoo's finger.

The army of wild dragons coming out of the darkness and the humongous dragon flying right behind them. It was so big that it looked like it was flying in slow motion. That monster was so mighty that even the combined force of all the hunters from around the world wouldn't inflict so much as a scratch on it. It could burn down everything across the land with one breath.

Jinchul hadn't been able to process the sight at first. Regardless of his own power or what rewards he was offered, he didn't have the confidence to take on such a creature.

I couldn't do it......

Jinchul had the utmost respect for Jinwoo not running away after discovering the dragon's existence.

Speaking of Hunter Sung, I wonder what he's doing now.

There was still some time left before all the representatives from the different countries would finish gathering. Jinchul was suddenly curious about how Jinwoo was spending his time.

He asked his subordinate before they left. "By the way, where is Hunter Sung now?"

"I believe he's at home resting."

* * *

"Ta-daaa!"

Jinah's face brightened as Jinwoo served her the kimchi stew he had made.

"Wow! It looks so good!"

Meanwhile, Kyunghye felt guilty for letting her busy son cook. "I could've made it for you......"

Jinwoo replied with a smile. "I wanted to show you the expert cooking skills that I've been honing."

He had finally managed to persuade his mom to surrender the kitchen to him. Jinwoo pestered his mom to taste his masterpiece. She picked up her spoon with a smile on her face.

"Hwoo……" She carefully blew on the stew before having a taste. Her eyes widened in surprise.

Jinah poked her for her thoughts. "So how is it, Mom? It's good, isn't it?"

"It is!"

Jinwoo grinned at his shocked mother.

"Who knew Jinwoo could cook, right? Try this, too, Mom. His perfectly seasoned side dishes." Jinah sang her brother's praises with a grain of rice stuck on her lip.

But as the look on Kyunghye's face slowly began to change, Jinwoo turned to her. "Mom?"

Kyunghye quietly put down her spoon. "Jinwoo……is something the matter?"

Jinwoo tried his best to keep a straight face. "What are you talking about?"

"Your father used to cook for me like this before he went on a dangerous mission."

"……"

Jinwoo hadn't cooked for her before he went to Japan to defeat those giants or when the huge gate opened in Seoul, but he was now. Kyunghye couldn't help but worry, as a mother's intuition was always correct.

I guess I am my father's son. I can't believe I'm doing the same thing he did……

Jinwoo internally shook his head before he answered his mother. "Nothing's the matter, Mom."

Kyunghye picked up her spoon again and smiled back. It was hard to tell whether it was because she actually believed her son or because she didn't want to pry at his strained smile.

Jinah held her spoon in her mouth as she observed the exchange between her mother and brother. She joined in the laughter as she went back to eating.

Toward the end of their meal, Jinwoo heard Bellion's voice in his head.

My lord. I have prepared the soldiers as you have commanded.

Got it.

Beru continued as if he had been waiting for Bellion to finish.

My king, accommodations for you have been prepared as well.

......I see. Thank you.

Jinwoo hadn't really asked for that, though. At any rate, he slowly rose from his chair following their report.

"I'm done eating."

As he began to put the dishes away, Jinwoo's hands froze when he heard a noise coming from outside.

Sounds like four sets of footsteps......

He could hear their hearts racing. Although it didn't matter to Jinwoo, he could tell that all four were ordinary people and not hunters.

What's up with them?

No thief would be crazy enough to try and rob the home of an S-rank hunter. And with Surveillance Team members assigned by President Woo guarding the lobby, no reporters could enter the building. Jinwoo was puzzled when the doorbell rang.

Ding-dong!

"Let me answer it." He stopped his mother from getting up and went to the door.

Kerchak.

Jinwoo opened the door to reveal three well-built young men in black.

They don't look like they're from the Hunter Command Center......

Jinwoo eyed their outfits. "What brings you here?"

The three young men stepped aside for an older man.

"Hunter Sung......my apologies for the unannounced visit, but may we please talk?"

Jinwoo's voice went up in surprise. "......Chairman Yoo?"

The chairman looked a bit of a mess. Whatever he wanted to talk about was not to be discussed here. Jinwoo thought about his mother and sister as he glanced toward the kitchen table. He then turned back to Chairman Yoo.

"......" Chairman Yoo anxiously awaited Jinwoo's response.

Jinwoo debated it for a bit before he answered. "As long as it's somewhere private......"

The chairman's face lit up. "Then I will escort you somewhere quiet. Please come with me."

Jinwoo went back inside to inform his mother and grab a jacket. He then followed Chairman Yoo and his men to the lobby of the building. As expected, reporters were camped just outside the entrance. It was possible the chairman had brought along the three bodyguards in order to get through the crowd.

The reporters yelled as they aggressively wrestled with the hunters of the Surveillance Team.

"Come on! You let the chairman of Yoojin Construction in but not us? That makes no sense!"

"You said Chairman Yoo was a guest of Hunter Sung's? Then why can't we be his guests? Fine, we're his guests. Are you happy now?"

"Oh, sure, the biggest sponsor of the association is fine, but no journalists?"

The reporters pushed so hard that they would've trampled the people in their way had they not been hunters.

"Please step aside!"

The Surveillance Team was starting to seem overwhelmed by the reporters.

"Hunter Sung has said no interviews!"

"I said, step aside!"

"You need permission from the association to see Hunter Sung!"

Unable to use their powers against ordinary citizens, the Surveillance Team struggled to keep the reporters in line. Feeling bad for them, Jinwoo decided to take matters into his own hands.

"Huh? What?"

The reporters found themselves suddenly floating in the air.

"H-help!"

This time, Jinwoo lifted the reporters ten meters up in the air. As he exited the building, he was enthusiastically greeted by the hunters.

"Hunter Sung, sir!"

"Hunter Sung!"

Used to his tactics, the hunters weren't all that surprised by the situation. On the other hand, Chairman Yoo and his three bodyguards couldn't believe their eyes.

"Oh my goodness......" Chairman Yoo stared at the reporters struggling in midair. For the first time ever, he felt bad for the members of the press as their faces grew pale.

The person in charge approached Jinwoo. Although he looked troubled, he couldn't help his smile. "Hunter Sung......we'll get in trouble if you keep doing this."

"They were growing too loud for me to ignore."

"Ha-ha!"

Contained in a tent of magic power, no one could hear the reporters screaming.

The person in charge glanced up at them. "So how long are you going to leave them up there this time?"

"I was thinking of giving them five minutes to settle down."

The hunters of the Surveillance Team guffawed at the new record.

Ha-ha-ha!

"Hush, hush!" The hunter in charge muffled his own laugh and tried to keep his subordinates in check. He turned to Jinwoo and made a polite request. "Please just make sure no one gets hurt."

"You don't need to worry about that."

Jinwoo had mastered Ruler's Authority, a skill involving the manipulation of mana just like moving an object in his own hands, quite some time ago. Even if he left the area, the mana would safely lower the reporters to the ground.

I can't help their nausea, though......

Jinwoo figured this was fair warning, considering the ruckus they were causing in front of his home.

Chairman Yoo's sedan pulled up to the curb, and Jinwoo and

Chairman Yoo got in the back seat. The car glided away from the apartment building and headed toward Chairman Yoo's mansion.

* * *

There was no place quieter than Chairman Yoo's drawing room. The chairman guided Jinwoo into the room, and the two men sat down facing each other.

"I would like to talk to Hunter Sung privately."

"Yes, sir."

As soon as Chairman Yoo's bodyguards left, Jinwoo spoke. "So how did you know?"

Jinwoo hadn't left any evidence that he'd helped him. How had he found out?

Jinwoo listened with interest as the chairman explained. "My daughter saw you leaving the hospital that day."

Chairman Yoo's daughter...... Jinwoo remembered running into Jinho's older sister just outside of the guild office. No wonder he had thought that she looked familiar. It hadn't clicked that she was the same person he had run into in front of the hospital. Despite the steps he'd taken to keep things secret, he'd been found out thanks to a tiny coincidence. He couldn't help but laugh to himself.

Chairman Yoo had been keeping an eye on Jinwoo's reaction. He was now able to relax.

What a relief.

Jinwoo might have done what he did for Chairman Yoo out of the kindness of his heart, but Chairman Yoo was still worried that Jinwoo might be upset at his secret being revealed. Had Jinwoo been mad about it, Chairman Yoo wouldn't have been able to look his savior in the eye. Thankfully, Jinwoo didn't seem too bothered.

"So it really was you, Hunter Sung."

"It was." Jinwoo didn't bother denying it.

The confirmation came as a shock to the chairman. Countless people had curried favor with Chairman Yoo for personal gain, sometimes without even trying to do an equal favor for the chairman in return.

But that wasn't the case with the young man sitting in front of him. He had saved a life, and not just any life but the life of the man who ran the largest corporation in Korea. Yet he didn't want anything in return.

If his daughter hadn't seen Jinwoo's face and merely walked by him, Chairman Yoo would've lived the rest of his life without knowing how he had recovered from his illness. The man known for his poker face was now overcome with emotion.

"But why......?" He tamped down his feelings and did his best to continue. "Why did you help me?"

Chairman Yoo had previously asked Jinwoo for help and even offered the hunter a huge amount of money, but Jinwoo had declined, saying he didn't have the power to help the chairman. So what had changed his mind? This was what Chairman Yoo really wanted to know.

Ba-dump, ba-dump, ba-dump!

Each second felt like ten minutes to him as he awaited an answer from Jinwoo.

"Because I concluded that you were a trustworthy person."

"......!"

The completely unexpected answer caught Chairman Yoo off-guard. "What do you mean......?"

"If you were the type of person who would do anything to get what you wanted, I wouldn't have put myself in a tricky situation for you."

"You mean......because I didn't try to use Jinho?"

"Yes." Jinwoo nodded.

As expected of the head of a global company, Chairman Yoo immediately understood what Jinwoo was getting at. Chairman Yoo had held a trump card he could've used on Jinwoo, and that was none other than Jinho Yoo, his son and the vice president of the Ahjin Guild. However, instead of resorting to dirty tricks, he had trusted that Jinwoo really didn't have the power.

Jinwoo believed in an eye for an eye and a tooth for a tooth, so he had repaid Chairman Yoo's trust in him with his own trust, even if it had taken some time for him to reach that conclusion.

I made the right call.

Jinwoo smiled. At the same time, tears fell from Chairman Yoo's eyes.

"I don't know how to express my gratitude to you." He wiped away his tears and then made a serious face. "Please let me pay you back even half, no, a quarter of what I've received. Please let me do this."

Chairman Yoo felt indebted to the man in front of him. "By any chance, is there anything you want?"

"There's nothing I want. Just......"

Chairman Yoo was all ears. If Jinwoo wanted money, Chairman Yoo would give him money. If Jinwoo wanted something else, Chairman Yoo would use everything in his power to get it. But Jinwoo's request was a little different from what Chairman Yoo was expecting.

"If anything was to happen to me......would you please take care of my mother and sister?" Jinwoo said after a bit of hesitation.

Jinwoo wanted Chairman Yoo to take care of his family if the worst-case scenario ever occurred. Jinwoo had saved up a lot of money, but money couldn't buy peace of mind. Chairman Yoo would be his family's safety net.

"......Is that really all you want, Hunter Sung?"

"That's plenty."

Chairman Yoo couldn't imagine anything ever happening to Jinwoo, but he nodded at once. "I will promise you that."

Their long conversation had come to an end.

"Well then......"

As Jinwoo made to get up from his seat, Chairman Yoo was a little disappointed that their meeting was over. He'd realized just how much he liked this young man. If Jinwoo could somehow become part of his family......

It had never crossed his mind that he'd use his beloved daughter as a lure for an arranged marriage, but he couldn't resist asking Jinwoo, "Incidentally, are you seeing anyone right now?"

Chairman Yoo would be happy to offer Jinhee's hand in marriage to Jinwoo. He was just that special.

But Jinwoo grinned. "There is someone I like."

"Oh......" Chairman Yoo flushed red as he realized how embarrassing his question was. But Chairman Yoo wasn't the type of person to obsess over something he couldn't have, so he lifted his head up high and laughed as he said good-bye to Jinwoo.

"I hope I won't need to fulfill my promise anytime soon."

Jinwoo rose from his seat with a smile. "I'll do my best not to let that happen."

* * *

Since all of Jinwoo's stats were maxed out, the only thing he could improve was the ability to command his army. He returned to the restricted area in Japan to train. The vast sea of trees devoid of any other humans lay in front of him.

Upon Jinwoo's command, Grand Marshal Bellion divided the entire army into three groups to be led by himself, Igris, and Beru. Jinwoo nodded as he surveyed the three units from the top of a hill. Based on the energy signatures coming from the soldiers, it looked like Bellion had paid strict attention to the division of power among the three groups.

Bellion bowed when he made eye contact with Jinwoo. He seemed to be a perfectionist just like Igris.

On the other hand......

Is he kidding me?

Jinwoo turned to look at the "small" shelter at the top of the hill.

"Beru, get your ass over here."

Zoom!

Beru ran over in a split second and dropped to his knees next to Jinwoo. "My king!"

"Assume the position." Beru slammed his head on the ground even before Jinwoo had finished his sentence.

Jinwoo exclaimed, "This is what you consider small?! Never mind its size! How is this a shelter?"

"Skree......" Beru pouted. "This is the least you deserve as our king......"

"......"

Jinwoo brought his palm to his face. He had forgotten that ants were builders. Considering the sizes of their homes relative to the sizes of their bodies, he should've expected something like this.

Jinwoo looked up and was overwhelmed by the grandness of the so-called small shelter. A huge white stone castle that stretched the length of the area had been constructed. It was so tall that Jinwoo had to crane his neck to look up at it.

Jinwoo rubbed his temples and sighed. "That black flag flapping at the top of the castle...... What were you thinking?"

Bellion quickly moved next to Beru and also assumed the position.

Boom!

Jinwoo was at a loss for words as he simply stared at the two marshals. He eventually turned around toward the other soldiers.

"Okay, let's just begin the drill, everyone!"

The thunderous cry of the shadow soldiers shook the ground.

"Raaaaaaaaah!"

9
PRIDE AND DELUSION

9

PRIDE AND DELUSION

One day. Two days. Three days. As three days passed since the first appearance of the multiple large gates over eight different countries, things began to grow critical for them and their neighboring countries. With no one offering any solutions to this crisis, angry citizens hit the streets to protest and demand some answers.

The news switched back and forth between showing the gates and reporting on the increasing number of demonstrations.

"It is hour seventy-five since these massive gates first appeared. The government has yet to......"

"I see a group of citizens marching and waving signs demanding some kind of response from the government!"

"The number of people joining these protests continues to grow. The demonstrations have gotten more intense. It's like a powder keg out there......"

This hadn't happened in Korea when the sole monolithic gate spawned. Experts were quick to analyze why, and the answer was simple. First, the Hunter's Association of Korea had made the decision to immediately assemble all their hunters as soon as the gate appeared.

Second, the Korean people had the peace of mind knowing that they had someone on their side who surpassed even national-level hunters.

An expert panelist on some TV special explained, "Hunter Jinwoo Sung handled two S-rank dungeon breaks, the ones with the ant- and giant-type magic beasts, almost entirely by himself. The two most infamous incidents in the past year were handled by Hunter Sung."

The entire world had paid close attention to the incidents in both Japan and Jeju Island. The network that had the exclusive broadcasting rights for the Jeju Island raid made three times their annual profits on that single day. What else needed to be said?

The host nodded in agreement as the expert tapped his temple with his finger.

"It's inevitable that South Korea would grow to believe that Hunter Sung is capable of dealing with any and all threats."

For this reason, the citizens of Korea had remained relatively calm despite the appearance of the monolithic gate in the sky above Seoul and its population of ten million people. The expert panelist ended by strongly emphasizing how the existence of Hunter Sung was an incredible blessing to Korea.

However, not every country was as lucky. Powerful hunters were rare and unevenly spread throughout the world. Naturally, countries where gates had appeared despite their hunter strength being on the lower end were having to deal with more riots. Many people were demanding the recruitment of as many high-rank hunters as possible, even if it meant that they had to pay higher taxes. Even wealthy citizens known for their distaste for taxes surprised their governments with offers of financial assistance in order to save their homeland.

As tensions mounted by the minute, bigwigs from all over the world gathered in Seoul as representatives of their respective countries per the request of the Hunter's Association of Korea. They were all after the same thing: information about the eight massive gates that had simultaneously appeared across the globe. They'd been informed that this information would come straight from Hunter Jinwoo Sung himself, so their expectations were quite high.

"Whew……" David Brannon let out a small sigh. The director of the Hunter Command Center had elected to go to Korea in order to escape the constant phone calls from the president of the United States. He looked at those around him as he wiped sweat from his forehead.

……*Tons of people came, I see.*

Presidents, secretaries of state, guild masters, and the heads of hunter's organizations. The director recognized most of the faces in the auditorium. They were individuals whose names were well-known by the general public.

Brannon wiped sweat off his chin as he surveyed the anxious faces of those around him.

Regardless of their title, everyone here is under a lot of pressure.

Although they were pretending to be calm and collected in their seats, Brannon knew very well that internally, they were biting their nails with worry. It was the same for him.

How wonderful would it be if Hunter Sung said that these gates were also not a big deal? If David could report that to his superiors, it would get the president off his back. This was a chance for him to salvage his dignity.

However, if it just so happened to be bad news…… The very thought of this made the director's heart sink. He checked the time in nervous anticipation.

It was 2:55. Five minutes until the scheduled announcement.

Tick, tock!

David grimaced as he listened to the unusually loud ticking of his watch.

* * *

Meanwhile, Jinwoo turned to Bellion after completing his inspection of the shadow army. "What happens to the armies without Monarchs?"

"The marshals of those armies will lead those soldiers."

Bellion elaborated that the army of giants whose king had been kidnapped by the Rulers had been led by the marshal for some time now.

Jinwoo nodded in understanding. A marshal being able to lead an army in place of its master explained why eight gates had still spawned despite the deaths of some of the Monarchs.

A question then popped into Jinwoo's head. "If I die, will you lead the shadow army?"

Bellion shook his head. "Our lives are yours, my lord. If you closed your eyes forever, we would also return to the void."

The soldiers would live for as long as their master did. The absolute loyalty of the shadow soldiers who existed for their master without a care for their own lives was one of the strengths of the shadow army. On the other hand, should their master meet his end, it would also be their end.

......

Strength and weakness were opposite sides of the same coin. Strengths could become weaknesses and vice versa. If this was something the enemy could take advantage of, then could Jinwoo not exploit it as well?

......

Jinwoo's eyes blazed as he was in deep thought. Just then, another voice came from next to him.

"My lord." It was Igris. "In the event of an all-out war, we stand no chance at victory."

His deep voice resonated in the space between them. Jinwoo had been communicating regularly with the knight, but he still wasn't used to hearing Igris's voice. Igris's armor looked light and sleek, but the voice that came out of it was a heavy bass befitting of a great knight who once led hundreds of soldiers when he was human, before the Shadow Monarch brought him back to life.

But I still can't get over the weird contrast......

Whether or not Igris was aware of Jinwoo's dilemma, he continued. "Unlike the previous Shadow Monarch, who had grown weary about the coming war and stopped maintaining his army, the Monarchs have kept at it all this time."

"What do you think the difference in combat power is?"

It was Bellion who replied. "We do not know for sure, but it will at least be a hundredfold."

Beru had no insight he could provide on the other armies, so he quietly listened to the exchange between his master and the other marshals.

Jinwoo looked grim. A hundredfold meant that the enemy had at least ten million soldiers.

"A hundredfold......," Jinwoo muttered. "I wasn't planning on a full-scale war, though."

He had never considered going head-to-head with the armies because the way he maneuvered his army wouldn't work if he did. Jinwoo mentally drew up his future battle plans.

Vrrr, vrrr!

Jinwoo pulled his vibrating phone out of his pocket. Before he could say anything, a familiar voice came from the other side.

"Hunter Sung, this is Jinchul Woo."

"Yes, President Woo."

"The representatives have gathered in the auditorium as you requested. Are you on your way here?"

Jinwoo looked over his shoulder before answering Jinchul. There lay evidence of a brutal battle. Fissures, cracks, and holes littered the ground as far as he could see. Trees that once dotted the forest were nowhere to be seen. This was the result of the simulations run by the shadow army after being split into three units. The mana-enhanced land was in ruins from the impact.

Jinwoo had informed the Hunter's Association of Japan about the practice in advance, but the supervisors who had been watching were unable to hide their shock at the clash of magic power. What they had witnessed was the true might of the shadow army. Jinwoo also bore witness to this power. From his vantage point, he was able to size up his army's abilities, and he was satisfied with the results.

Jinwoo's eyes moved from what was behind him to what was in front of him. More than a hundred thousand soldiers knelt before Jinwoo. They stayed perfectly still as they awaited his command.

When Jinwoo took too long to answer, Jinchul carefully called his name.

"......**Hunter Sung?**"

Jinwoo grinned. "Yes. I just got here."

* * *

"You've arrived? When did you......?"

Jinchul had ordered his subordinates to let him know as soon as Jinwoo arrived. As he turned around, he found Jinwoo standing directly behind him.

"Oh!" Jinchul gasped and stood there blinking for a moment. He then smiled and hung up. "......I guess it's pointless to ask for an ETA."

Jinwoo gave a shrug and a smile in response.

The two men stood in the waiting room of the auditorium. Beyond the door, the seats were filled with representatives from different countries dying to see Jinwoo.

Jinchul checked the time on his phone. It was two minutes to showtime. There was still a little time left.

Jinchul somehow felt relieved as he looked at Jinwoo. "Hunter Sung, are you planning to tell them the truth?"

"Yes, I am."

"If civilians learn the truth, it will be chaos. Some countries won't be able to handle that chaos, either."

"I know."

That much was obvious. Even the Rulers had been aware that this would occur, which was why they had kept their intentions secret until the very end. But if the end of the world was nigh, didn't the people have a right to know?

Wouldn't that be better than dying in ignorance?

Thus, Jinwoo had decided to tell the truth. He wasn't the only one who would need to mentally prepare.

Seeing the determination on Jinwoo's face, Jinchul nodded. "I understand. If that's what you really think......"

Jinwoo walked past Jinchul and toward the door leading into the auditorium. But then Jinchul realized something and urgently called to him.

"Excuse me, Hunter Sung!"

......?

Jinwoo turned around with a puzzled look as Jinchul pursed his lips. "There are reporters out there, too."

"Oh." Jinwoo looked at his clothes. He was filthy from the training he'd been doing with his soldiers.

What should I do......?

He didn't want to make a big fuss and go somewhere else just to change clothes. And he couldn't buy clothes from the system's shop like before.

......Wait a minute.

The system's shop? He could no longer use the shop because the system was gone, but the power used to sustain the shop had been the Shadow Monarch's. Theoretically, he should be able to make clothes, then. And there was one set he was confident he could make at this time.

Fwoosh......

Black smoke filled the room and wrapped around Jinwoo's body as if it were alive.

"Huh?!" Jinchul jerked back in surprise.

The black smoke transformed into black armor.

"How's this?"

Hunters often wore armor to protect themselves against powerful magic beasts. When a mighty hunter like Jinwoo put on armor, it made him seem even more unapproachable.

Jinchul was rendered speechless for a second at Jinwoo's majestic appearance. "It s-s-suits you."

Jinwoo smiled dryly. "I'll take that as a compliment."

Jinwoo returned his attention to the door and slowly made his way into the auditorium. The buzzing room was quieted immediately.

Hunter Jinwoo Sung......!

He's here.

Everyone was focused on the person at the podium.

Jinwoo organized the different thoughts that crossed his mind as he scanned the crowd. He was about to tell these people what was going to happen in the near future. That eight powerful armies bent on the destruction of the world were on their way. That each of those armies was made up of soldiers from the World of Chaos. And that humanity didn't stand a chance against them.

......

How would the eagerly awaiting representatives react once they learned the truth? Jinwoo's expression turned a little grim as the nerves got to him.

"......"

Everyone held their breath and strained to hear him. One could hear a pin drop in the auditorium.

After a beat or two, Jinwoo focused mana on his vocal cords so that he wouldn't need a mic. "It will be a difficult time for everyone."

His voice gently echoed throughout the quiet auditorium. He could hear the representatives swallow nervously as their hearts raced. Strangely, as their heartbeats got faster, his own stabilized.

......I'm feeling calmer.

Jinwoo smoothly continued his explanation. "But no one can ignore this. They will appear before you and destroy everything you love."

How were these representatives supposed to take this? By the time he finished, they were unable to hide the panic on their faces. Even the carefully vetted reporters had completely forgotten their jobs and were preoccupied with exchanging helpless looks. The auditorium exploded with noise.

Finally, one fearful representative couldn't hold himself back and yelled at Jinwoo. "Do y-you seriously expect us to believe that?"

How could anyone accept that horrifying beings who were powerful enough to destroy everything on this planet were on their way?

The older man desperately shouted, "Show...... Show us the evidence! I won't believe you until you do!"

"That's right!"

"What an absurd theory!"

"You claim hundreds of magic beasts like Kamish will appear. That makes no sense!"

It was human nature to become enraged or dismissive when faced with the incomprehensible. The representatives directed their rage at the man behind the podium, willfully erasing the many miracles Jinwoo had shown them up to now.

But Jinwoo silenced them with a single gesture.

"Gah!"

"......!"

Multiple gates appeared behind Jinwoo. Gates were doorways that connected various dimensions, and Jinwoo was able to create dozens of them by using the Shadow Monarch's power.

It's faster for me to move through shadows, so there's no reason for me to use gates, but......

He couldn't think of a more efficient way to drive his point home, so he easily conjured up numerous human-size ones. He returned his attention to the audience.

Sure enough, everyone, whether they were the representatives, reporters, or employees of the Hunter's Association of Korea, was gawking at the gates.

"Th-those are all gates, right?"

"H-how......?"

Hunter Jinwoo Sung made dozens of gates at once! And in front of all these people!

Even David Brannon, who had witnessed a dragon emerging from a dungeon break, kept rubbing his eyes in disbelief.

It's definitely working.

Satisfied with people's reactions from his display of the Shadow Monarch's power, Jinwoo closed the gates. They vanished in the blink of an eye, as if they had never been there.

Oh no!

One devastated reporter quickly turned to another reporter. "D-did anyone film those gates? It doesn't matter if it's a cell phone or a camera! Did anyone get that on video?!"

"Oh!"

Reporters buried their faces in their hands and let out disappointed cries. It had happened so quickly, and they hadn't been thinking straight. No one had thought to record any of it.

The regretful moans of the reporters signaled the start of the outcry. The auditorium exploded with debates and discussions.

"Hunter Jinwoo Sung!" The representative from England suddenly stood up and shouted shrilly, "Maybe you're one of them! Those soldiers from the first massive gate—maybe you summoned them here to kill us!"

Everyone froze at his accusation as they considered this terrifying possibility. The irrational fear that Jinwoo might be one of the enemies spread in people's minds like a plague. After all, gates represented a power from another world that led to fear and the deaths of so many.

"......" Jinwoo silently stared at the English representative.

Soon, the representative realized that he had made a mistake. If Jinwoo was their ally, that had been a huge faux pas. If not, the representative had just put a target on his own back.

"Of course, I do trust you one hundred percent......" His voice trailed off as his face turned pale.

Jinwoo sighed and gave him a look that let him know just how pathetic he was. "Hmm......"

Jinwoo had already done his duty. He didn't feel the need to appease any of them. "Whether you believe me or not, accept what I've said or not, that's your choice. I've said what I've come here to say, so it's now on you."

The reporters realized the presentation was coming to an end and hurriedly shook off their shock to start snapping some pictures.

Ka-shak, ka-shak, ka-shak!

As Jinwoo turned from the audience, the hand of the director of the Hunter Command Center shot up.

Jinwoo acknowledged David, since he knew the man. "Director Brannon?"

The director slowly rose from his seat. Once again, the auditorium grew quiet. Everyone here recognized the leader of the Hunter Command Center.

"It's been a while, Hunter Sung." David politely bowed his head, and Jinwoo returned the gesture. The director continued. "We now understand what will come out of those gates."

Tens of thousands of black magic beasts had come out from the first gate. Fortunately, they had been the soldiers sworn to serve Hunter Sung, who had coincidentally gained the Shadow Monarch's power. Those soldiers had submitted to the S-rank hunter right away.

But they had received confirmation today that the ones appearing through the other gates would not be as friendly to humans. How, then, was humanity supposed to respond to those creatures?

The director took a deep breath and asked, "How should we proceed?"

Jinwoo looked at him, then slowly scanned the audience. He picked up on the concern, uneasiness, anxiety, fear, shock, and confusion on their faces and in their eyes. Possessing superhuman perception wasn't always a good thing.

......

Jinwoo made up his mind and gave the best advice he could. "Please keep away from the gates. Put as much distance between them and yourselves as you can."

* * *

The ripple effect of Jinwoo's announcement was tremendous. After all, this wasn't an announcement made by any random person. This was an announcement by Jinwoo Sung, the man who had accomplished jaw-dropping feats at the first massive gate.

At his warning that the number of magic beasts projected to pour out of the gates would be difficult for humanity to deal with, people scrambled in fear to get as far away from said gates as possible. Every road was congested with cars, and the streets were filled with the ear-piercing honking of traffic. Jinwoo's picture graced the front page of every newspaper with the same six-word caption.

"Run as far as you can!"

It was enough to mobilize the whole world.

However, as the number of people fleeing grew, so did opposition to it. Not everyone trusted Jinwoo's words.

Jay Mills, a hunter stationed in Canada where the biggest among the eight gates had appeared, boldly spoke out against Jinwoo.

"Tell him to stop spewing bullshit."

The top Canadian hunter criticized Jinwoo in front of a live audience as a panelist on the Hunter Channel.

"If I knew how to reach Hunter Jinwoo Sung, I would've told him that myself. Anyone watching this can tell him for me."

The host forced a smile to try to lighten the mood. "Ha-ha......
Hold your horses there. Hunter Sung is one of the best hunters in the world, isn't he? How can we ignore a warning from a hunter of that caliber?"

Jay was ranked seventeenth in the world. As a newbie with only three years of experience, he could not compare to Jinwoo. He had no choice but to acknowledge this disparity.

"Yeah, of course Hunter Sung is a great hunter. He's powerful enough to knock down Thomas, and he has countless minions...... But it doesn't matter how great the hunter is. We shouldn't trust every little thing he says."

"What evidence do you have that what he said isn't reliable, Hunter Mills?"

Jay smirked. "What evidence does *he* have that it's all true?"

As the host tried to come up with a rebuttal, Jay looked straight at the camera.

"Here's what I think: The only reason those horrifying black creatures bowed down to Jinwoo Sung was because he was standing right in front of that gate in Seoul. Those magic beasts might've submitted to any hunter standing there."

Jay pointed at the camera as if he was speaking directly to Jinwoo.

"Hunter Sung, you don't get to hog all these gates for yourself. Other people may have been spooked by your bullshit, but you don't scare me. Not one bit."

Beep.

Jinchul turned off the TV, quietly put down the remote control, and looked to where Jinwoo was sitting. "Hunters in Canada are rallying behind Jay Mills. It also looks like India and a few other countries with powerful enough hunters are preparing for raids of their own."

Jinwoo just nodded quietly. The choice was theirs. As for him, it was time to focus on the battle against the Monarchs.

"The United States is watching your every move. It's not an exaggeration to say that the whole world is keeping an eye out for your next step." Jinchul dithered before getting to the heart of the matter. "What are you planning to do, Hunter Sung?" Jinchul watched Jinwoo for a reaction.

We must not get in his way.

The truth was, he'd been hiding something from Jinwoo. The whole world was sending out SOS signals, asking for Jinwoo's help. There were so many requests that it was keeping him from focusing on his actual work. In particular, the United States, which shared a border with Canada, was begging for assistance.

But the Hunter's Association's purpose was to assist hunters so that they could concentrate on hunting magic beasts. In accordance with the principles President Go had laid out, Jinchul said nothing and awaited Jinwoo's decision.

And Jinwoo had already made up his mind.

It's impossible to fight all eight armies at once.

In that case, he elected to take care of the threat closest to South Korea, where his family lived. He would deal with the other Monarchs later. His chance at victory would increase with each successive battle anyway.

First up is......

Jinwoo turned to Jinchul. "I'm going to China."

* * *

THE HERO OF THE REPUBLIC OF KOREA, CHINA WELCOMES YOU!

1.5 BILLION PEOPLE THANK YOU, HUNTER SUNG!

MAY KOREA AND CHINA'S FRIENDSHIP LAST FOREVER!

There were banners hung all over the airport, written in Korean so Jinwoo could read them. Zhigang Liu, who was there to welcome Jinwoo, frowned at the banners covering every millimeter of the airport. It wasn't the sentiment that rubbed him the wrong way.

China was ecstatic that Jinwoo had chosen them out of the eight countries with massive gates. Zhigang himself was immensely grateful to have Jinwoo to fight alongside him when the magic beasts emerged from the gate. Rather, he was disgruntled over how drastically different the people of China were reacting compared to when he'd stepped forward to help Korea.

Do these people have no shame?

The same people who had dared to label him a traitor were unanimously praising Jinwoo. That's why Zhigang couldn't help but glare at the banners littering the airport.

Had I not gone to Korea with our hunters back then, I wouldn't be able to face Hunter Sung right now……

He clicked his tongue and turned toward a plane making its landing. He could tell that Hunter Sung was on that airplane. He felt a chill coming from the plane that made every hair on his body stand up. There was only one person in the world who could make him feel that way.

Sure enough, government officials and executives from the Hunter's Association of China chattered excitedly as they got up from their seats at the news that Hunter Sung had arrived.

No…… This isn't right.

Already annoyed by the banners, Zhigang was even less impressed by everyone's behavior. These were the same people who had opposed him when he had insisted on helping Korea. If it wasn't for the fact that he was a seven-star-ranked hunter, they would've stopped him by using force. He couldn't let these cowards welcome the warrior who was risking his own life to save theirs.

Zhigang turned to his assistant. "Tell the president to cancel all welcoming plans. I will personally welcome and escort Hunter Sung."

"Pardon me, sir? But they……"

The assistant hesitated and looked over his shoulder at the officials and executives behind them. The eavesdropping officials pretended to cough and feign ignorance.

Zhigang burst out laughing and walked up to them. "I want you all out of my sight right now. Does anyone have any objections?"

Well aware of Zhigang's bad temper, every single one of the officials and executives hightailed it out of there. The completely empty waiting area put a satisfied look on Zhigang's face.

"Now then, you were saying?"

"R-right! I will inform the president, sir."

As his assistant hurriedly made the call, Zhigang walked toward the arrival gate as travelers poured out.

"Hunter Sung is coming!"

"Get a picture of him!"

Ka-shak, ka-shak, ka-shak, ka-shak, ka-shak, ka-shak!

Reporters had camped out at the airport all day in order to secure a good spot. Camera flashes went off as soon as they spotted Jinwoo.

He scanned the airport with a puzzled look on his face.

Didn't they say around a hundred officials would be here......?

The handler from the Hunter's Association of Korea accompanying him was just as flustered at the lack of an escort from the Hunter's Association of China.

But then Jinwoo smiled when he spotted a familiar face approaching.

"Hunter Liu."

"Hunter Sung."

The two men exchanged a short, firm handshake befitting two warriors preparing for battle.

"So......where is everyone?"

A grin spread across Zhigang's face as he listened to the interpreter.

"Well, they do say that Chinese people are quite impatient. They couldn't wait for you any longer and left, so I'll be escorting you, Hunter Sung."

Jinwoo felt like Zhigang was leaving out a big part of the story, but he didn't press him any further, since he got along just fine with Zhigang. Relieved that Jinwoo was okay with this, Zhigang led him toward the exit.

"This way, please."

However, Jinwoo stopped after a few steps. Zhigang paused as well. Outside the airport's glass walls, Jinwoo could see part of the massive gate covering the sky.

"That's......"

Jinwoo's expression grew grim.

Zhigang solemnly said, "I don't have the power to deal with that thing."

If Zhigang couldn't take care of it, there was no need to even mention other Chinese hunters, so he'd been beyond happy when he heard Jinwoo was coming. In order to express his gratitude, he carefully chose his next words and spoke with sincerity.

"I can't speak for the rest of China, but I, Zhigang Liu, will never forget your aid."

* * *

As the hour of the dungeon break crept closer and closer, news continued to break throughout the world.

Hunter Jinwoo Sung Chooses China!
Japan and Russia have announced that they will send support for Hunter Sung......
The airplane transporting hunters is scheduled to depart this afternoon......

Meanwhile, it has been revealed that the white castle discovered in an abandoned Japanese forest has nothing to do with the gates......
With five hours left before the dungeon break, will Hunter Sung's warning be proven true? Or......

Jay Mills ranted, "Japan and Russia are kissing Jinwoo Sung's ass!"

To him, the reason why those two countries were helping China was obvious. They clearly wanted to curry favor with Jinwoo and score some brownie points in case they ran into trouble and needed his help in the future. China, Japan, and Russia were all weak. How could the hunters from those countries even call themselves hunters if they couldn't protect their own homeland?

Meanwhile, Canadian hunters had assembled of their own volition in order to protect their country.

We stand on guard for thee!

Jay looked proudly upon the tens of thousands of hunters who had voluntarily gathered for this raid. The lies about running away from the gates hadn't fazed any of them.

"Yeaaaaah!"

Their morale was so high, it pierced the sky. Canadian civilians had also gathered to support them from a distance.

CANADA NEVER GIVES UP!

WE DON'T RUN AWAY!

OUR HUNTERS WILL PROTECT US AND THIS LAND!

The cheering people waved their signs to show their support for the hunters. As he looked up at the massive gate, Jay was confident in their victory.

We'll defeat whatever magic beasts come out of there!

Completely psyched, he turned to the other hunters and raised his hands.

"Yeaaaaah!"

* * *

China was ready as well. The raid team consisting of hunters from several countries surrounded the area below the gate just as they'd done in Seoul. The mightiest force among them were the elite hunters from China. As expected of the country boasting the most hunters, there were more than a hundred thousand Chinese hunters here even after choosing only high-rank individuals. Although Jinwoo had warned them that besting the oncoming armies would be difficult for humans, the hunters started to hope that it might be possible with these numbers.

As if challenging this assumption, Jinwoo summoned his shadow soldiers.

Come out.

Jinwoo had purposefully left room behind him for his army of 130,000 to fill.

Whoooosh......

The spine-chilling energy that came from these soldiers made it harder for the hunters to breathe and broke them into a cold sweat.

Th-they're on a whole other level......

Things like that will fall from the sky? Here?

No way......

They were struck with an overwhelming fear. Since they were high-rank hunters, they had extremely well-developed senses of perception, which were currently warning them of the danger posed by the beings before their very eyes.

Zhigang was not an easy man to surprise, but even he couldn't help but gasp. "Are all of these your minions, Hunter Sung......?"

Jinwoo nodded. He sensed that his soldiers' fighting spirits were as sharp as a knife.

Good.

Jinwoo looked up at the sky. Only a few minutes remained before the gate opened. He needed to not only win this battle but also make as many of these soldiers from the World of Chaos into his own. That would be the first stage of the war.

The boisterous group of hunters went silent after the appearance of the shadow army. Everyone sensed that the big battle was imminent. Tension pressed down on their shoulders.

Jinwoo swallowed hard. What kind of magic beasts would fall out of this gate? At that moment......

"My lord." Bellion informed his master that it was time.

Jinwoo responded quietly, "I know."

Zhigang was taken aback to see Jinwoo making casual conversation with his minion. "Hunter Sung, you can communicate with your......?"

Beru, who felt that Zhigang was standing too close to Jinwoo, zipped in front of Zhigang.

"Grrr!"

Zhigang felt murderous intent coming from the ant soldier.

"Whoa!" Zhigang shuddered and quickly stepped back.

But Jinwoo knocked Beru on the back of his head. "He's on our side."

Beru continuously bowed at Jinwoo as he retreated. Jinwoo apologized to Zhigang on Beru's behalf.

"Sorry. He's just on edge because of this upcoming fight."

"I-it's okay." Zhigang gave up on trying to understand Jinwoo. He had a strong feeling that he'd never be able to apply common sense to the Korean man anyway.

"It's opening!"

Everyone looked up at the sky at the yell.

Jinwoo's eyes narrowed.

The entrance to the gate was slowly opening. The hunters' chests tightened at the nerve-racking moment.

But nothing happened.

Jinwoo was the one most surprised by this. He focused his perception but didn't detect any presence from the other side of the gate. It was completely empty.

What?

Jinwoo felt goose bumps on the back of his neck as he thought of a possibility he'd never considered before. Could it be? He grew more uneasy as he became surer of his theory with each passing second.

"What?"

Hunters began to realize that something was wrong. Zhigang urgently turned to the hunter in charge of communications.

"What about the other locations?"

"The other gates are the same. Nothing's happened."

"Are you saying all the other gates are empty, too?"

"I'm...... I'm not sure......"

Zhigang spun to look at Jinwoo, but he couldn't bring himself to talk to him. The Korean man had frozen in place, stunned. Did he look like that because he had been wrong? No, Jinwoo's expression looked too intense for that to be all that was bothering him.

I......I made a mistake.

Jinwoo bit his lower lip as he realized he had made a miscalculation.

Why? Why had Jinwoo underestimated the Monarchs like this? They already knew he would use the strength of the shadow army.

If Jinwoo was right......

He headed straight to the hunter in charge of communications. "How about Canada?"

"Pardon?"

Upset, Jinwoo yelled at him, "I said, how about Canada?!"

* * *

At around the same time, the gate opened in Canada. Just like the other locations, nothing happened. The hunters who were raring to go looked curiously at one another.

"What's going on?"

"Didn't he say magic beasts would fall like rain?"

"Was Jinwoo Sung exaggerating?"

Suddenly, Jay spotted something and yelled at the other hunters. "Quiet!"

He was the strongest hunter among them, and his command was laced with magic power. It compelled the others to shut their mouths.

As the area fell into silence, Jay glared at the gate. Sure enough, a lone humanoid creature leisurely descended from it.

No, not just a humanoid creature. It's an actual human.

As the creature landed gently, Jay stopped the other hunters and approached the creature alone. He swallowed nervously.

As he drew closer, Jay was able to clearly see that his opponent was a middle-aged man with dark-red hair and a beard. He wore beautiful armor of silver and red that covered him from head to toe.

The man looked at Jay as he approached.

Are you the king?

Although the man hadn't opened his mouth, his voice echoed inside Jay's head. Jay automatically understood him as if he had spoken in a human language.

Jay's heart started racing. "Yes! I knew it! I totally called it!"

This was how Jinwoo had been able to take the soldiers under his command. He had probably communicated with them just like this.

"That fraud! I told you something was up!"

He was exhilarated at being correct. Unable to contain his excitement, he raised his fist up toward the other hunters. They raised their fists as well and cheered.

"Whooooo!"

Jay turned back toward the man who had been waiting quietly.

So he asks the first person he sees if they're the king, and he submits to them if they say yes......

He eyed the mystery man, unsure whether he was truly a human or if he was a magic beast. He then smirked.

"What if I say that I am?"

Jay could claim he was the king, since he was the leader of the hunters gathered here. There was a bold confidence in his voice.

It seems he's not here.

The man blinked, revealing bloodthirsty, reptilian eyes.

10
THE ADVENT OF THE DRAGON KING

10

THE ADVENT OF THE
DRAGON KING

"I—I haven't heard from Canada yet......," the hunter in charge of communications stammered.

Frustrated, Jinwoo pulled out his cell phone. He knew someone who could give him the answer he was looking for in a timely manner. Jinwoo went through his contacts and called up Special Agent Adam White of the Asian Branch of the Hunter Command Center. Considering everything that was going on right this second, Jinwoo was worried that his call wouldn't go through.

"Hunter Sung!"

A nervous voice picked up the call. There was no time to exchange greetings, so Jinwoo got straight to the point.

"Adam, what's going on with the gate in Canada......?"

Just then, Jinwoo heard cheering through the phone. It was faint enough that he barely managed to pick it up even with his excellent hearing, but it was enough to confirm his suspicions.

"Where are you now?"

"I'm at the gate in Canada. I'm here with other American agents to support the raid."

"Why the hell are you there?!"

Adam was taken aback by the disbelief in Jinwoo's voice.

"We're not exactly in a position where we can sit back and watch what happens...... A lot of American agents are here with me."

He also added that he was far enough from ground zero that he could evacuate in time should things go south. Regardless, Jinwoo couldn't help but be exasperated.

Didn't I warn them......?

People had no idea of the enormity of the situation. But there was still hope that his prediction was wrong, since Adam was safe and sound.

He collected himself and continued calmly. "Have there been any......changes with the gate?"

"No, it looks like the gate is empty just like everywhere else. It's quiet here."

Jinwoo was relieved. He would rather be criticized for spreading false information. He let out a sigh of relief.

Whew......

It seemed he'd had the wrong idea.

"Huh? Hang on......"

Adam sounded rattled, which sent a chill up Jinwoo's spine. Why did bad feelings always come true?

Adam quickly reported, "Someone......! Something is coming out of the gate right now. Huh? What? It's...... It's a single person!"

Jinwoo's heart began to race once again.

Just one person......?

Jinwoo felt as if his hair was standing on end as he blurted out, "His hair?!"

Adam was a safe distance from the gate, so he wouldn't be able to check the man's pupils, but he could see his hair.

"What color is his hair?"

"H-hold on......"

Adam borrowed some kind of special equipment from an agent nearby.

"Looks black and red......? His hair is dark red."

Oh, crap. Jinwoo's eyes widened.

"Adam! Get out of there! Get in a car or whatever! Just get out *now!*"

"What?"

But before Adam could ask Jinwoo for clarification......

Kra-koooom!

An explosion came from the other side of the phone.

"Oh my God!"

Adam started screaming.

"Adam!"

Jinwoo's voice snapped Adam out of his shock. He sobbed into the receiver.

"The hunters! All the high-rank hunters on the front lines are turning to ash! Their bodies are still on fire. Oh my God......"

"Adam! Adam, it's okay, just get out of there now! You need to get out of there immediately!"

Jinwoo tried to calm Adam down, but the agent was already half out of his mind.

"Oh no......"

Through his sobbing, Adam managed to describe everything to Jinwoo as if it was his duty.

"Dragons are descending...... An endless horde of dragons and other magic beasts is coming! There are all kinds of magic beasts...... How is this happening......?"

At the sorrow in Adam's voice, Jinwoo could no longer bring himself to simply listen. As risky as it was, he tapped in to the shadow soldier attached to Adam. He was able to see what Adam was seeing.

It was as if the apocalypse had come. The envoys of destruction blanketed out the sky as they descended from the yawning gate. Horrifying monsters occupied both land and air. The roar of four-legged beasts shook the earth while flying creatures flapped their wings overhead. Even before the magic beasts hit the ground, the hunters who had gathered to oppose them had vanished with a snap of the fingers from the Monarch of Destruction who preceded them.

Everyone else was in a panic and trying to escape, but their chances at survival were dreadfully slim.

But......

Jinwoo could at least save Adam. The high orc shadow soldier controlled by Jinwoo grabbed a fearful Adam by the wrist.

"A-ahhh!"

Adam screamed at the sight of the high orc in black armor, but he soon noticed the shadow of a familiar-looking man in his eyes.

"H-Hunter Sung?"

There was no time to explain. Jinwoo could debrief Adam after teleporting him. While possessing the high orc's body, Jinwoo tried to drag Adam into the shadow beneath his feet.

But someone suddenly came up from behind and grabbed the high orc by the shoulder.

Whap.

The high orc looked back and saw a middle-aged man with creepy reptilian eyes glaring at him.

Where do you think you're going, shadow?

The man opened his mouth wide, charging up powerful energy.

Jinwoo looked at Adam. Adam seemed to realize something and stared the high orc controlled by Jinwoo dead in the eye.

"Hunter Sung, I—"

Fwaaaaaaaah!

The man unleashed the fire in his mouth, and the shadow soldier disintegrated into nothing.

"Argh!"

Jinwoo felt like his body was on fire and writhed at the intense pain. He was able to escape, since only his senses had been connected to the high orc, but it was a different story for Adam.

Jinwoo had witnessed the agent's final moment. Jinwoo ground his teeth as he thought about the look in Adam's eyes as he caught fire and turned to ash.

Bam!

Jinwoo slammed his fist into the ground and shook the entire area.

Dammit......

Jinwoo should've known. With their enemy being the Shadow Monarch, who would grow stronger as the war dragged on, the enemy would minimize the battlefield and focus their attacks on one target at a time. The Monarchs had faked him out with their original plan to open all eight gates at once.

And they sent their entire force to the gate farthest from me.

Jinwoo had made a painful mistake. His plan to increase his shadow army while the other gates were being attacked had gone up in smoke.

Realizing something awful must have occurred, Zhigang cautiously approached Jinwoo. "Hunter Sung......"

It was then that the hunter in charge of communication walked up to them, the blood having drained from his face.

"H-Hunter Sung, Hunter Liu...... Canada has been......"

Jinwoo didn't need to hear the rest. When he looked up, the gate covering the sky was slowly vanishing, having completed its purpose.

* * *

A shadow soldier and the human next to him were burned away, as the fiery breath of destruction could melt even an immortal soldier with one blow.

......

The Dragon King looked down over the ashes at his feet, satisfied with the results. He then turned to look at the soldiers of the World of Chaos. Stuck in the gap between dimensions for far too long, they were now taking to the use of their powers and their newfound freedom like fish to water.

The Dragon King closed his eyes, spread his arms out wide, and relished his own freedom. The heartbeats of living creatures. Their screams. The sounds of those creatures being destroyed. It was music to his ears.

Thud!

The ancient dragons landed forcefully on the ground, followed by two Monarchs. The Monarchs were then followed by several marshals. In a show of respect, they knelt before the most powerful Monarch.

The Dragon King smiled and grabbed at some mana vibrating in the air. The mana that had been released into this world in order to enhance it was also a boon to those who knew how to use it.

Their preparations were complete.

"Gya-ha-ha-ha!"

The Dragon King let out a laugh powerful enough to make the ground shake. He cried out to the soldiers who continued to pour from the gate.

"We have but one mission! Destroy everything!"

Hundreds of dragons rocketed past him overhead and rained flames down below.

Fwooooosh!

* * *

David Brannon sat alone in the director's office with the lights off. He ignored the countless reports and phone calls from his higher-ups and drank the expensive booze he had been saving for his eldest daughter's wedding.

The muted TV screen flickered in the dark. Now and then, magic beasts came up on-screen. David knew why the network kept airing the same footage.

They're probably all dead.

Just like the Hunter Command Center's agents who had been sent to Canada to support the raid, it was likely that no one had survived. Hunters, agents, and reporters covering the story were all dead, every last one of them. But thanks to the cameraman who had risked his life to get this footage, people had an idea of what they were dealing with.

"It's all over!" the director screamed.

Jinwoo hadn't been exaggerating. The dragons alone numbered in the hundreds. They were followed by a tsunami of giants, wild beasts, and bugs. These magic beasts were walking disasters no human had the power of stopping.

David now understood why Jinwoo had repeatedly emphasized evacuation. It was the end of the world.

"That crazy bastard!"

Jinwoo had gone to China with his minions to confront those terrifying things, hadn't he? Why would he even consider engaging those creatures, knowing what he knew about them? The director wanted to crack open Jinwoo's head and inspect his brain if he could.

But my skull would be shattered into dozens of pieces before I could make that happen.

"Heh-heh!"

As he laughed in spite of himself, he pulled out a picture from the inner pocket of his jacket. It was an image of him looking annoyed next to his daughter wearing a party hat.

Is she sixteen in this photo?

Had he known his daughter would become the victim of a dungeon break in the year after that, he would've spent more time with her and taken more pictures with her. Heck, he would've quit his job to do so. David was dejected that this was the only picture he had of the two of them together.

He emptied another glass. When his daughter was buried, he thought he'd never open this bottle. He smacked his lips bitterly and shook the bottle. It was already half-empty.

"Yes…… It's over now."

Half of Canada had apparently been devastated already, and that was merely an estimate. No one knew how quickly those magic beasts were advancing on the United States.

The director angrily pulled off his tie. "I won't die at the hands of those bastards."

He'd sworn on his daughter's grave that he'd never let those magic beasts kill him. At the very least, David wanted to choose how he died.

His decision made, he stood at a window from which he could see the ground way down below. A cool breeze blew on his sweaty forehead.

……I hope I'll see my daughter again.

He squeezed his eyes shut and leaned forward.

Someone grabbed his shoulder.

"Ah!" David's eyes flew open to see a familiar face behind him. "H-Hunter Sung?"

The director paled like he had seen a ghost.

Jinwoo spoke. "I'm looking for something."

What was Jinwoo looking for as the world was about to end? More importantly, was this person in front of David really Jinwoo? The director shook his head to clear it, thinking that he must be hallucinating. But as Jinwoo came more and more into focus, he quickly realized that it was Hunter Sung in the flesh.

David sobered up instantly. "Wh-what are you looking for?"

"A rune stone," Jinwoo clarified. "Please give me the rune stone Kamish left behind."

"......!" The director's surprise didn't last long. He shook his head out of reflex. "As you know, the Hunter Command Center has been......"

David's mouth snapped shut. Damn his habits. What about the Hunter Command Center? Never mind that! The entire country was going to be decimated, so who cared about the rune stone?

I think I'm still drunk.

The director slapped both his cheeks hard. He started to think straight as his cheeks heated up. Once his eyes cleared, he determined that Jinwoo's reason for wanting the rune stone was more important than whatever it was worth to the Hunter Command Center and the United States.

After a bit of thought, the director cautiously probed Jinwoo. "I can give you the rune stone. But may I ask why you need it?"

Jinwoo answered without hesitation. "I'm going to use it for a counterattack."

* * *

Jinwoo had seen the skill locked within the rune stone through the system. It contained the power of a dragon, but he previously hadn't been interested in the rune stone because of the skill's obvious disadvantage. Jinwoo hadn't needed it.

But......times change.

Jinwoo and the director descended to the ninth underground level within the Hunter Command Center headquarters. They soon arrived in front of the tempered-glass display case housing the rune stone.

Without the system, Jinwoo now looked over the skill contained in the stone using his own eyes and perception. It was as he had remembered—a terrifying power. However, this incredible power was worth any drawbacks, especially in this situation.

Ba-dump!

Jinwoo's heart pounded in his chest.

After staring at the rune stone for a moment, David posed a question. "You said these so-called Rulers sent magic beasts here, right?"

"Yes."

"Why are these rune stones in the bodies of magic beasts?"

"They're gifts of sorts from the Rulers to help us hunt magic beasts more efficiently."

The Rulers had wanted to release mana into this world through violent clashes between humans and magic beasts. The sacrifice of humans was an unfortunate side effect, not their ultimate goal. Having rune stones seal a magic beast's power when it died was their attempt at sympathy for the humans' plight.

That was how Kamish's power had come to be stored in this rune stone. Jinwoo took hold of the key for his counterattack.

The director swallowed as he nervously watched Jinwoo with the rune stone in his hand. "Can......can you really stop those magic beasts with that?"

"I'll have to try at least."

Even at this very moment, the armies led by the Dragon King continued their advance and destruction of everything in sight. Thanks to the Rulers reinforcing the world with mana, the armies could only move so fast. However, that was just buying time. Before long, the whole planet would be on fire.

Jinwoo couldn't very well just watch the world come to an end, now could he?

The enemy very much feared the power of the Shadow Monarch. They wanted to disrupt that power even if it meant plotting against the Shadow Monarch behind his back. Jinwoo was going to show them how a weak creature could wield that power.

"I'm going to do everything I can."

The determination in Jinwoo's eyes hit the director right in the heart. Jinwoo had never backed down from a fight, regardless of how powerful his opponent was. Meanwhile, David had spent much of his time trying to avoid the threat. Standing in Jinwoo's presence, the director felt utterly inadequate.

Was I really thinking of joining my daughter? How pathetic of me......

David was ashamed of himself. Now he wanted to bear witness to Jinwoo's battle, regardless of the outcome.

"I have no right to ask this of you, but......please stop those monsters!" The director sobbed.

Perhaps all David had really wanted was to avoid dying at the hands of those magic beasts. As the head of the Hunter Command Center, he should have led the charge against them, but he didn't have the courage to watch countless Americans die. But even if they were merely hanging on by a thread, Brannon wanted to grab on to it no matter what. He continued to tear up as he summoned this newfound courage.

Jinwoo gently put his hand on the director's shoulder. "......"

To David, this gesture felt more dependable than a thousand words of reassurance. He wiped away his tears.

"How embarrassing. I'm sorry, Hunter Sung."

Jinwoo waited until Brannon was calmer before he spoke. "One more thing. There's somebody I need to find."

* * *

Jinwoo followed the director into an apartment building not far from the headquarters of the Hunter Command Center.

"She lives nearby?"

"The Hunter Command Center believes it's best to keep close the people they need to protect."

It looked like she lived on a lower floor, since David chose to take the stairs. David was just starting to sweat when he stopped at a door on the fourth floor.

"We're here."

Jinwoo nodded.

Knock, knock.

Brannon gently knocked on the door twice instead of ringing the bell, like it had been previously agreed upon. After a brief silence, an agent inside confirmed that it was David and then opened the door.

"Director Brannon?" The agent's nose crinkled at the smell of alcohol; then he jumped back in surprise as soon as he spotted Jinwoo. "......!"

At least he didn't pull a gun on Jinwoo as he had during their first meeting. The agent did instinctively put his hand on his waist after seeing that there was an unexpected visitor. But he soon looked flustered as he remembered what had happened the last time he'd tried that on Jinwoo.

"Hunter Sung......?"

There was no time to ascertain why the world's most powerful hunter was standing there. The director and his guest entered the apartment. The other agent assigned as a guard came out to see David.

"Where is she?"

"She's inside— Whoa!" This agent was also startled to see Jinwoo. "Director Brannon, that's......?"

"I brought him here because he wished to see her. Please tell her Hunter Sung is here."

"......Yes, sir."

"I wasn't expecting to receive visitors at this time."

The door to a bedroom opened just then, and Norma Sellner walked into the room. She was the Upgrader and former psychic who could increase a hunter's power beyond their limits.

Jinwoo moved one step forward and politely bowed to Mrs. Sellner.

"Please come in." She led Jinwoo inside the bedroom. When the director attempted to follow them, Mrs. Sellner gently stopped him. "Hunter Sung probably wants to have a private conversation with me."

When she turned to Jinwoo, he nodded in agreement. The door closed on the director, who cleared his throat and straightened out his clothes.

With the door completely shut, Mrs. Sellner slowly turned toward the man waiting for her in one corner of the room. She gasped after getting a good look at him from head to toe.

"My goodness!"

Jinwoo looked totally different from the last time she had seen him.

"You......you are not the person I knew."

Mrs. Sellner was incredulous. She had previously seen the darkness deep inside Jinwoo, but now he was the darkness itself. The power of the dead encompassing Jinwoo was quite evident to her.

Jinwoo shook his head. "I'm the same person. The only difference is now, the darkness and I have become one."

"Ahhh......"

There were no words to describe this wondrous sight. The power of a god was nestled inside a human. Mrs. Sellner marveled at the power oozing from Jinwoo's every pore. But she soon snapped back to her senses and picked her jaw up from off the floor.

"I......cannot be of help to you, Hunter Sung."

Nobody in the world could help this superhuman. But Jinwoo had a different wish. He carefully approached the fearful Mrs. Sellner.

"You said you could see into the future."

"In a way......"

"Then could you please look into mine?"

Jinwoo wanted to see the end of this war through Mrs. Sellner's eyes before entering the fray in earnest. Whatever the answer, it would put his mind at ease.

Mrs. Sellner hesitated at first but eventually nodded slowly. She reached out to take Jinwoo's hands and then closed her eyes. She needed to muster up the courage to stare into the darkness. But she also knew Jinwoo himself would need an inordinate amount of more courage to go into battle. She could not deny the brave warrior this request.

Time flew by quickly. When Mrs. Sellner opened her eyes, she couldn't help but weep.

"You...... Are you really going to carry this burden all by yourself?"

"......" Jinwoo didn't answer.

"How......how could one person bear such a burden......? Are you planning to save everyone and everything with your sacrifice?"

Jinwoo's face brightened. "It's good to hear I'll get that far."

"Good?! No one will remember you. You will fight a lonely war!"

Jinwoo let go of her hands even as she tried to dissuade him. He had prepared for this ever since he decided to fight the Monarchs. He took a step back from her and wished her farewell.

"My apologies for the sudden visit and for asking such a huge favor."

"Hunter Sung!"

Jinwoo disappeared into the shadow beneath his feet even before she finished her frantic cry. The agents rushed into the room at her scream, but Jinwoo was already gone.

* * *

......

Jinwoo stood on the roof of the tallest building downtown and sharpened his senses to search for an energy signature, the same way he'd located Jinho when he was kidnapped. He sensed a countless number of soldiers making their way south from the northern tip of the country. He couldn't sense a single living creature left in their wake. Everyone had been devoured by the denizens of chaos.

Byunggu Min, Gunhee Go, Adam White, and Jinwoo's father. The faces of all the victims who had been sacrificed in this fight flashed through Jinwoo's mind. Fury clawed at and engulfed his heart.

Jinwoo closed his eyes to search for the Dragon King within the huge army. It wasn't difficult to locate the eye of a storm that was consuming everything in its path.

......*Found you.*

Jinwoo and the Dragon King spotted each other at the same time. He sensed the energy scanning him and knew that only one person possessed that kind of power. The emperor stopped dead in his tracks and glared in Jinwoo's direction. Having located his true enemy, his reptilian eyes stared into the darkness for quite some time.

......

......

The Shadow Monarch and the Monarch of Destruction met each other's eyes even from that distance. The Monarch of Destruction was the first to bare his fangs.

"I am right here!" A dreadful roar like hundreds of thousands of lightning bolts striking at once shook the sky. "Tens of millions of your kind are already dead. How long are you going to hide like that?"

Jinwoo's eyes flashed with rage.

I'm coming for you. And when I get my hands on you......

Jinwoo swallowed the rest of his words and silently sank into the shadows.

HAVE YOU BEEN TURNED ON TO LIGHT NOVELS YET?

86—EIGHTY-SIX, VOL. 1–11

In truth, there is no such thing as a bloodless war. Beyond the fortified walls protecting the eighty-five Republic Sectors lies the "nonexistent" Eighty-Sixth Sector. The young men and women of this forsaken land are branded the Eighty-Six and, stripped of their humanity, pilot "unmanned" weapons into battle...

Manga adaptation available now!

WOLF & PARCHMENT, VOL. 1–6

The young man Col dreams of one day joining the holy clergy and departs on a journey from the bathhouse, Spice and Wolf. Winfiel Kingdom's prince has invited him to help correct the sins of the Church. But as his travels begin, Col discovers in his luggage a young girl with a wolf's ears and tail named Myuri, who stowed away for the ride!

Manga adaptation available now!

SOLO LEVELING, VOL. 1–7

E-rank hunter Jinwoo Sung has no money, no talent, and no prospects to speak of—and apparently, no luck, either! When he enters a hidden double dungeon one fateful day, he's abandoned by his party and left to die at the hands of some of the most horrific monsters he's ever encountered.

Comic adaptation available now!